AF437990

THE MARK OF CAIN

A SOUTHERN NOIR

TYLER KEITH

The Mark of Cain
by Tyler Keith

Published 2022 by Cool Dog Sound LLC

P.O. Box 454 • Water Valley, MS 38965

www.cooldogsound.com

For more information contact tim.lee@bark-loud.com.

ISBN 979-8-218-07064-9 (paperback)

Book design by Susan Bauer Lee
Author photo by John Rash

This book is dedicated to my mother, Rosalie Riley, for teaching me to read and write, and to my father, George Keith, for telling me about our family's past.

AND THE LORD said unto him, Therefore whosoever slayeth Cain, vengeance shall be taken on him sevenfold. And the LORD set a mark upon Cain, lest any finding him should kill him. … And Cain went out from the presence of the LORD, and dwelt in the land of Nod, on the east of Eden.

— Genesis 4:15-16

PROLOGUE

HOLMES COUNTY FLORIDA *is a mean place. A hard place. After they took the trees. The long leaf pine made some outsiders rich. Gave people work for a few years.*

Then it was gone.

Two options left: Dirt farming Christian with no sense of humor, or dangerous outlaw, not very funny either. Some families have both, a father from one side and a mother from the other. Then the offspring is ripped apart by competing tendencies. That could be me. Third option: you leave. But you always take that place with you. And Holmes County is always waiting for you to come back. Somebody there can put you to work ... doing something wrong.

My dad's people came from the outlaw side. Way back. 1820s, maybe. They've been making whiskey for over a hundred years. Brought the recipe with them from wherever, Scotland, I guess. The Choctahatchee River is clean and pure, springs and deep holes of crystal clear water feed into it. Everybody knows the key to good whiskey starts with the water. And the Choctahatchee River leads into a bay and then out to the Gulf of Mexico. You can just take it right out.

During Prohibition, Holmes County was the center of the moonshine world. Dad's family held a whole section of the river around East Pittman, just south of the Alabama line. People were killed, both revenuers and outlaws. There were feuds.

My father took a different path, the church. Even the hard-ass outlaw communities had their own churches. Usually some crazy preachers. Tongues. Strychnine. Snakes. Even the ones called by the Lord thrived on danger and chaos. Key to faith is action. "Faith without works is dead." James 2:26. Daddy fell under the spell of one of these preachers, Reverend Vernon Harrison, maybe a second or third cousin. He was almost a John the Baptist character. Locust and wild honey. Maybe sometimes pure grain alcohol. He held services in a brush arbor, or sometimes in an old wooden church in the woods.

The Rev was a bit too wild and visceral for most folks, but a group of outcasts formed around him. Serious people. Women who had gifts of the spirit. Men searching for a father figure, a leader. The man had a command of the scripture. That's how my father fell under his spell. Daddy loved to read and the Bible was his book. He could recite entire chapters. Tell all the stories.

But the Rev was just a man. He ran off at one point. With men's wives. Made them shave their heads. Wear all black. Sometimes put shit on their faces. Ashes. It was a repenting thing. Who knows? Most of the women trickled back to Holmes County after a few months, in shame, some indignant. My grandmother, mom's mother, was one. When she came back she was plain mean, always clutching an old Bible.

Even if you were a man of the cloth, you couldn't escape trouble. It was a family business. If they needed you, they got you. My uncle, Albert Harrison, my dad's oldest brother, ran things. He was a dangerous man. Ruthless. Violent. Scoffed at my dad's religion. Abused him. Beat the shit out of him. Maybe other things. Finally forced our family to leave Holmes County and move to Pensacola. I guess I was about seven years old. My maternal grandfather had moved years earlier to find work, and get away from the family business. Maybe he was run out.

My closest childhood friend, before we moved, was Albert Jr. Everybody called him Junior. He was my age. His father had a special hatred for him. Beat him. He nearly killed him once. Served a year hard labor for it. He came back even meaner. I'd see Junior in the summers when I'd go down to see family, and stay for month or so. He was always scared of his daddy, always running from him. He drowned. Nobody knows what happened, but everybody knows who was responsible. Nobody

Tyler Keith

saw anything. Someone found his body floating in the river. He was thirteen.

After my daddy disappeared, we didn't see Albert Sr. much when we went back to visit. I didn't go back for the summers anymore. Just sometimes to see some of mom's kin. Nobody fucked with Albert. Everybody was scared of him. He still ran things down there. Had a few men that did his bidding. The moonshine expanded to marijuana. Money came in. I knew there was always work for me if I wanted it. Driving. Security. Family was always preferred to outsiders. In high school, I'd drive over and pick up some weed and sell it to friends, just enough to keep some for myself.

After high school, I drove a truck for a number of years. Moved with my wife and daughter to Gulf Breeze. We had it good for a while, a nice little ranch-style house with a yard full of stickers. The gas crunch took some of the money and work out of trucking. I was having some trouble getting steady work. One night I ran into a cousin at a bar on Pensacola Beach. He told me if I wanted work in the family business, they were hiring, always, especially for kin. I could drive a truck or drive whatever. I could make some real money.

I started working for them, driving at first. Tammy thought I was long-hauling it. I was bringing home good money. She didn't ask too many questions. I worked for my uncle. Didn't see him much. I mostly answered to his oldest son, Charles. He and some of Albert's other kids took care of the day to day. Some cousins. The Harrisons ran everything in the county.

We started expanding and trading goods with some people in South Florida. I'd drive a rig down there, drop off, pick up, and come back. Sketchy people showed up. There was guns and paranoia. Things got weird. I stayed out of any decisions. Never asked what I was carrying. It was easier on the mind not to know too much. Not that I didn't know, but …

There was more money. More violence. More heat. I got put away before it got too bad, before the drug laws changed. Got harsher. But you could see it coming.

I don't want to go back there. But there's a gravity to

the place, something that pulls me back, a voice that calls me. Memory. Something in my blood. There's the river and the land. It's the place of my childhood, the place of my ancestors. It's the last place on earth. There are things that have not been done. Unfinished business. The dead won't rest 'til things even out. Maybe I don't have to go back.

Tyler Keith

1

THEY LET ME out of the Federal Prison Camp, FPC, in Pensacola on a Friday morning. I stopped just past the gate and gazed towards the sun with my eyes closed, feeling the crisp sunlight on my face, and that Florida breeze.

"So long, Ronnie," someone behind me said. "Stay outta trouble."

Without looking back, I gave him a half wave. He laughed.

I'd been inside for six years on a twenty-year sentence. Paroled. It was August, 1986. The War on Drugs ran full tilt, and they wanted to make room for all the new drug thugs, so they were letting all the old convicts with good prison records out early.

Good behavior? I wouldn't call my behavior good … or bad really. Just nothing. I hadn't expected to get out so soon. I had a fresh pack of Marlboro Reds, $382, and the same set of clothes I had on when I went in: Wrangler blue jeans, blue jean jacket, black denim shirt, a pair of brown, zip-up, Jensen cowboy boots, and cheap sunglasses.

I knocked out a cigarette from the pack of Marlboros and stuck it in my mouth. I patted down my denim jacket and fumbled out an old pack of matches from my upper pocket. The matches were old and crusty, but I managed to put two together and get a light. I thought of nothing as I took a long drag on the cigarette. I exhaled: part smoke, part sigh of relief. My first free moment in six years. An invisible burden seemed to drop off my back. I rolled my

head around in a circle and began to walk with nowhere
to go.

My wife gave up and left about three years in. Hadn't
heard from her much. I had a grown daughter but we
were estranged. We wrote some letters for a while, but I'd
let it fall off. My mother died while I was locked up. I had
the contact number for a halfway house in Gulf Breeze
called Camp Eden. They put up ex-cons 'til they could
get on their feet. You had to do some work in exchange
for housing and food. It was loosely affiliated with a local
Pentecostal Church, so you also had to attend church three
times a week. That thought, going to church three times
a week, didn't thrill me, but I didn't have much choice.
After surviving six years in prison, I guessed I could
handle going to church three times a week. Maybe.

I figured I'd get down there and stay and work for
a few weeks 'til I could get some real work and a place
of my own. I had a loose plan: take a bus from the jail to
downtown Pensacola and call the guy from there. Get
directions and details. Maybe a ride. But for now I just
started walking, feeling the sun beating down on my face,
chain smoking, lighting one cigarette off the last, and my
eyes behind dark sunglasses, barely open.

I passed bus stops. I passed strip malls. Old motor
court motels. A day-care enclosed in a tall chain-linked
fence. An office building built in the sixties. A Church's
Fried Chicken closed and boarded up. An old country-
and-western dance hall called RODEO, the old sign falling
off its pedestal. I had a flash of memory about a night I'd
spent in that place many years ago. Drinking and fighting
with my ex-wife. I didn't dwell on it. Just kept walking.

When I finally stopped and stood still for a moment, I
took a deep breath and looked around to see where I was.
It was just empty parking lots with tall weeds growing
up through the concrete, and empty businesses with
taped-up, tinted windows. Across the four-lane highway,
I saw a small bar next to a motor court painted seafoam

                                                      Tyler Keith

green and coral with a wooden fence around it so you
could barely see inside the circular courtyard. The sign
flashed PARADISE MOTEL, parts of the neon burnt out.
Weekly/Hourly Rates it said underneath. The bar had
a flashing Pabst Blue Ribbon sign in the window. The
moment I caught sight of the sign, an intense thirst rose up
inside me. I threw my cigarette down and hurried towards
the bar across the highway.

The warped sound of a car horn brought me back
to earth. I realized I might get killed crossing the road
so I kept an eye on the cars and half-jogged across the
road. I stood in front of the place for a few seconds and
looked around. To my right, a lady in a black mini-skirt,
half a mile down the cracked sidewalk, walked back and
forth. The sign on top of the bar above the door read Fire
and Fiddle, a violin bulging out of a campfire. The place,
like the motel next door, had seen its best day sometime
around 1976. I looked at the flashing Pabst Blue Ribbon
sign and opened the heavy green door and went inside.
Thick smoke hung in the air, steel guitars whined in the
background, and I smelled that stale-beer, rotten smell I
hadn't smelt in six years. I took a deep breath through my
nose without making a big show of it.

Three men bellied up to the bar, two about halfway
down and one at the far end below the exit sign above the
backdoor. A woman leaned over an old Rock-Ola jukebox,
punching out songs. They all looked my way and took me
in. When they realized they didn't know me, they went
back to their drinks and the glow of the jukebox.

I sat at the bar, second stool closest to the door. The
bartender, an older, large woman, waddled over to me.

She didn't speak.

I said, "Budweiser."

She turned around and shuffled over to the silver
cooler, slid open the top, and pulled out a Bud longneck;
opened it on the side of the cooler, wrapped the beer in a
white bar napkin and set it in front of me.

"One dollar," she said.

I fished out the wad of cash from my pocket and took two dollar bills and set them on the bar next to the beer. She took the money, placing one of the dollars in a plastic pitcher with a hand drawn sign for tips. She turned and ambled halfway down the bar and put the other bill in an old cash register.

I studied the beer for a few seconds then hoisted it to my mouth and drank about half of it in slow swallows. Letting out an uncontrollable "aahh," I set the beer down in front of me. My eyes watered, slightly. I'd thought about this moment for six years. The bittersweet taste. The warm feeling. I took a deep breath and finished the rest of my beer. As I shook out a cigarette, I swear "A Satisfied Mind" played on the jukebox. I smiled.

As soon as I caught the bartender's eyes, I held up the Budweiser bottle and tipped it towards her. She brought me another one, offered a pained smile, and I gave her another two bucks.

A little plan began to form in my head. I'd just drink some beers here tonight and get a room at the motel next door; then in the morning I'd make my way to Camp Eden and get settled in. They wouldn't let you in those places with beer on your breath anyhow. So I finished off my second beer and ordered another one. I felt a contentment I hadn't felt in six years. "Behind Closed Doors" played on the jukebox.

The next few hours passed in a drunken blur. I remember the music getting wilder. I swear I heard "The Girls All Get Prettier at Closing Time" spinning on the jukebox. I got drunker. The girl from the jukebox got friendlier. I thought she may be a working girl. That didn't excite me much, although it didn't make me turn her away either. A person who's never been in prison for any length of time might have it in their head that by the time you get out, you can't wait to have a woman. But it's not like that, at least not for me. I'd pushed those thoughts so far back in my

Tyler Keith

mind, and avoided the pictures and the porn inside that the thought of having a woman wasn't in my head yet.

When I first went in I was thirty-seven years old, half ugly and raw boned. I'd kept to myself. Didn't make friends with the guards. Nobody seemed to notice me after a while. When I first got to prison, I had a few fights. I suppose I won. Although I've never been a brawler, I've also never been afraid to fight. I guess the other inmates could see that and let me be. I wasn't a prize to fight over.

All that being said, the jukebox lady, Darleen, made the hard press. I started to come around to the idea too. *Fuck it*. But I knew women like Darleen. I'd spent many nights in bars just like this one. Even if I'd never met Darleen, I knew her. She could probably tell that I'd just gotten out of prison. She'd be trying to get my money. At some point in the evening, in the bathroom stall, I put a wad of cash in my boot. Left a good deal in my front, right pocket.

One thing about bars like the Fire and Fiddle, it might be part of the appeal, they exist in a vacuum, no space and time. After coming out of the bathroom, I figured I'd better go over to the motel and get a room while I had the money and the ability. The bar had no windows, and when I opened the door to go outside, I realized it wasn't even dark outside yet. The sunset shone on the concrete wasteland. Light sparkled off the weeds in the vacant lots. It seemed to bounce off of the roofs of the passing big rigs.

I took it in for a second. Took a big breath of fresh air. That smile crept up again. I strolled over to the Paradise Motel with a slight wobble. I was drunk. My mind was still clear but my body unsure, like stepping off of a boat after a deep sea fishing trip.

I entered the coral-colored office at the Paradise, trying to straighten out my drunken smile. Nobody manned the desk. The lobby had a damp smell of mildew and cigarettes. Some electrical device, maybe a window unit, made a loud hum. The paint flaked off the wall in places and a couple of beachscape paintings hung randomly around the room.

I hit the bell on the counter and after a few seconds, I heard something moaning behind the door. An old man came out of the back room, his face contorted in an almost comic way, a caricature of an old man, chomping on his gums.

"Can I help you," he asked.

"Yeah. I need a room. One room. One bed."

The old man fumbled around underneath the counter and pulled up an orange keychain with the number 9 on it. "How long?"

"Just one night."

"No drugs," he said. "Twenty-two dollars. Checkout's at noon."

My mind eased up a bit knowing I had a room. *A real bed,* I thought, and then *more beer,* and *Darleen.* I paid the man, and without saying anything or looking at him, I turned and walked out the door and back down the sidewalk towards the Fire and Fiddle. I stopped about halfway and thought for a moment. *Maybe I should go to the room. Check it out. Sleep.* But I went on back to the bar. The neon sign above the bar blinked, first "Fire" then "Fiddle," then both together.

I sat back down at the bar and ordered another beer. Darleen sauntered back over, placing her arm on the back of my chair, and putting one foot up on the bottom rung of my barstool. She leaned into me, her waist and crotch slightly rubbing against my knee and the side of my leg, the upper part of her shoulder and the edge of her breast sometimes brushing my elbow and upper arm. I felt myself leaning towards her, almost moving my shoulder to touch her body. I can't remember ever wanting someone more in all my life.

"I thought you might've left," she said, looking me right in the eyes, a little smile. Her face had a plainness to it, light freckles scattered about. Her eyes were green

                                    Tyler Keith

or maybe blue and her crow's feet somehow suggested a gentleness. She'd spent time in the sun. Maybe kept a small garden. Her mouth seemed small but she had full lips with little wrinkles above that showed her age, mid-40s. Her hair hung limp down to her shoulders, a dirty blonde, like muddy water in a tire track.

She wasn't a street walker, I thought. Maybe she turned a trick now and then, when desperate for cash. Or she had a rich older man. Probably not rich, just lonely with extra money to give her in exchange for a night of drinks and a little time in bed.

All of these thoughts and ideas about her flashed through my mind in the few seconds our eyes met.

"I just needed some air," I said.

"When did you get out?" she asked.

"Just today," I said. "Is it that obvious?"

"There's a certain pallor to the skin. I've seen it before."

"I'm supposed to be heading to this place in Gulf Breeze called Camp Eden," I said. "It's a halfway house run by Pentecostals or something."

"Those places are about the same as prison," she said. "My ex-husband stayed in a place in Memphis that was worse than prison. This place had freshly released convicts — it didn't matter if you were a killer or rapist — along with homeless men and teenage drug addicts. It was set up in a big warehouse with beds out in the open. They locked everybody in at night with hardly anybody on guard. He said it was scarier than prison when the lights went out for the night. They worked the shit out of him, too. He was supposed to stay in there for six months but he took off after three or four days. Broke his parole. He was a son of a bitch."

"Jesus, I can't wait," I said. A wave of foreboding swept over me. It almost sobered me up.

"Two shots. Tequila," I motioned to the bartender.

"Why not," she said.

More drinks came after that. She talked. I listened.

Sort of. She had an estranged daughter and a dead son. She cleaned houses but wanted more steady work. She'd waited tables for years. Bartended. But she preferred the other side of the bar now.

She kept leaning closer, rubbing her body against me nonchalantly. My mind twisted around itself with booze and insane lust.

"I've got a room next door," I finally said.

She smiled and said, "One more round."

We stumbled into the room with our mouths on each other's mouths and hands groping each other's bodies through our clothes. I didn't have time to check out the room except to notice that the walls looked like some hula skirts were stapled up everywhere, a small TV with the antenna in a V and an old black rotary phone sitting on the table next to the bed. The only light came from a lamp with an eggshell shade and a dim light bulb.

As we fell together on the bed, I grabbed her between the legs and rubbed as she bit my bottom lip. She fondled my bulge and rubbed, too. Then we both struggled to unbutton each other's jeans, finally giving up and concentrating on our own.

She managed to get out of her jeans and took me in her hand. I couldn't get my pants all the way off because my boots were still on. She just straddled me and guided me inside her. I slid in. Grabbed her hips. I caught her eyes for a moment and we kissed again.

I saw something in her eyes so hungry and lost, a loneliness so deep, I felt a sadness overcome me for a second. Everything I'd put aside in prison, all the loneliness I'd sheltered and hidden came rushing out. I wanted to burst into tears, or flames. My heart banged and I almost gasped for breath.

Just then my dick slipped out. Darleen quickly put me back in. My pants were around my knees and I couldn't get the right torque. My mind raced everywhere. She straightened things out for a second then it happened again. I flipped her off me and tried to get on top but my legs were stuck. I panicked and tried to get my boots off.

I lost it. I ran out of breath and I laid back struggling to breathe. Darleen leaned over me and kissed my neck. Tried to fondle me. But it was too late. All the feelings I'd just had evaporated in an instant. Not to mention my dick went as limp as a wet bar towel.

I sighed and closed my eyes and pushed her away.

"I'm sorry," I said. "I can't right now."

"Oh baby, it's okay. We've got all night."

I felt ashamed. I wanted this lady. Right now. But something wouldn't let me. My mind wasn't ready. I stared at the ceiling and then closed my eyes, not wanting to look at her. But then I did, and she smiled at me and kissed me. I put my arm around her and she turned on her side and put her arm across my chest.

"I really hate you have to go to that halfway house," she said. "Don't you have any family you could stay with?"

"My ex-wife divorced me while I was locked up, and I lost touch with my kid. She's grown now. She may help me, but I'm going to have to track her down. Getting out was a bit of a surprise. I forgot to get my shit together," I said.

"What about your mamma and daddy? Can't they put you up?"

"My mother died when I was incarcerated. She's been dead two years now. Daddy took off when I was a kid. Never heard from him again."

"At least he didn't beat on you every day like mine did. You ever think about looking for him?" she asked.

"I thought on it a lot. I've had the time to think here lately," I said. "Something must of happened to him. It's hard for me to believe he wouldn't say one word for all these years. He comes from rough people. Anything could've happened to him."

"What kind of man was he?" she asked.

"He was a preacher," I said.

"Oh, lord," she said.

"Oh, lord, is right."

She lit a cigarette and started back talking about her family. The world began to slip away and my eyelids grew heavy.

I woke up just after daylight and she was gone. A piece of paper, torn from the Gideon's Bible, with her name and number scrawled on it, lay by the phone. It read, "call me, Darleen."

WHEN I CHECKED out of the room, an old woman took
my room key, looked me up and down and said, "You
need a ride?"

Without letting me answer, she said, "Bus stop's
about half-a-mile down there," and pointed.

"Thanks," I said.

I pondered on how she knew I needed a ride, but then
I looked out into the parking lot of the motor court and
realized there were only a few cars in the lot. I stumbled
back out into the bright sunlight. It seemed to reflect off all
the broken things, and the white concrete. I began moving
with a deliberate pace towards the bus stop. The scenery
struck me again, the crumbling storefronts, cracked pavement, and trash.

I thought about what Darleen had asked me last
night, "Don't you have any family?" as I sat in the back of
the bus headed downtown. *Maybe if I could get back with
my ex-wife. Get in touch with my daughter. Stay out of bars.*
But I knew my ex-wife, Tammy, was done with me. She'd
had to be. She still had time to make a good life for herself.
She was still good-looking, and smart. I'd heard she'd
started working as a secretary for a big real-estate man. He
bought and built a lot of condos on Pensacola Beach and
Sand Destin. She'd been seeing him. I was glad she had
some financial stability, but I figured he was an asshole.

As the bus made its way downtown, we passed
familiar streets and landmarks, places from my past, stores

and churches of my youth and early family life. Maybe that's why I thought about Tammy. But I knew that reconciliation with her wasn't much of an option for me. I'd put it away in the back of my mind with all the other broken dreams and failures. But our daughter, Tina, that name meant hope. She was fourteen when I went in. I could find her. Get in touch. Reconnect. *If I could stay out of trouble.*

We passed through Brownsville, West Pensacola, through a tunnel of ancient live oaks covered in Spanish moss, hanging like grey stalactites. Then we passed my grandfather's old house. He died the year I went to prison. A few years after his death, the house had sold. I could just see the edge of the yard. Broken down cars and bits of trash lay scattered about. The side of the house looked dingy and the paint peeled back in spots. It barely looked like the same house. The thought that the house my grandfather built with his own hands 50 years ago, where all my aunts and uncles grew up, where I ran free through the yard with all my cousins, could fall apart in a few short years, filled me shame and guilt.

My mind whirled around in the past. I stared blankly out the window, not seeing anything. Then, right as the bus began to move again, I realized where I was. I pulled the cord, and hurried off in downtown Pensacola.

I found a pay phone on Palafox Street, and put in a call to Camp Eden, the place that promised me a safe haven until I could get back on my feet and join society again.

"Hello," a husky voice answered.

"Hello, Is Mr. Speed there?"

"Speaking," the voice said.

"Hello, Mr. Speed, this is Ronnie Harrison. Reverend Wilkins gave me your phone number. I'm looking to stay at Camp Eden?" I said in a questioning voice.

"Yes, Mr. Harrison, Reverend Wilkins told me you'd be coming. I thought you'd be here yesterday."

"Yes sir. I got sidetracked a day. I stayed in a motel."

"Well, where are you now? Do you have a way to get here?" he asked, almost pissed off.

"I'm in downtown Pensacola. Palafox and Cervantes. I don't have a ride," I replied.

"If you can be at that same spot at two this afternoon, I'll pick you up there."

"I'll be here."

"Mr. Harrison, I'm not sure what you did yesterday, and I don't want to know, but we don't allow drinking and drugs here at Camp Eden. So If I smell anything on you, or if you seem intoxicated in any way, I'm going to leave you there to fend for yourself."

"Yes sir. I understand."

"I'll see you at two."

I tapped out a cigarette, stuck it in my mouth, pulled out a pack of matches that said "Fire and Fiddle" on the back. I took two matches, struck them, and lit my cigarette. I took a long drag and exhaled through my mouth and nose. I slowly perused Cervantes Street, not really thinking where I should go, or anything else. In prison I'd learned to keep a calm, still presence that projected a peaceful demeanor, a stoic pose. But it was only a mask of calm. Underneath the mask it wasn't exactly calm. It was more like nothing. Maybe way in the back of myself, almost imperceptible, there was fear. Anger maybe. I wondered how bad Camp Eden would be. The man I spoke to on the phone sounded like a hard-ass. I guess he'd have to be to deal with folks he'd have to deal with.

I had some lunch at an old Greek place called George's, a place I'd been with my father as a kid. I ate red snapper with George's Special Greek Sauce. After a slice of key lime pie and a cup of coffee, I walked back to Palafox and Cervantes. I sat on a bench under the shade of a big magnolia tree on the edge of a small park. Without wanting to, I fell into a quick sleep. Not long enough to dream.

The man looked me straight in the eyes, a smile on his face like a drill sergeant's shit-eating grin. He was short, built like a stump, with a crew cut, hands on his hips, muscles bulging from his black Izod shirt, tight jeans, and red Asics Tiger tennis shoes.

"Mr. Harrison," he said.

"How'd you guess?"

"I know a convict when I see one."

"Ex-convict," I said.

"Let's hope you stay that way," he said with that smile. He patted me on the shoulder and his threatening demeanor loosened a bit. He motioned towards an old white Econoline van parked by the sidewalk. A sign on the driver's side door read "Eden Ministries, Gulf Breeze FL," and a handful of men sat in the bench seats in the back.

"I've got you in the front seat so we can talk on the way to the camp."

I followed him to the van, walking around the front to get in the passenger side door. I looked back at the men for just a second. I still had that prison mentality not to stare or look anyone in the eyes if you could help it. But these men looked serious. Tired. Quiet. A black man, two old white men, and one younger white kid.

"These guys got lucky and got some extra work today. Pretty lucky, right, men?" he looked to the men with that smile.

"Right?" he said again.

"Right."

"Yes, sir."

"Right."

"Right," said the driver. "See, a man can get extra work if he's got skills and gets his life right."

As he put the van in gear and headed down towards the Pensacola Bay Bridge, he looked sideways towards me. I caught it out of the corner of my eye, but kept looking straight ahead. This place wasn't going to be a pleasant retreat to help ex-cons cycle back into society. I could see that right away by the look of the men in back, and the look of Mr. Speed. The thing is, they won't parole

                                        Tyler Keith

someone unless you have a place to go, with family. I was thinking, now that I sat in the front seat of this grim van, maybe I should've tried harder to contact my daughter. She'd be 20 now. Maybe she'd have room for her old man. But for now it was going to be Camp Eden. Eden Ministries. That prison fear and paranoia still gripped my gut. *Good thing*, I thought. *I best be on my toes.*

"You see, Mr. Harrison, the more work you do, the less trouble you cause, the better you have it here at Eden Ministries. I heard from the Reverend Wilkins that you're not a troublemaker. He said you worked as much as you could in there. Stayed out of trouble. Is that right?" He looked me in the eyes again, his bullshit plan to intimidate me into telling the truth.

"Yeah," I said. I looked at him briefly but turned back and stared out the window. My jaw clenched. I'd done my time as quiet as I could. Work made the time go by quicker than just sitting in my cell.

"He also told me you drove a truck, and could work just about any vehicle — front-end loader, forklift. You did some of that work before. Is that right?"

"Yes, sir. I've used all of those. Not in six years, though."

"If you can keep it together, you'll be making better pay than most. You'll have plenty of work."

"What are the rules on coming and going?" I asked.

"Due to the class of people we have staying at Eden Ministries, we can't let everyone come and go as they please. It's just not safe or practical. We've found a few bad apples spoil the barrel for the rest. Understand? But you can go off campus with family as long as you schedule a meeting before hand. And after a time, with hard work and good behavior, you can leave weekends. But if you want to leave for good, and you're certainly welcome to leave anytime you feel like it, you can't come back. And we're obliged by law and our charter to inform your parole officer of your decision."

I cracked my window and smelled the salt air and

looked out at the Pensacola Bay. I pulled out a cigarette, lit it, and took a long drag, exhaling slowly. Mr. Speed smiled again, looking my way.

"Listen Mr. Harrison, let me you tell a little about Eden. I'm going to give you my testimony — tell you a little about myself. Maybe it will shed some light on the value of Eden and the good things it can do in your life. As you've probably guessed, I'm ex-military. I served my country proudly in Vietnam. Two tours. When I got back to the States I stayed in for a while. I liked the structure. But I had problems with people, some of the college-boy type officers that had no idea of what went on in the real world. Hadn't seen any combat. I went a little wild. Got out of the service. Got a little crazy. I'm not going into too much detail, but let's say there was violence involved. I did my time and then came to Eden when I got out. It was hard to adjust to the outside world at first, but Eden helped me find that stability I longed for. I needed. Like in the service. And they gave me work to do. So I decided to stick around and help if I could. Do my part to help men who wanted it, and maybe protect the good men from those men that might impede the progress of those who wanted to change and better their lives. The Lord gives me strength to do this, and help those who want it and deal with those men who seek to hamper his ministry."

He tried to make his smile merciful. But it wasn't mercy I saw in his eyes. He gave me a wink and turned up the radio, which blared a screaming preacher.

I looked back at the other men. They all stared out the window. I looked out and saw a giant sign that pointed towards Pensacola Beach and pictured an enormous sailfish in mid-jump with rainbows shooting out of it. It brought me back to my youth and family trips to Pensacola Beach, back when the sign was new. Back then the beach had an unspoiled quiet beauty. Just people with umbrellas and picnic baskets. No buildings. One pier that families crowded around with their blankets and men

                                    Tyler Keith

stood tightly packed together fishing for speckled trout, or snapper, and throwing nets to catch mullet. The memories just seemed like faded postcards to me now.

Then we passed that exit, heading to the outskirts of Gulf Breeze to the place called Eden. It felt like back in the days, when I was a boy swimming in the Gulf of Mexico, and the undertow would take you down and keep you there, and the current would carry you farther down the shore away from the safety of your family.

Camp Eden appeared to be an old 1950s motor lodge with a front building/office surrounded by small bungalows aligned in a semi-circle. Behind the bungalows stood tall pines, and behind that, the Bay could just be seen. I could smell the water and could almost see the knotty beach, covered with pine straw, and hear the steady splash of the waves. This place must have been a welcome sight for travelers once, back when Highway 98 served the desolate area of the Panhandle, hundreds of miles of sandy road with no place to stay.

It didn't seem so welcoming to me. Now the old motor court stood behind a tall barbed-wire fence. As we drove up to the gate, a young man walked up to the window of the van.

Speed rolled down the window and said, "Hey Jessie, everything okay today, son?"

"Yes sir, Sarge," Jessie said with an energetic voice.

I thought for a second the kid might've had a pistol on his belt. That seemed strange. "Thank you, son," Mr. Speed said looking at Jessie, then back at me. "People here call me 'Sarge,' I'm sure you can guess why."

Sarge parked the van in front of the office. We all got out and I stood and stretched and rolled my neck in a circle, taking in my first view of the property. Although the buildings looked a bit dated, the grounds were neatly manicured. All the cabins seemed to have a fresh coat of paint. A few men were working around the grounds.

Speed came around the front of the van and yelled

at two of the men walking towards the cabins. "Davis! Beasley!" A middle-aged black man with an athletic build, and an old white man with a slight hunch stopped and turned towards us. They walked back to Sarge.

"Yes, sir," said Beasley.

Davis just looked at him with a long weary look.

"This is your new roommate, Ronnie Harrison. He'll be coming over to the cabin shortly, so make sure it's clean and he's got an open bunk."

"Hey, Harrison," Davis said, giving my hand a hard squeeze and a short shake. "It's the cabin on the back corner there." He pointed.

"Call me Sam," said Beasley. He shook my hand and gave me a big smile. He sounded a bit like Walter Brennan in *Rio Bravo*.

"You smoke?" he asked.

"Yes, sir."

"Got a cigarette for an old man?"

"Sure, Sam." I took out the pack of cigarettes from my jacket pocket, thumped out a cigarette and handed it to the old man.

"I like this man already, Sarge." He took my cigarette, put it behind his ear, and walked towards the cabin in the corner of the complex. I swear he whistled "Dixie."

"Those are some of the best men in Eden, Harrison," Sarge said. "They've been here quite awhile and they know how things work. They don't cause trouble either. I can see you don't have anything with you. You'll need some toiletries, sheets, and some more work clothes, socks and underwear. Let's stop in the office and we'll get you taken care of and get you to your room as quick as we can."

I followed Sarge into the office. He sat down behind a desk and started rifling through the desk drawers, finally bringing up some papers and a manila envelope, and laying it on the neat desk.

"We need you to fill out some paperwork. Most of it is

                                        Tyler Keith

routine insurance, disclaimer stuff," He said, handing me some papers.

I flipped through them, signing by the x mark at the bottom of the pages. I paused at the last sheet, reading.

"Look, Harrison, it's very expensive to feed all these convicts here. We sign everyone up for food stamps. It defrays the cost," he said, his face blank, head cocked to the side. "Just sign it and move on."

"Ex-convicts," I said. Looking him in the eyes, I signed the papers. I was used to six years of being told what to do. I just did whatever people told me to. It bothered me. It built something up inside. Resentment. Anger. For the past few years I'd been clenching my jaw. Grinding my teeth. Even in my sleep. I didn't notice it at first. I saw a dentist in prison. He said my front teeth were being ground down. I chew gum. Smoke when I can. That seems to help. But I hadn't gotten to the point of telling people "no" yet.

"Alright, Harrison, let's get you outfitted. Looks like you need some work clothes. Socks. Skivvies. I bet you need a carton of cigarettes," he said this as he walked over to a cage that led into a closet. He looked at me over his back while he took a set of keys off of a hook on his pants like he was protecting a secret. He opened the cage door and walked in. I could've shut the door and locked him in right then. Maybe I should have. But I thought about my daughter. I knew no matter what I had to do, I was going to see her this week.

Sarge turned around with a stack of white t-shirts and handed them to me.

"What's your pants size, Harrison?"

"34-30."

He turned back around and pulled out two pair of worn but clean dark blue Dickies work pants and two long sleeve work shirts. Then a paper bag with some used but laundered white socks and white underwear. He took another key off his belt and opened an old school locker on the other side of the cage. The locker appeared jam packed with cigarette cartons. He pulled out a carton of Marlboro Reds and handed them to me. I looked at them for a second, almost shaking with joy. The first time I had my own carton in years. I felt an odd, almost overwhelming, sense of relief flow through my body. Sarge could see my expression.

"Listen, Harrison, you'd better keep an eye on that carton. You know you still live among thieves. And we don't investigate petty theft here at Eden. If your smokes come up missing, don't even mention it. It's better that way. If I were you, I'd keep all my valuables with me at all times. Take them to work. Put them under your pillow at night. You know what you're dealing with here. Some people can't help themselves. They do wrong as a matter of course. They're broken. Don't give them the chance to act like themselves."

"I can't believe I'm getting free cigarettes," I said to no one. "Jesus."

"These cigarettes aren't free. We'll take this stuff out of your work earnings each week."

"I'll bet I'm getting a real bargain on these smokes."

"Beats prison," he said.

I put the carton in the bag with my socks and underwear. As I turned to walk towards the door Sarge said, "We've got dinner at 6:30 sharp. If you're not there at 6:30, you don't eat. And be prepared to stay after and do some dishes. This food's not bad. Beats the hell out of prison food. But it makes a hell of a good mess. See you at 6:30."

As I turned to walk out the door, I gave Sarge a half salute.

I stood outside the office door for moment, lighting up, perusing the grounds. For a second it felt like a Vietnamese prison camp from some movie about POWs. I saw Jesse lurking around the big metal building, mindlessly swinging a police mag-light. Again, I thought about just walking out the front gate. But instead I made a beeline across the compound towards my cabin with the same confident strut I'd cultivated in the prison yard.

I stopped at my cabin door, labeled #9. I listened for a moment. Hearing nothing, I knocked a few times. Nothing. I opened the door slowly. Peeked my head in then entered with some caution. The old motel room had the appearance of a prison cell. Not the comfort a traveller would want after a long day on the road. The walls were painted grey. A grey window shade covered a small window. The floor was a slightly darker grey linoleum with white specks. The room did seem well scrubbed and smelled like Pine-Sol and sweat. Two bunk beds stood against each wall. On the right hand side the two men I'd met occupied the bunks, Davis on the bottom and Beasley on the top. Both men stared at me blankly. I stood still looking back for an awkward moment. Finally, right before things got too weird, Beasley said, "Pick a bunk, Harrison," pointing to the bunk across from them.

"I like the top. Reminds me of being in the Navy," said Beasley.

Before the old man could start into a story, Davis said, "Why don't you let the man get settled in for awhile before you start in with the Navy stories?" He paused, briefly, as Beasley muttered to himself.

"Me, I like the bottom bunk," Davis said. "You can store your shit under the bed. It's easier to keep track of."

"You should have no stuff in here to put under there," Beasley said to me.

I nodded to Beasley, then to Davis, and walked slowly to the bottom bunk. I sat on the edge of the bed for a second with the bag still in my arm. I set the bag on the floor by my left leg then slowly pushed it under my bed. I knocked three cigs out of my pack and offered each of them one. Beasley said, "Yes sir," and opened his two hands in a catching motion. I tossed one up to him and he caught it.

"I told you this guy was alright," he said, putting the smoke in his work shirt pocket.

I motioned in Davis' direction with one of the smokes. "Don't smoke."

"Mind if I do?" I said, sticking the cigarette in my mouth, about to light it.

"Be my guest."

I laughed at that line for a second, and then I lit up and took a big drag and laid back on my bed. Stared up at the wire bottom of the bunk above me. On the table between the two bunks there was a black plastic ashtray. I ashed. Took a few drags and closed my eyes. I could feel a heaviness on me, an immense fatigue. I stubbed my cigarette out. Closed my eyes again. Right before I crashed I heard, "Yep, reminds me of the Navy."

I woke up with a start, Beasley shaking me.

"Might want to get ready for dinner, Harrison," he said. "If you ain't there at 6:30, they shut the door. They're having spaghetti tonight. Every Saturday night. Not too bad. I imagine they got you on dishes tonight. Newcomer's job. If you find any bread left that's still good, bring me a piece."

He was looking down at me. Crowding me. I motioned him to back up, and when he did I sat up and turned and sat on the side of the bed. I thumped out a cigarette, lit it, and took a deep drag.

"I got time to take a shower?" I asked.

"Yeah, you got time," Beasley replied.

Davis said, "That's what really separates this place from prison. We've got our own shower. Shower as much as you want here. I take two a day, at least. You haven't done much today to need a shower though."

"Let's just say I had a hell of a night," I said. "And I took a shower this morning but I don't think it took."

"What'd you do last night, Harrison? Let's hear all the details. Was there ladies involved?" Beasley asked and looked at me with a sideways smile.

                                        Tyler Keith

"I'll tell you some other time."

I stood up and grabbed the white threadbare towel at the foot of my bed. Started towards the bathroom.

"That's not how it works here, Harrison. We share here. Bible says, 'Share and share alike.' "

"I don't remember that verse."

"Well, not in those exact words, but the same principle," Beasley said.

"Later," I said.

"I don't want to hear none of that shit," Davis murmured.

"You don't have to listen, J.D.," Beasley said.

"Later," I said over my shoulder as I stepped into the bathroom.

The dining hall was a large metal building with a polished concrete floor and green wooden picnic tables set up in three rows, nine altogether. A line of three fold-up tables at the back of the hall served as a buffet line. It smelled like freshly heated French bread, cooked ground beef, and the slight smell of bleach. The first table had Styrofoam plates and real silverware. The second table had one large vat of red meat sauce and one pot of spaghetti noodles and a pan of French bread next to it. The third table had Styrofoam cups of ice with a pitcher of Kool-Aid and an urn of unsweetened tea. My first thought was *these dishes won't be too bad to wash. No plates. Lots of forks, but no glasses.*

I got a big plate of spaghetti, a piece of bread, and some unsweetened tea, and sat at the table with Beasley and Davis. I started in with a big forkful of spaghetti but looked around just as I began to chew and noticed no one else had started eating. I slurped up a long piece of noodle and stopped eating. I noticed Sarge standing up at his table.

"Before we say the prayer and eat this food, I just want to introduce you to our new man. Ronnie Harrison, will you stand up for a second?" I stopped swallowing and half stood up. I gave a little wave without really looking around.

"Who wants to say the blessing?" he asked.

Jessie sat at the opposite end of the table across from Sarge. He raised his hand with enthusiasm.

"Eager boy," whispered Beasley.

"All right, Jessie," Sarge said.

Jessie stood up and clasped his hands together in front of his bowed head like a child and began his prayer. "Dear Jesus, thank you for the food we're about to receive. And thank you for these men that need your help and guidance. Protect us from evil men and our own wickedness. And thank you for Camp Eden and the shelter it provides. Forgive us our sins, Lord. Amen."

"Thank you, son," said Sarge.

I looked around at Davis and Beasley. They chuckled and shook their heads. I heard other men say "amen." Some prayed their own prayer a little longer with their heads bowed and then began to eat.

"All these men aren't ex-cons, huh," I asked Beasley.

"No. Some are just men with nowhere to go. Maybe they're just here for a few days. Some stay a good long while. Some of them might have done time years and years back."

"You can tell the ex-cons by the way they guard their plate and hold their fork," Davis said.

"You want your bread?" Beasley asked.

"Yeah, I do."

I looked around and figured there was about eighteen to twenty men here, all together. Maybe ten looked to be convicts. A few others might have been, but not in awhile. A few looked like old transients. You could tell by their faces. The wrinkles. There was something stoic and wind-blown about them. Their eyes seemed to have a clarity, not the suspicion and paranoia you could see in the eyes of the ex-cons.

Everyone ate quickly and headed outside to smoke.

This place probably made a fortune just off selling cigarettes to the men who stayed here. I swear every man but Davis smoked.

I took about an hour and a half to finish the dishes. Scrubbed the saucepot with a steel wool pad. Silverware just took time. I turned off the lights, pulled the door to, and stood outside the back door, smoking. A light shined in my face. I shielded my eyes with my left hand, looking towards the light.

"What are you doing out here?" a voice said. Jessie.

"Washing dishes. Smoking," I said.

"Well, it's getting late. Sarge likes everybody to be in by nine or so, or at least in front of their rooms. Are you done yet?"

"Yeah. I'm done."

I tossed my cigarette on the ground and stomped it out. I walked around the side of the mess hall, back towards the rooms along the fence line. Jessie followed me, shining the light on my back. This part of the complex paralleled a dead-end circle. A four-door maroon Chrysler New Yorker drove towards us then turned around at the end of the circle and came along next to us. The back window rolled down and cigarette smoke poured out but I couldn't see any faces in the back. I looked back at Jessie and he had his head down. He turned off the flashlight.

"Hey, Jessie," a voice from the back window said.

Jessie kept walking, maybe a little faster.

"Jessie, you can't stay up in there forever. Come on kid, you're like family to me. We'll forget everything. Let's just talk."

Jessie made a quick turn on the side of a cabin, headed through the yard to his room near the office.

"We'll be seeing you, Jessie," the man said.

I squinted to see if I could see in the back window.

"What the fuck are you looking at?" someone said from the back of the window.

The Chrysler sped off down the dead end street, turned onto 98 and sped off into the darkness.

In the room, Davis and Beasley laid on their beds. I tossed a piece of French bread I'd saved off a plate to Beasley.

"Damn, Harrison, you're too much."

"Dishwashing man," said Davis.

I laid down on my bunk and got out a cigarette. "I met a few of Jessie's old friends on the way back here just now."

"I seen them. Big red car?" Beasley asked.

"Yeah."

"Now you might see where Jessie's devotion comes from, and why he likes to keep close to Sarge," said Davis.

"Everybody's got their reasons for being in here," Beasley said. "And their reasons for staying."

"What about you, Beasley? How long you been here?" I asked.

"I've been here a number of years. I can't do too good out there. I get in trouble. I ain't got no family neither. Plus, you here long enough they let you out for a weekend. You can get some kicks. A bottle. Maybe a woman. Your own room. Then they let you come back on Monday. By Monday I'm ready. I just get in trouble the longer I'm out there."

"What about you, Davis? You've been here a good long while too."

"I've got my reasons. If I feel like you need to know, I'll tell you."

"I'm out of here as soon as I can get a place."

"Yeah, we'll see how long you got," Davis said with a quiet chuckle.

I kicked off my shoes, stubbed out my smoke and rolled over away from the other two, facing the wall. I was asleep right away, a red New Yorker cruising through my dreams.

3

SUNDAY MEANT CHURCH. Cornerstone Pentecostal Independent. We took two vans down 98 towards Navarre Beach and Fort Walton. Veered off towards Niceville, then turned off on a dirt road, lined with old live oaks covered in Spanish moss. Passed a few trailers and a few old dogtrot cabins along the way.

We arrived at a whitewashed A-frame church shaded by a big oak and a few large pines in the back of the building. We parked the vans on the grass on the left side of the church. Sarge got out, clutching a light brown duffle bag and a large Bible with bits of paper and bookmarks sticking out. Jessie got out of the front seat, carrying a small white New Testament. He wore a blue sports coat and a blue dress shirt buttoned up to the top. The other men just wore their regular clothes with their collars loose at the neck and old sports coats. We all got out and stood around between the vans. Sarge came around the side. He wore a green sports coat, white shirt, and red tie and tan Sansabelt slacks. He looked at us and shook his head.

"Try and stay awake at least," he said. "And we're staying after for dinner on the grounds. Be polite. Let everybody else eat first."

He turned and walked up the steps and opened the door, holding it so we could go in.

We sat in the last two rows on each side of the aisle. The church reminded me of the places my father preached in before he took off. Wooden churches. Hand-built pews.

Places that could've been built a hundred years ago. They had some sort of natural comfort … until the preaching started. The fear of God entered me in these churches. I could've been in this church before.

I remember hearing my father and other preachers screaming, "worms shall eat your flesh!" and "all the drops of sand down there on those beaches, they don't make up one fraction of eternity!" and "your flesh shall burn for eternity!" I do thank the Lord that after my dad left my mother gave up church for good, even though she replaced it with bad men and liquor. And my dad always comforted me with the knowledge that once you're saved, you're always saved. I never had any more involvement with church until prison. It helped me stay out of trouble and I knew it would help with the parole board. I guess it led me back here again.

People started filling up the rest of the pews, country people, women with their long skirts and long straight hair, clutching Bibles. I sat in the very last pew in the corner, next to Davis and Beasley. A few men came through a back door behind the pulpit. Speed got up with his duffle bag and went up to one of the men and shook hands, and disappeared out the back door with the man. He came back a few minutes later without the bag.

"Who was that guy?" I asked.

"That was Reverend James Milford. Excuse me, Doctor James Milford. Owns Camp Eden. Matter of fact, owns eight or ten camps in the South," said Davis.

"What the hell just happened?"

"The Lord's business. I wouldn't worry about it if I was you."

"Eight or ten camps?"

"Yeah. You never heard of him? Doctor James Milford. Got a radio station. A TV show. A big church in Pensacola. He shows up here every four or five weeks. But he's usually traveling. Evangelizing. He's got some pull in state politics here. Where you been? Oh yeah, prison."

                                                      Tyler Keith

He looked at me like I was stupid and I should shut up. So I did.

Behind the pulpit, there was a drum set, a guitar amp, bass amp, and a piano. A few young men wandered onto the stage and plugged in instruments. They started playing. Part tuning, part one chord vamp. A young man sitting on the first pew came onto the stage and up to the pulpit. The band stopped for a brief moment. Then the piano player, a young man with wild hair and a white shirt with a black leather vest, ran through a chord from left to right. Paused on the highest note. The snare cracked and the band, the young assistant, and a good part of the audience, broke into song.

I'm in the way/ the bright and shining way/I'm in the glory land way/and I'm telling the world/Jesus Christ died today/I'm in the glory land way

The congregation rose to their feet, clapping their hands, and a few stomped their feet. We all rose, too. I felt a shock in my veins for a moment, a rush of memory. Guilt, pleasure, remorse, and joy rolled up my spine like I'd touched a live wire. I drew myself back, away from those feelings. I watched it flow through others as we repeated the words over and over. When that song ended, it never really stopped. The hum of the electric band reverberated through the wooden building. The young assistant pastor let out a "Thank you, Jesus!" Eyes were closed. Hands were raised to the ceiling. Others did the same. Some repeated phrases. "Holy God! Holy God!" "Praise Him! Praise Him!" Some burst out with unknown tongues. "Hobotto! Somosetto! Mallasatta!"

A slight pause came over everything and the pastor started singing the old spiritual "I'll Fly Away."

The band jumped back in with wild abandon. The congregation began to clap and sing along.

The door in the back corner behind the pulpit swung open. The Reverend Doctor Milford appeared, bible in one hand, the other hand raised to the heavens. He sang with his eyes closed for a moment. He made his way to the pulpit. Put his hand on the pastor's shoulder. The pastor, smiling, handed him the microphone. The Reverend Doctor sang one last verse then motioned for the band to bring it down.

"I'm sanctified! I'm saved! Though I once wore the mark of Cain, I'm saved!"

"Amens" rang out. He placed his Bible on the pulpit, raising a hand towards the congregation. He began to recite the scripture from memory.

" 'And Adam knew Eve, his wife; and she conceived and bore Cain, and said, I have gotten a man from the Lord. And she bore his brother Abel. And Abel was a keeper of sheep, but Cain was a tiller of the ground.'

"We all know the story. God accepted Abel's sacrifice of his finest flock but did not take Cain's sacrifice of his crop. Abel's was a sacrifice of blood. The best of his flock. The Lord was pleased. Cain's was not accepted. This made Cain very mad!

" 'And Cain talked with Abel, his brother; and it came to pass, when they were in the field, that Cain rose up against Abel, his brother, and slew him! And the Lord said unto Cain, 'Where is Abel, thy brother?' and He said ' I know not: Am I my brother's keeper?' And He said, 'What hast thou done? the voice of thy brother cryeth from the ground … And now art though cursed from the earth, which hath opened her mouth to receive thy brother's blood from thy hand.' "

The preacher went on …

"The Lord put a curse on Cain, making him a 'fugitive and a vagabond' forced to wander the earth. Nothing Cain would plant would grow. He might have to beg to live. Traveling from place to place."

The Reverend Doctor paced the stage like a prize-fighter before the bell of the first round.

"No one wanted him because of what he had done!

                                        Tyler Keith

'And the Lord set a mark on Cain! The Lord set a mark on Cain!' Genesis 4:15, 'The Lord set a mark on Cain!' "

He seemed to point back to the last rows where the men from Eden sat.

" 'The Lord set a mark on Cain!' I myself once bore the mark! Because my heart wasn't pure. Because my heart wasn't pure. There was no blood in my offering to the Lord! My offering had no respect from God. God's rejection made me an angry young man. I was full of hate! I did wrong and wore the mark! I was given a number in prison! Shackles on my feet! I bore the mark. But I found the Lord there. The Lord Jesus Christ gave me a new covenant! I found the Lord Jesus there. The old mark of Cain was replaced with the love of Jesus! My new mark became the gifts of God! The gifts given on the Day of Pentecost! Acts 2:2, 'And suddenly there came a sound from heaven as of a rushing mighty wind, and it filled the house where they were sitting. And there appeared unto them cloven tongues like as fire, and it sat upon each of them!' "

The band still vamped. A few members of the congregation repeated phrases, "Holy God! Holy God!" Some shouted in tongues, "Bosssostta! Holy Massattaa!"

The Reverend Doctor blurted out, "Mallhalla! Candonaa quantoamoda!"

He continued: " 'And they were filled with the Holy Ghost, and began to speak with other tongues, as the Spirit gave them utterance!' Many of the non-believers there that day thought they were drunk. Bosos matte beso! Acts 2:17, 'And it shall come to pass in the last days, saith God, I will pour out my Spirit upon all flesh. And you your sons and daughters shall prophesy, and your young men shall see visions, and your old men shall dream dreams.'

"You can get rid of that mark of Cain! You can get a new mark! You can get a new mark! You can one day enter the new city. You can be sanctified and filled with the Holy Ghost. Acts 2:21, 'And it shall come to pass, that whosoever shall call on the name of the Lord shall be saved.'

Acts 2: 24-25, 'Whom God hath raised up having loosed the pains of death, because it was possible that he should be holden to it. For David speaketh concerning him, I foresaw the Lord always before my face, for he is on my right hand, that I should not be moved!' "

He stopped for a brief moment and just looked at the congregation, a blank mask across his face. Just looked everyone over good. He started singing a cappella:

I shall not be, I shall not be moved
like a tree planted by the waters
I shall not be moved.

The band began to thump quietly as he repeated that verse.

I shall not be, I shall not be moved
like a tree planted by the waters
I shall not be moved.

The aisles filled and some folk moved towards the front.

I'm on my way to glory land
I shall not be moved

Some sang. Some prayed. The Reverend Doctor motioned for the associate pastor to come to the stage. He passed the microphone and raised his hand in the air then towards the congregation. Slowly backing away towards the door. He seemed to mouth, "Thank you, Lord," eyes closed. Then he opened the door and then his eyes and hurried out into the daylight.

The rest of the congregation and the young pastor kept singing for a good ten to fifteen minutes. Some danced. The song seemed to naturally wind down until the pastor began a benediction, the band almost silent except for a few random guitar chords.

"Father God, we thank you for this church. We thank you for these people, this congregation. Lord God, bosotto masa setto, the church is not the wood and concrete that make up this building. It's the congregation that make a church. 'Whenever two or more of us are gathered

                                    Tyler Keith

together, there am I in the midst.' Thank you for these men who once wore the mark of Cain!"

Me and Davis looked at each other and almost cracked a smile. "Let them now wear your mark. Let them receive your gifts, Lord. And thank you for the ministry of Doctor Milford. All the great things he does here and all over the world. Keep us safe from Satan who 'walketh about like roaring lion, seeking whom he may devour.' Father God, thank you for the food we will eat and the hands that prepared it. Amen."

After the service we all wandered outside. Some of the ladies of the church had set up tables with red and blue checkered tablecloths, a long row of food stretched out before us. The smell of cornbread, fried chicken, field peas, mashed potatoes, mac and cheese, cabbage, chicken and dumplings, dinner rolls, and buttermilk biscuits floated through the air like a heavenly cloud. The desserts sat in a row: banana pudding, blackberry cobbler, pecan pie, and carrot cake. *Maybe there is a god,* I thought. This kind of food you couldn't think about in jail. It would drive you to do something stupid. Maybe hatch an escape plan.

We let everyone go first; then we stacked our plates until they almost gave way under the weight of food. We all sat down in metal folding chairs, or leaned up against the side of the church. Us men did wear the mark of Cain. The ex-con. The regular folks could see it on us. They were friendly enough. Some nodded recognition. A few spoke. Small talk. "Great Sermon. We're glad you're here." But most kept their distance. Didn't look us in the eye. The ex-con wears the mark of Cain. I guessed the Reverend Doctor was ex-con. Now he has a ministry to help his fellow Cains. The man could preach, I'll give him that. I had a natural skepticism about preachers, though. Most with money and power seemed full of shit. Many of those had great talents and gifts.

I walked over to Davis who was sitting under a large oak with an empty paper plate next to him.

"Where's the Reverend Doctor, I wonder?" I asked.

"Must've had more of the Lord's business somewhere else. 'Collections' we used to call it."

"Yeah, right. The man can preach a bit, I guess."

"He's got the spirit all right. But I could never get down with the tongues, myself. Kind of gives me the creeps. Like demonic or something."

I walked over to the aluminum trashcan and dumped my plate and empty iced tea cup in the can. Then I walked over to the van and had a smoke. The smoke almost made me believe in God.

On the ride back to Camp Eden, on Highway 98, we passed a billboard advertising "Dolphin Realty — Looking for a beach house or a new family home in Tiger Point subdivision? Call Dolphin Realty." It gave a number. I memorized it on first look. That's where my ex-wife worked. I'd be calling there tomorrow. Not for a beach house, but to get my daughter's number. I shall not be moved.

Later that night after dinner, finishing up the dishes, the radio played: *Slip Away, Slip Away.*

"That was the Clarence Carter classic 'Slip Away' from 1968. We've got a tropical storm just southeast of the Keys headed into the Gulf. Seems to be growing in power ..."

I turned off the radio above the sink. Turned off the lights and knocked a cigarette out of the pack. Pulled the back door to and locked it. I stood there smoking for a second. Jesse came around the corner and shined his light on me. Once he saw it was me, he cut off the light and quickly turned back towards the rooms, towards the lights. I looked down at the end of the circle. Saw a car barely in silhouette.

This guy is serious, I thought. *Wonder what the poor kid did. No doubt something stupid. The mark of Cain, 'stupidity.' This kid had the mark of Cain. Kept everybody from killing him. That New Yorker might be Jesse's final ride.*

I walked back towards my room. The wind lifted for a moment, a relief from the heat. I thought about that storm in the Gulf, maybe it'd be here by the end of the week. I repeated the phone number from the billboard in my head. I stood outside my room smoking another cigarette. Sarge strolled out of the office, saw me smoking in front of my room and made a beeline.

"Evening, Sarge."

"Harrison, you got all the dishes done already?"

"Sir, yes Sir."

"Well, get some sleep. You've got work tomorrow. It won't be easy."

"But it beats prison, huh Sarge?" I said sarcastically.

"You know what, Harrison? You've got an attitude problem. You just might need an attitude adjustment. And it just so happens I have years of experience in that field."

"Yeah, my attitude needs some work, sir. I bet you could help me," I paused and looked at him. "You've got a nice little set up here at Eden, don't you? You got Little Jessie and some of these boys helping you."

"I won't need any help with you though. You know Harrison, you've only got a small chance out here. Out of prison. At your age. What if you were in a wheel-chair? How much worse would it be? What if you were a cripple? Had a busted back. You would long for a place like Eden. But you'll be down on the corner wearing your army jacket, in your chair begging for change."

"Hey Sarge, here comes your friend, Jessie, now."

"Everything all right here, Sarge?" Jessie said. He could tell Sarge was agitated.

"Everything's fine, Jessie. Just explaining to Harrison here we've got a big work day tomorrow."

"In that case, I'm going to turn in. Night, Jessie. Night, Sarge." I saluted.

I went inside and laid down on my bunk. Davis and Beasley barely noticed. As I laid there I could hear the wind blow outside. Seemed to build. Clarence Carter played in my head. I turned on my side and faced the wall, finally drifting off to sleep.

4

I WOKE BEFORE daylight, and laid in bed thinking about
Tammy, my ex-wife, and the Saturday mornings when we
first lived together. I drove a truck back then. Sometimes
I'd come in late Friday night and crawl in bed with her.
She'd be laying on her side facing the wall. Sleeping in just
a t-shirt and cotton panties. I'd slide in beside her and slip
my arm around her. She'd tighten her arms around mine.
Her skin felt warm and smooth and she smelled clean and
fresh, just the smell of soap and some simple skin lotion.
My body fit right into hers. I would kiss her neck and she
would slowly turn her head, without opening her eyes,
and we would kiss. Her mouth was so warm and delicate.
   Tammy was the only woman I ever really loved. She
was so different from anyone I'd met. She was honest
and kind. But she had a toughness that let you know that
she'd be on your side no matter who was on the other.
She worked hard, too. I wanted to give her everything. I
wanted to be as good as her. That's why I'd had to let her
go when I went to prison. I knew she'd stand by me until
the end. But I didn't know how long that would be. What
would happen to me inside. What I'd become. It was the
hardest thing I've ever had to do, letting go of her. And I
knew she was still with me somewhere deep inside. She
always would be.
   Our daughter, Tina, had a lot of her mom in her, the
true-blue honesty, and the loyalty. She never lied as a
child. She was leery of strangers, always clinging to my

legs looking out at them. I hadn't talked to her in two-and-a-half years. I'd let her go too. Part of it was for their own good. Part of it was for mine. The aching loneliness and misery I felt, being separated from them, proved too much to bear. My bones ached when I laid down in my cell bunk at night. I saw guys go through the same thing. It oftentimes led to violence or reckless behavior. After a few years I'd had to get rid of the pictures and the letters. I'd tried to get rid of the memories but that was impossible. So I tucked them away in the deepest part of my mind. If they ever came up I'd shake them away, like shaking away the image of a car wreck that might pop into your mind for no reason.

It felt good to think about Tammy again now that I was on the outside. Maybe something could happen. Maybe she'd still want me even though I had nothing. No money. No jobs or prospects. I doubted if I was even me anymore. I'd put myself in suspended animation for so long I couldn't remember who I used to be. All I knew was, that when the prison doors opened it also opened up a flood of the deepest pent-up emotions that I'd hidden away for so long. But not in an organized way, just a chaotic flinging open of the doors setting everything loose: fear, anger, aggression, regret, anguish, revenge. I could barely keep these feelings in check.

As I laid on my bunk at Camp Eden, I started to cry. No noise, just tears, tears of rage and sadness. I heard Davis and Beasley starting to wake and get up. I reached over and grabbed a cigarette, first of the day. The freedom of being able to smoke whenever I wanted felt good. Beasley came out of the bathroom and Davis went in right after. Beasley put on some work pants and his work shirt and some brown work boots.

"You better get up, Harrison. Breakfast. You need to eat. It's going to be a long, shitty day. You know what they say, 'It's the most important meal.' "

I looked at him and finished my cigarette. Then

Tyler Keith

waited another minute, staring up at the bottom of the top bunk.

Powdered eggs, instant grits, toast and coffee, breakfast of champions. Felt good to have a full stomach. We met Sarge by the van to head to our job. I had no idea what we'd be doing or where we'd be going. I smoked outside the van while Beasley, Davis, and four other men got in the van. I thought the work couldn't be too hard if these four old guys were going to do it. These were men that were through with life but not ready for convalescence. Didn't have anything anyway. Just lived at Eden, waiting to not wake up one day. Maybe smoke a few more thousand cigarettes before then. They probably hoped to drift off to sleep and never wake up.

We drove from Gulf Breeze over the Bob Sykes Bridge to Pensacola, the day already hot under the cloudless blue sky. Traveling over that bridge always made my mind wander and my imagination spark. I thought about the possibility of getting my family back together. Have a home. Maybe back in Gulf Breeze. I laughed out loud, knowing how far fetched that was. Just on the other side of the bridge I saw another billboard advertising Dolphin Realty. "We'll swim circles around the competition," it read. I smiled a crooked smile and looked down at my feet.

We took Scenic Highway, with its view of the bay giving it its name. L & M Marble stood off the highway behind a chain-link fence, just a metal building with a two garage loading dock with the doors open and a smaller door with the logo on it. Sarge pulled up and kept the van running. Me, Davis, and Beasley got out. The other men stayed in the van. Sarge looked at me.

"Don't work too hard. See you at lunch."

"Where are they going?" I asked Davis.

"They got the cush gig at the Camp Eden Thrift store."

L & M was set up like a factory. Two rows with marble sinks lined up, an industrial buffer set up that could reach three sinks, the idea being you buff out any scratches or blemishes from the sink tops. You put some brown liquid on the blemish, then, with the buffer on full blast, you apply force and the blemish disappears. After Davis schooled me on the best method, which he said was constant pressure, a bell rang, like the half-time bell at a high school basketball game. Everybody started on their sinks.

I got the hang of it pretty quickly. Didn't seem too bad. The noise and the constant motion caused the rest of the world to go away, until my arm muscles began to burn, and the physical nature of the work set in. I stopped my buffer for a second and looked around. Davis worked at a furious pace. He'd already finished four or five sinks more than I had. And he wasn't slowing down. Beasley worked at the same pace as Davis. He looked up at me and gave me a big knowing smile, and got back to work.

At 10 a.m., the bell rang again. All the workers put down their buffers and headed to the break room. Some of the men bought sodas from the machine. A few had thermoses, and some had things stashed in an old fridge. I went straight to the pay phone. My arms were sore from the buffer as I picked up the phone. I wedged it between my head and shoulder. Although I remembered the number, I pulled out a sheet of paper out of my back pocket. It was quiet in the room. No one talked except for a mumbled sentence every now and then, too much work to do yet.

I took a deep breath and dialed the number. I was afraid.

"Hello, Dolphin Realty. This is Tammy. How can I help you?" Her voice …

"Tammy, it's Ronnie." I squeezed my eyes shut in fear and anticipation.

"Ronnie. Why?" She hesitated, her voice unsure. Anger? Bewilderment? "Why are you calling, Ronnie?"

It felt so good to hear her voice.

"I'm out. On Parole."

"How did you get paroled after only six years? I thought you had more time."

                                                  Tyler Keith

"Population explosion. They needed more room. I got lucky, Tammy."

"Yeah, lucky. You could've told me earlier. Called me or something."

"I know. I should've done a lot of things. I thought I had at least six more years before I even came up for parole. Probably another two before I even had a chance. I couldn't keep you on a chain that long. It wasn't fair to you and Tina."

"Well Tina didn't understand your plan. She thought you abandoned her. She went through hell. She needed you."

"Can I get her number? I want to see her now. Explain things to her."

"Things have changed, Ronnie. Did you know you're a grandfather? You have a granddaughter. Her name is Ruby."

I paused for a long time.

"I need her number, Tammy."

"I'll give you her number, but she's married now. Did you even know that?"

"Please, just give me her number."

"He's a Navy guy. He's not the most pleasant man. She's usually home without him from 3:30 to 5. I'd try calling her then."

She gave me the number and we sat in silence for a second.

"What about you? Can I see you? I'm out. I'm staying at this Christian camp, Camp Eden. I'm working already …" She cut me off.

"Ronnie, I'm married. I got remarried about four months ago. You wanted me to move on and I did."

We sat in silence again. Before I could speak the whistle blew. The men started towards their posts. I searched for words. She'd heard the whistle.

"Look Ronnie, I'm glad you're out. Really I am. I'm at work now too. You can't call me anymore. Try calling Tina, but don't get your hopes up. Now I've really got to go. Goodbye, Ronnie."

She hung up. I stood with the phone in my hand. Just staring at the wall.

"Time to get back to it, Harrison," Beasley said. "Don't worry, the lunch bell will ring before you know it."

I wanted to smash the receiver, and sit down and cry. Just leave the job site. Wander off. But I just went back to my station and started working, in shock. The crazy realization came into my head as I buffed out a blemish on a piece of pink marble. *I'm a grandfather.* I couldn't help grinning. I pushed the buffer over the marble, annihilating the bad spot in the pink sink. I worked at a furious pace, almost keeping up with Davis and Beasley. Kept waiting for the whistle to blow. I wanted to get back to Eden and call Tina.

Four o'clock came. Sarge came back around eventually and went into the office with the foreman. I could see them together behind the glass. The foreman handed him an envelope. Maybe that was our pay. Who knows? We kept working until about 5:30. Just when I was about to put down the damn buffer and walk out to the highway, the whistle blew.

5

ON THE RIDE back, staring out at the bay, my thoughts turned from Tina back to Tammy. Hearing her voice again brought back so many memories — our wedding, our little honeymoon, and our daughter's birth.

After Tammy got pregnant, we decided to get married. Not really a shotgun wedding because her father seemed pretty indifferent. Seemed like the right thing to do. It was October 1966. I'd known her all my life. We went to grade school together. And we weren't the popular kids, just the quiet kids on the outside, sort of invisible. Never really belonged to any group. Feels like I just looked over at one of these dances and there she was. Then we were together. I guessed I loved her. Never really learned what that meant until the prison doors closed on me. Separation. That's when you know for sure. But by the time you know for sure it's too late.

There wasn't going to be a fancy wedding. We didn't have any money. Didn't have any common friends. She had some old girlfriends from school and childhood. I had a few beer-drinking buddies. Under the circumstances, no need to bring them into it. We decided to go to the justice of the peace. Tammy did have one stipulation: she wanted to get married on the beach. Navarre Beach. Although she wasn't one of these beach babes, she did have a deep love for the sand and sea. She seemed so at home there. She seemed to fit as a natural part of the landscape.

I wore black jeans, white snap western shirt, black

leather western cut sports coat, and a turquoise and silver bolo tie that belonged to my dad. I'd found it in a utility drawer after he left. Kept it in my box of things in a closet. Thinking on it now, I guess the box of odds and ends were the few things that had belonged to him: the tie, the picture of us fishing, an old Camillus knife, black rubber change purse, a rusted .22 pistol with a cracked pearl handle. Random stuff. The bolo tie was the nicest thing I owned. My hair was combed back in a medium pompadour.

Tammy wore a simple white silk dress with short sleeves and a bow on the front. Maybe frilly shoulders? She looked so natural and beautiful. It was a cloudy October morning. It was just her dad and mom, and my mother. Tammy took off her heels and we walked down the sand to the water. It was a quick service. Afterwards my mother hugged me and whispered in my ear, "Don't be like your father."

"I won't," I lied.

Her father shook my hand and slipped me a fifty-dollar bill.

"You'd better take care of my little girl," he said. Barely cracked a smile. "Here's a little something for your honeymoon."

I stuck the bill in my pocket and said, "I'll spend it all on her, Walter."

I really didn't care for the man. He was generally concerned with his next drink, like my mother.

We stood around the parking lot for a few minutes. I held Tammy around the waist. We kissed a few times, both of us smiling. I had a thought flash through my head: *You're an adult now, buddy,* which made me feel a little shaky.

For our honeymoon, we decided to just drive south. See some Florida. Not make too many plans. Mess around for three days then drive back from wherever we ended up. We did have our first destination in mind, Wakulla Springs. It had an old hotel built in the '20s. At the time I had a beat up 1958 Ford F100 truck, black with white front

Tyler Keith

grill. I'd thrown some camping gear in the back. Tammy had a white Samsonite suitcase and a matching make-up case. I had a green canvas duffle bag with some socks, underwear, a t- shirt, and cut-off jeans for swimming.

We took 98 to FL-293 and then 20 almost all the way there. The closer we got to Wakulla the more the landscape turned mysterious, jungle-like, a thick smell of black, wet dirt hung in the air. The foliage seemed to be a darker green than normal. The road became a tunnel of ancient oaks draped with Spanish moss. Out of the tunnel of trees the lodge appeared, Spanish style with a red stucco roof. Two protruding buildings jutted out from the main building.

The lobby looked like something out of a 1920s dream: old oriental rugs on the floor, tall ceilings with dusty crystal chandeliers, dark wood furniture. Seemed to me this would've been the perfect place for a gangster to hide out, like something out of an old movie. *Must've been paid for in whisky,* I thought. Wakulla Springs led out to the Apalachee Bay and out to the Gulf. Easy way to get the whisky out. The main attraction in the lobby was an eleven foot stuffed alligator. I guess it was there to let you know what's out there in all that beautiful clear water. A sign around its neck read "Old Joe."

We came in still dressed in our wedding clothes. Got a room on the second floor. Elevator was the old kind. You pulled the gate back, and pulled the lever. We got to our room and I carried her through the door and laid her on the bed. Closed the door. Took off my bolo tie, my jacket and shirt, and laid down beside her. We kissed. Made love. The afternoon light came through the window onto the old bed. We held each other for a while, quiet.

After we slept, we walked out back to the spring for a swim. The spring had a large roped off area for swimming. Signs warned, "Whatever you do, do not swim outside the ropes." There was a large diving platform with three levels: one about six-feet, one about fifteen, and one at about thirty. We dove from the six-foot platform, the water

so clear you could see all the forty feet to the bottom.
We dove off the fifteen-foot, but Tammy only did once.
I decided to try the tallest level and climbed to the top.
I looked out over the vast jungle. Looked down into the
clear water. I felt dizzy. I could see Tammy down below in
the water, waving her hands. "Come on, Ronnie, jump!"
I stepped away from the edge for a moment. Behind me
someone was waiting on the ladder. I couldn't turn back.
Without thinking more about it, I ran off the end swinging
my arms and legs. I heard a scream and realized it was me.
Didn't come near the bottom. Swam over to Tammy. We
embraced, doggy paddling. We kissed, struggling to keep
our heads above water. She looked so young, her face clear
and white with light brown freckles, her eyes, a crystal
green, reflecting the rest of the world, the green trees and
the water. That moment was the closest I ever felt to her.
Her legs wrapped around my waist as I kicked like crazy
to keep us afloat. I think she saw me as a strong man who
could take care of her. Keep her safe. Provide. That's what
I wanted to be for her too. Just then I felt like I could.

That night we had dinner at the lodge: fried catfish,
fried alligator tail, hushpuppies, slaw, grits. We slept late
the next morning. Went for a quick swim and then headed
to our next destination. We looked at the map as we drove
and picked out Homosassa Springs for an afternoon
jungle-boat ride to see some manatees and gators, then on
to Cedar Key for dinner. Maybe find a campsite.

We packed a cooler with some sandwiches, and
a few Pepsis for her. I packed a few beers. We ate and
drank as we traveled further south. Although we'd been
together for a while, I didn't know much about her or her
family. It's funny, thinking back on it now, how little we
knew each other. We were both quiet types. She only said
necessary things. Not much for gossip or idle chatter. I
think that's what I liked most about her. On the car ride
to Homosassa Springs, she told me about her father. He
owned a hardware store in Milton. He worked until five,

                                    Tyler Keith

came home and started drinking. He was a quiet drunk, just mostly blissful but out of it. Never beat the wife or kids. Just listen to baseball on the radio and have drinks every day. Her mother was a homemaker. She liked a drink, too. Tammy seemed to be so well adjusted. She hardly drank, at least not in a way that damages a person. She just wasn't interested. Not like I was.

After high school, she took some courses at Pensacola Junior College, secretary training. That's when she got pregnant. But she made sure she finished. After Tina started kindergarten, she worked steady. She's like no one I've known. During my trial, she came to court every day. Sat right behind me, dressed in a nice business suit like she wore to work. But she let me know I was a fool. Let me know it hurt her to stand by me. She told me as much. But she said she'd made a vow and intended to keep it. She probably would've waited for me forever. She's loyal. But when I told her to forget about me, she was mad enough to do it.

That afternoon we took the jungle cruise on the glass bottom boats at Homosassa Springs. Saw the gentle, cow-like manatees and giant gators. Every few years some kid or fisherman will disappear off a pier and not be seen again. Just a shoe or a tackle box left behind.

That night we ate dinner at a restaurant at the end of the pier on the Gulf in Cedar Key. Cedar Key is a sleepy little village. A green paradise. Just a quiet little town. Maybe a good place to disappear. We ate raw oysters, steamed blue crab legs, fried speckled trout, a salad, and rice and gravy. The lights on the pier and the blinking red lights on the buoy reflected off the water. The smell of the seafood and the salty breeze blew in on the deck. I got a little drunk on beer and we decided to get a room instead of camping. We had that money from her dad. We stayed at the Breezewood Acres Motel. The rooms were clean and they had a pool. That night, we laid together in bed.

Looked at the map. We decided to get up early and drive to Sanibel Island, famous for its beautiful shell beaches.

Tammy fell asleep early. I laid next to her, drinking my last beer. "You're the Only World I Know" by Sonny James played softly on the Silvertone radio next to the bed. Being away from home with Tammy, I imagined a new life for us. Away from the people we knew. The history. I felt so free just then.

"We should start over down here. Get shed of all those people," I mumbled.

She put her hand on my leg but didn't open her eyes. There were jobs down here. Opportunities. But I didn't know how to do it. I just let things happen to me. Just did things without making plans.

Marty Robbins' "Ribbon of Darkness" played on the radio. I smoked one more cigarette and finished the last of my beer. As I slipped off, I heard Marty whistle in the Florida night.

We woke up early. Took a quick swim in the pool, and then hit the highway south towards Naples and Sanibel Island. I was quiet for the first part of the ride. Tammy talked the most I'd ever heard her. I wanted to ask her about moving. But she talked about friends, her classes, where she'd send the kids to school, her folks. I knew she was tied to home. I kept quiet, a mistake, as it turned out, and maybe in some ways, the worst mistake. Cowardice. I think about what could've been if we'd left.

Later, as we laid on the beach, my mind drifted back home. I shifted my mind back to the way we normally lived and forgot about the idea of moving south. A kind of inertia set in. *Just let it all happen.* I did ...

Now that Tammy was remarried, I knew she was gone forever. In prison, even though I'd known we weren't together, and I'd even told her to move on, I didn't believe it in the back of my mind. Back there, she said she'd always love me. *How can you ever stop loving someone?* I thought. But now I knew she had moved on.

                                        Tyler Keith

Riding back to Camp Eden, I finally knew it was over. She'd done what I'd told her to. But talking to her on the phone, I'd wanted to protest and say, "Remember, I'll never love anyone else." I smiled at that thought. Smiled at what I knew she'd say to that. "*Now* you say that? Go to hell, Ronnie." Then I was angry again. The old feelings were coming up. The self-hatred. I didn't know how to keep the feelings down. *Maybe I still have Tina*, I thought.

When things were new, there was the chance for happiness. That day on Sanibel Island, we laid on the beach. Swam some. Held each other. Laid in the sun some more. After awhile, Tammy said, "This is one of the most beautiful beaches I've ever seen. But you know what? It's just not very comfortable. All these damn shells."

"Damn, I love you," I said.

"I love you too, Ronnie."

We looked at each other and laughed.

"You want to get out of here?" she asked.

"Yes, I do."

We stayed in a new Holiday Inn that night. Got up early and headed back. As we pulled out of town, we tried to sing along with Dell Reeves on his song, "Girl on the Billboard," with the windows of the Ford rolled down, the wind blowing through our hair.

BACK AT EDEN, I went directly to the pay phone by Sarge's office. I hoped Tina would answer, but it was after six by now. Maybe the husband wouldn't answer.

"Hello," a male voice answered, kind of husky but in a put-on way, like someone trying to have a deep voice.

"Hello, can I speak to Tina?"

"That depends. Who is this?"

"It's Ronnie Harrison."

Not sure why I said my name. I guess I was nervous. Wanted to assert my identity.

There was a long pause on his end. Then I heard him yell, "Tina." After a second, I heard her voice. I think I detected happiness, but maybe it was awkward surprise. She wasn't expecting to hear from me. Maybe her mom called her.

"Hello?" she said.

"Hey Tina, it's your dad."

I paused. She paused.

"I'm out now."

Silence.

"How are you?" I asked in a pathetic way. It just came out. Everything I'd planned to say slipped away.

"Daddy. You're alive?" she asked without wanting an answer.

"Yeah. I'm sorry I lost touch," I said. I wanted to say more. But I didn't say anything.

There was another long pause.

"I needed you, daddy," Tina said. "A lot of bad things happened. I wrote you letters but they all came back."

She paused again.

"I forgave you, though," she said. "I knew you were suffering. I knew my trouble would only make things worse for you. So I stopped writing. And I found David. He saved me. He's a good man. He's a Navy man. He's very protective, but he loves me. And we have a daughter. Her name is Ruby. You're a grandfather."

She stopped for a minute. I wiped away a couple of tears.

"I want to see you, Tina. I want to see my granddaughter. I'm down at Camp Eden off 98. You're in Gulf Breeze, right?"

"Yes sir. We want to see you too, Daddy. I missed you so much. I worried about you every day. We can come Wednesday after six. Will that be okay?"

"Yeah, baby. That'll be great. I've missed you too. More than you'll ever know."

"I love you, Daddy. I'll see you Wednesday."

She hung up. I stood with the phone in my hand. I felt a second of joy. I had something to look forward to now.

As I smoked a cigarette on the front porch, I looked in the office window and noticed Sarge putting cash from the envelope and a ledger in a small green safe behind him. When he turned around, I wasn't sure if he saw me but I tried to play it off, like I didn't see nothing. Sarge came out.

"Harrison, can I see you in my office?"

I came in the office and sat in a folding metal chair in front of his desk. Sarge sat behind his desk. I thought he might be trying to find a way to explain what he was doing. He leaned back in his chair. Bouncing. Smiling at me.

"You know Harrison, I'm very close with most of these cons, I mean ex-cons, parole officers. Real close."

He looked at me for a response. I just stared back without smiling.

"It turns out you have the same officer as some of the other men. Beasley and Davis."

His smile faded. He leaned forward. I didn't know if this was a veiled threat or just his style.

"Mrs. Blankenship. She'll be coming by tomorrow. The place you worked today. You can have a little meeting there."

I didn't respond. Just met his eyes.

"From the reports I got today, you worked your ass off." He paused again. "I don't really like you, Harrison. I think you might've noticed. But if you work hard and don't stir shit up, you won't have any problems with me. See what I mean? It's easy. You work hard and stay out of trouble. No problem. Like I said, I'm real close friends with Mrs. Blankenship."

There was another pause.

"You understand, right Harrison?"

I wanted to reach up and slap his face, but I thought about Tammy.

"Yes, sir. My daughter's coming to see me Wednesday at six."

"Well, you need to check with me before you make appointments with family." He didn't look at me. Just started to do some paperwork. I raised up with a quick rage, into almost a squared off fighting stance.

He quickly looked at me, and maybe he understood this wouldn't be a place to make a point or assert his authority.

"Wednesday will be fine. Just ask next time." He didn't look at me again. I stared down at him.

"You can go now."

I stood outside my room, leaning against the doorway, smoking. It started to rain lightly. The wind picked up. You could smell the salt water from the bay. I stared at the office thinking about things: about the envelopes of money, the work, the safe, my daughter, Tammy, my ex-wife. Just random thoughts. Pieces of questions.

Mumbled things to myself. "How much money's he got in there?"

"What's this husband like?"

"Probably an asshole," I answered myself.

Car headlights appeared at the gate. Nobody was there. Jessie must've gone inside out of the rain. The headlights pointed straight ahead. I couldn't see the make of the car or anyone inside. A hulking, round figure got out of the passenger side door and walked up to the gate, a little hunched over like trying to keep dry although he had no jacket or umbrella. The rain came down a little harder. The car honked three times and backed away, and pulled off down 98.

Sarge came out of the office and unlocked the gate. Both men hurried to the office. I couldn't see who the man was. Camp Eden seemed more like prison every day. New people coming in you didn't want to see. Inside the room the radio DJ played songs for a rainy day. The Cascades sang about the rhythm of the rain and about being a fool.

7

IN THE MORNING, the usual crew met by the Econoline, smoking cigarettes. Sarge and the man I'd seen the night before came out of the office laughing. They walked up to the van where the men stood by the sliding door.

"Some of you men might remember Travis Campbell," Sarge said and nodded towards Beasley and Davis.

"Campbell," Beasley said, tipping his ball cap. Davis gave him an almost invisible nod.

He was a guy I knew only by reputation. After I went to prison, Travis Campbell showed up in Holmes County. I'd heard about him. He was away in prison when I worked down there. Came out as I was going in. He had a reputation for violence. Big personality. Liked to party. Unpredictable. He was close to my uncle. I heard stories about his doings when I was inside, but I stopped listening to stories about Holmes County after a few years in. When what I'd done set in. I thought about what went down the day I got busted. Who got hurt. Then I decided to scratch everything from my mind.

Everything I was. Just keep my family, Tammy and Tina, and my mom. Then, when I thought I might not make it out, I let them go too.

But I remembered the name, Travis Campbell. *Why was he here?*

Campbell had a goofy grin on his fat face. He had a ruddy complexion, with light brown hair parted to the side, down to his eyebrows.

"This is a new man here," Sarge pointed to me. "Ronnie Harrison. I understand you might know some of his people from over in Holmes County." Sarge looked at me with something like respect and hatred. Maybe he realized something he hadn't known about me before, who my uncle was. He was still not that impressed.

Travis Campbell stepped towards me, slung his head sideways to get the hair out of his eyes, almost like an uncontrollable twitch, stuck out his hand. Looked me in the eye, and said, "Travis Campbell. Glad to know you, Ronnie. I believe I did some work for your Uncle Albert over in Holmes County for a number of years."

He held his hand out for about five seconds. Then I shook it. He smiled and squeezed my hand like a vice grip. I did the same.

"Hey. I believe I've heard of you," was all I said. I just took him in a bit. Wondered what he was doing here.

"Your uncle's quite a hard man. Not the sentimental type for sure. All the same, I bet he'd like to talk to you."

"Maybe I'll send him a post card from Camp Eden," I said with a little laugh. I couldn't help it. The thought of sending my Uncle a postcard forced a laugh.

Travis gave a chuckle too.

"That would be funny," he said, adding, "Yeah, he don't have much of a sense of humor."

The morning sun beat down on us with an intense heat. But on the edge of the horizon, from the southwest, silver and grey clouds gathered. One long thunder roll pierced the awkward silence. A swift breeze blew through the tall pines for a moment. Then it was still again. I could smell the ocean and hear the cicadas hum.

"All right, ladies, let's go to work," yelled Sarge, like he enjoyed it. Like we were his recruits.

Back at the marble factory, back with the soft metallic hum of the buffers, and the blurred vision of the safety glasses, I sunk back into my mind. My thoughts. *Darleen*. She was already a fuzzy memory. I couldn't

                                    Tyler Keith

bring up a clear image of her face, just an image in hazy light, like looking into that dirty hotel room from the outside. Steam fogged the glass. I could see our two bodies entwined. I remember the smell of the room: some floral perfume, sweat and cigarettes. I could almost taste the booze on her lips. I felt a flash of shame for being too drunk and guilt for being there at all. More than anything, I felt a crushing loneliness. I wanted to touch her again. Her phone number ran through my brain as I buffed out the blemishes on the pink marble. I caught myself, and remembered where I was and what I was doing. I looked around the factory floor to see if anybody noticed my thoughts somehow.

I caught Campbell's eye. He was standing up straight with his buffer resting on the sink in front of him. He gave me a wry smile and a slight shrug. We just looked at each other for an awkward moment. Then the factory air horn blew signaling the morning break.

I got coffee and sat on the end of the long bench next to Beasley and Davis. We looked at each other then stared down at our coffee.

"I've had worse coffee," said Beasley.

"I've had better," said Davis.

"Some of the coffee inside was so bad," Beasley started on like a whole story was about to come out.

"Let's not talk about prison today," Davis said without looking up from his coffee.

"Shit, there goes half my life story, J.D.," Beasley replied.

Campbell made himself a cup of coffee; added nothing; looked our way and headed towards us.

"Here comes your friend," Davis said, looking towards Campbell. He gulped down his coffee and headed towards the bathroom. He mumbled something to Campbell as he brushed by him. Campbell crowed, raising his coffee cup high in the air so he wouldn't spill it. He made a clown face towards me and Beasley.

"He must be giving his morning offering to the porcelain gods," he said as he sat down across from me.

"He's a regular guy, alright," chuckled Beasley.

Campbell half smiled at Beasley and looked him in the eye.

"I reckon I am too."

Beasley got up and walked out of the breakroom into the factory floor where the bathrooms were.

"Looks like it's just me and you, Hoss," Campbell looked at me with that grin.

"Wonderful," I said glancing at his face and then back to my coffee.

"Your uncle said you were a man of few words."

I just looked at him again, and didn't say anything.

"You like this kind of work?" he asked.

"I don't mind it too much. It lets a man think. Don't have to talk to nobody."

"Shit, I can't think with all that noise and clanging going on. And this goddamn heat. Sweating like a fucking pig. I guess I could lose a few pounds."

He paused. I didn't say anything. Just thought I should probably steer clear of this guy. I knew he was dangerous. Trouble. I knew he was still in touch with my uncle Albert, and that I didn't want to be.

"I know a place where you can find some other kind of work," he said.

I looked up from my coffee.

"I'll be back to work over there real soon," he said.

"I don't feel like I've got to tell you anything, but I'm gonna say this: I'm getting my shit straight and I'm staying the hell out of Holmes County."

"Hey, I hear ya. I wish you the best. But your uncle wants to talk to you. See if you need some money. Or anything."

I just stared at him. Took a long sip of my coffee. The bullhorn blew a long piercing scream.

During the next two hours, I thought about what I

                                        Tyler Keith

wanted to happen next in my life. I knew if I stayed in Eden too long, there'd be trouble. Especially with this character Travis Campbell. He was the door back to my old life in Holmes County. I didn't want to go back there. It was an option that I'd told myself I'd never consider, but there it was … the thought. It was in my head now. It wasn't such a bad life in many ways. Having a pocket full of money always felt good. Seeing the wife in new clothes. A new Easter outfit with white patent leather shoes for the kid. A shiny bike on Christmas morning. A house in Gulf Breeze bought and paid for, six miles from Pensacola Beach. I was gone a lot … then I was gone for six years.

But I'd seen guys coming into prison the last few years I was in with extra long sentences. Heard about the so-called "war on drugs." If I got busted while I was on parole I'd have to do my whole twenty years, plus whatever else they'd give me. Might be a death sentence for a man in his forties. No. I had to keep straight. Tina was my shot. If she put me up, I could work steady, and just be a grandfather.

My mind wandered back to my own childhood, before my dad disappeared. He took me out fishing on our neighbor's boat. We went out to the pass where the Pensacola Bay and the Gulf of Mexico meet. We had a rough time getting out there. It was like a washing machine. I puked a few times over the rail into the dark water. I wanted to go back. I whined and cried.

My dad knelt down close to me and whispered, "Listen, son, we're not going back 'til after daylight. You can either cry and moan or you can catch some fish. It's your choice."

That's all he said.

The redfish were running in the pass. My dad and the neighbor had already pulled in a few. They lay still breathing in the well of the boat. Big ones, thirty- to forty-pounders. Then I got mine. The rod doubled over and I almost pitched down into the pass. Both the other men helped me straighten up and reel in a few feet of line. I panicked but the adrenaline kept me from showing it. Time stood still. I worked the fish up to the boat then it ran back out. My little arm muscles burned. The two hours it took to get the fish in seemed like weeks. Seeing the thirty-five-pound red-and-silver creature flopping inside the boat sent a calmness over me. The calmness of pride. My father and the neighbor patted me on the back in congratulations. Time slowed then too as the fish flopped up and down for its last few times.

When we got home in the daylight and displayed the fish on the concrete driveway, we took a picture. I felt close to my dad that day. That moment. I had that picture in my room for years after he left. When I looked at it, I could almost hear the background noises, my mom and the neighbors laughing and congratulating me. Smell the salt water. Some point, in my teen years, I put the picture away in my closet with my old baseball glove and my skates.

I kept working. About 11:45 a woman came into the place with Sarge. White lady in a pants suit. Late thirties. Then I remembered Sarge saying the parole officer would be here today. Sarge wore a white short sleeve shirt and a brown tie and brown polyester slacks. He looked almost respectable. He put a hand on her back and pointed her in the direction of the break room. He opened the door for her. She went inside with her briefcase and sat on one of the benches.

"Harrison!" Sarge yelled, waving me over.

I took off my safety goggles and walked over to him.

"Your parole officer is here to talk to you. Why don't you take off that apron, go to the john and clean up, then get in there."

"All right, Sarge," I said with a fake smile. I washed my hands and face. Looked myself in the mirror. Be friendly and cool. This woman can help you … or send you back to prison.

I walked into the break room and sat down in front

of the lady. She had a folder out and open. She read some pages, flipped through, glasses on the end of her nose.

"Ronald Raymond Harrison," she said in a loud serious tone.

"Yes, ma'am," I said, trying to half-smile.

She just looked at me for a second over her glasses.

"I'm Mrs. Blankenship," she said. "You have a nice clean prison record, almost no trouble after the first two years. That's a good sign. I've had a good report from Sarge here. Although he said you arrived a day late. What was that about, Mr. Harrison?"

She looked up at me.

"Well, Mrs. Blankenship, I missed my ride downtown so I just got a room for the night. Just slept."

"Okay, Mr. Harrison. I'm going to let that slide. During this period, the State needs to know your whereabouts at all times. If you have a job, we need to know where and when you work. Of course, you're not allowed in bars or even allowed to consume alcoholic beverages. This is why Camp Eden is a good place for you right now. It's a good Christian environment and it keeps you out of trouble."

I wanted to laugh out loud. But I just smiled and gave a silent chuckle.

"Is something funny, Mr. Harrison?" she asked.

"Oh, no ma'am. I love it at Camp Eden."

I stopped smiling.

"It's helped a lot of men like you in the past. If you give a man a safe place to live, a job, and a place to worship, great things can happen. I'm very close friends with the Reverend. I work with many of the men who come through Eden. But, of course, Mr. Harrison, there's only so much we can do if the man doesn't want to make things right."

"Believe me, Mrs. Blankenship, I'm ready. I feel I'm ready now. I think I could be on my own now. What's needed for me to do that? To leave Camp Eden?" I asked with a sincere face.

"Mr. Harrison, the only way, at this point, to be able to leave Camp Eden is with a direct family member. Do you have anyone like that?"

"Yes, ma'am. I have a grown daughter. Tina."

"If she can take you in, and has a stable home, we will consider it. But if you want my advice, Mr. Harrison, you should consider staying at Camp Eden for a while. It certainly would be a comfort to me as your parole officer," she said, writing in my file. "I need you to sign these few papers, and then would you call in the next man? A Mr. Travis Campbell."

"Yes, ma'am."

I scrawled my name next to the x on a couple of pages.

The rest of the day at the factory I thought about Tina and my granddaughter. Taking them fishing. Getting away from these people. No ex-con roommates. No overlords. No parole officers. Just peace. I had an old friend that owned a lawn service, landscaping, and maintenance. Maybe he'd get me working forty hours. Mowing lawns. Digging ditches in the sun. I'd get in shape. Have a good tan. Six months in I'd be running a crew, getting Slurpees at 7-11.

Why can't that happen? I asked myself.

On the ride back to Eden, Travis Campbell babbled non-stop. I ignored him and looked out the window.

"Right, Ronnie?" Campbell asked with that crooked grin.

"Right," I said. I had no idea what he asked me.

"See, I told you, Sarge."

"Harrison, I want you to help Campbell with the dishes tonight. Your reprieve just came from the Governor," Sarge barked, trying to be nice. He couldn't be.

"Sir, yes sir," I said and saluted.

"All right, Harrison. We gonna have some fun tonight!" Campbell tried to give me a high five. I half pretended I didn't see it. I popped a cigarette in my mouth. Wagged my finger in a circle and half smiled.

"Woohoo."

I lit my smoke.

When we got back to Eden, I walked straight to the cabin. Grabbed my towel hanging on my bed frame and went into the bathroom. I turned the hot water on in the shower and let it run. I took my clothes off and gazed at my reflection in the mirror. The blurry image began to melt away in the steam.

Beasley banged on the door.

"Hurry up, Harrison. I got to see a man about a horse," he yelled.

After the shower, I put on a clean white t-shirt and my jeans and laid back on my bed. Had a smoke. Davis laid on his bunk across the way.

"So this guy Campbell's been here before?" I asked.

"Yeah. He was here a while back. He caused some trouble. Got drunk up in here one night. Tore some shit up. But the thing was, he didn't get sent out. Instead, the Reverend himself came down here and picked him up."

He looked over at me. His eyebrows raised.

"What the fuck?" I asked.

"Yeah, man, Campbell was like a guilty puppy too. All that bravado was gone."

Beasley came in.

"Come on boys, It's dinner time. Pepper steak night. Gosh damn, I'm hungry."

Davis and I looked at each other. I shrugged.

After I finished eating, I dumped my tea and started putting some silver in the bus tub. Everybody filed out but me and Travis.

"You gonna do all my work for me?" he joked.

"Just want to get this done."

"Hold up a second. There ain't no rush. We got all night. Unless you go out to the courtyard and listen to some old man strum Kumbaya."

He laughed, then lit a smoke.

"Come smoke one with me out back," he said. "I wanna show you something."

I didn't say anything, just lit a cigarette and followed him outside. We stood outside under a blue light.

"You look thirsty." Travis reached behind the opened back door and pulled up a plastic water jug.

"I'm not thirsty. Had my fill of tea."

"Oh, you gonna want some of this."

He took the cap off and brought it to my face for me to smell. I knew what it was before it even got close.

"Goddamn!" I said and pushed it away. He smiled and took a long swig.

"That's the Holmes County shit. I snuck it in in this water jug. It's crystal clear."

"Alright," I paused, "give it here."

I took it and turned it up. Took a deep slug. It burned like gasoline. I closed my eyes and took another deep drink.

"Damn, that's good."

We sat there and passed the jug back and forth for a few minutes. Laughed like we were in junior high school getting away with something.

"Shit, let's get these dishes done before it's too late," I said. "Sarge might make us do push- ups."

"Fuck that guy," Travis said. "I'll make him eat shit." He laughed.

We finished the dishes in record time. I was drunk. It felt good to be drunk. A weight lifted for a moment. I forgot about everything. I laughed. After we locked up, we stood in silence. Jesse turned the corner and shined the light on us.

"That you, Harrison?" Jesse asked.

"Yeah," I said. "And Travis."

"What are ya'll doing out here?"

"The dishes. Like every night."

As if on cue, the red Chrysler New Yorker turned off of Highway 98 and started down the dead end street, cruising slow.

"Your friends are here, Jesse," I shouted.

Tyler Keith

"Fuck you, Harrison." He hurried back around the corner towards the other side of the camp. Travis and I looked at each other and laughed.

"Too bad this ol' New Yorker don't know about the hole in the fence back down in the corner," Travis said and pointed to the corner of the lot. "Made it myself last Halloween."

We both laughed again.

"Shit, Travis, I'm kind of tight. I better hit it. It's about lights out for me."

I'd warmed to him a bit. Maybe it was the booze. Maybe the need for something connected to something somewhere.

"You gonna leave me to drink alone?" he asked.

"I guess so."

I grabbed the jug and took one last chug.

"Look, Ronnie, you really should think about calling your uncle. He'd really like to get you back to work. It's rough finding good help these days. He likes having family around."

"Tell that to Albert Jr."

I pushed myself off of the wall of the metal building and stumbled towards the cabin.

"What do you mean by that?" he asked while I walked away.

I just shot him the bird, backwards, over my head.

"All right, Ronnie. We'll see you tomorrow."

I stumbled into the room. It was dark except for a lamp that Davis read by. I flopped down face first onto my bunk. I didn't move.

"I see you got the dishes done," Davis said.

I flipped him off without looking up.

"I'm serious about this, Harrison. That man, Campbell, is no good."

I heard him just before my lights went out for the night.

Tyler Keith

8

THE NEXT MORNING I woke up with barely enough time to get a shower before we left for work. I had only a few cigarettes left, but I smoked one anyway. Sarge came out of his office and got into the driver's seat of the white Econoline van.

He honked the horn and yelled, "Let's go, people!"

No sign of Travis. Maybe the bastard called in sick.

"Where's Campbell?" Beasley asked.

"He's sick. Now let's go."

Sarge revved up the van.

"Sick of work after one day. What a lazy bastard," Davis said out of the side of his mouth.

The first two hours of work, I sweated like I was in Hell. Hit the water fountain a few times. A bit before the break, I started to feel better. My brain cleared and I started to think about Tina. I wondered what she looked like. *Would I recognize her?* I worried about her husband. *What he would think about our reunion.*

Probably not much. She was coming at six. I needed to tell Sarge to make sure we got there. He usually came back through with sandwiches and cold drinks at the noon break.

The bullhorn blew at ten. I got some coffee and a large glass of water from the fountain. My headache was gone, but I felt tired and wrung out. I sat on the bench across from Davis and next to Beasley. We sat in silence.

Beasley finally broke it. "We got a storm coming," he said. "Should be here by the weekend. Radio says it might be more towards Mobile or Biloxi. Maybe we'll get out of work Friday."

Me and Davis didn't say anything for a minute.

"Man, you look like shit, Harrison," Davis finally said.

I've felt better, I thought. Then I remembered what Davis said right before I went out last night.

"So what did this character, Campbell, do last time he was here?" I asked Davis.

"He raised hell," Davis said.

"He beat the shit out of a friend of mine, too," Beasley added "Hurt him real bad. An older fella, Bob Littlejohn. They was drinking real slyly back behind the Fellowship Hall. They got in a dispute over some cigarettes. Fellow Bob accused Campbell of takin' his last pack. Campbell takes offense, even though he probably did take 'em, breaks his nose real bad. Bloodied his face up. Broke his dentures. Then when he falls to the ground in pain, he kicks him twice in the ribs. Broke a few. Laid old Bob up for a few weeks. Couldn't hardly laugh without crying. Campbell took off for a few hours. Came back to sleep it off in his bunk. Next morning, instead of the cops showing up, the blessed Reverend took him away in his big Cadillac. This was about six months ago."

"I think they must be kin or something. Sarge is always talking about calling Mrs. Blankenship, but he called the Rev instead," Davis said.

"You can take the men out of prison but you can't take the prison out of the men," I said.

"That's for damn sure," Beasley said.

"Mr. Campbell's also not a fan of the black race. That's why I steer clear of him. I don't trust myself. My tolerance for bullshit is fairly low. He won't be here too long, I'd wager."

There was an awkward silence.

Davis picked up his coffee. Took a drink. Looked at me. "You knew him before, huh?" he asked.

"I knew *of* him," I said. "He worked for my uncle after I got busted. Over in Holmes County."

"What kind of work did he do?" Davis asked.

"I don't know. The kind of work you'd think he'd do. Muscle. Thievin'. Leadership. Motivation. Outreach."

There was quiet again. I wondered what he was really doing back at Camp Eden. Maybe he came back for me, to take me back to Holmes County. *I wasn't going*, I told myself. I was deep in this thought when Beasley said, "You gonna see your daughter today?"

I looked up from my coffee. "Yeah." I said and smiled.

The bullhorn blew loud and long.

A few minutes before noon, Sarge came in with his usual small cooler and satchel. I stopped and looked at him. Looked around. Waited for the whistle. When it blew, I sat down my buffer and made a b-line for him. Caught him right outside the break room. I tapped him on the shoulder. He turned around.

"Sarge, my daughter is coming to the camp today at six o'clock. I can't really work late."

I spoke a little fast.

"Harrison, you're supposed to make all visits through me," he said looking away.

"I told you about it yesterday," I said.

"You didn't," he answered and turned around to pick up the cooler.

"My fucking daughter is coming at six. I'm gonna be there."

I grabbed his shoulder. In one fluid motion he spun back towards me, knocked my hand from his shoulder, and stood in a semi-crouched fighting pose. I naturally raised my hands in defense.

"Don't fucking touch me, Harrison. Not when my back is turned."

Beasley and Davis came up beside me. All the workers stood still.

"Not ever. You hear me?"

I didn't move. He could see my face turning red. Knew it wasn't time. My rage was too close to the surface. And the other men stood around me. They had families they had lost. They might jump in on a fight like this.

"We've got Wednesday dinner and prayer meeting starting at 6:30, he said. "You've got until then. Next time clear it with me first."

No one said anything for a few seconds.

"Have a fucking sandwich," he said, kicking the cooler sitting next to him and walking out of the building.

We left the factory a few minutes later than normal. I think Sarge did it on purpose. Just to make me sweat. I chain-smoked. Ground my teeth. Smiled. I was on the edge of my seat. We were set to get back to Camp Eden by 6:05. I hoped to god she wouldn't leave.

When we turned the corner, I could see the gate was open. An early eighties Mustang was parked by the office. I could see three figures in the car. A man in the driver's seat, a child in the middle, and a woman in the passenger seat. The van pulled around the right side of the Mustang and before it came to a stop, I jumped out and ran around the front of the van. Tina got out of the Mustang. She seemed so tall and thin. She wore a short sleeveless blue dress with flowers on it. Her dark hair was cut short to about her shoulders. She wore sunglasses. We walked slowly toward each other. Not afraid.

She said, "Oh, Daddy," and embraced me with a full hug. I held her tight. Squeezed my neck into hers. She still smelled the same. Clean, some kind of lotion, like her mom. She seemed to have always smelled that way. The embrace lasted almost a full minute.

"Harrison, you've got fifteen minutes," Sarge said.

I felt a brief rising rage but let it go.

"Daddy, you look old," Tina said, wiping a tear from underneath her sunglasses.

Then she took them off.

"I am old, Tina," I half cried, half laughed.

We stood in silence just looking at each other.

"You're a beautiful woman now. You really are. I'm so proud of you."

"Thank you, daddy. I'm happy. I'm married to David, there," she looked back to the car and pointed to the man in the driver's seat. "He's in the Navy. He's a good provider, but he's gone some."

David had a bushy mustache. Hair shaved on the side. Tan Navy uniform with white undershirt. His hands gripped the wheel. He didn't look happy. He didn't smile or wave back. I nodded.

"And of course, I've got the love of my life, little Ruby. Look at her, daddy, your granddaughter. Isn't she beautiful?"

The little girl crawled on the front seat, patting the dashboard of the Mustang.

"You want to meet her? She wants to meet you."

"Of course."

She walked back to the passenger side door in a lanky gate. She seemed so tall.

She opened the door and picked up the child. "Mommy," she said.

"Hey there, Miss Ruby. Let's go meet granddaddy."

She walked back to me with the child on her hip. She looked at me with a little smile that seemed to say, "do you believe this?" She looked at the child. Ruby had little red curls, rosy complexion, and skin pure white. The little girl looked at me then back at her mother.

"Ruby, this is your granddaddy. Daddy this is Ruby. You want to hold her?" she asked.

"I'd love to," I said.

I held out my arms to take her. She hid her face in her mom's neck.

"She's shy."

I heard the car door open and slam shut. David came around the front of the car and stood next to Tina with his hands on his hips.

"Tina, take Ruby and get in the car," he said and

pointed to the Mustang without looking at them. Just stared at me.

"Why? What are you doing, David?" Tina asked. She looked at him with a pleading look.

"I mean it, Tina. I'll talk to you later. Get in the car." He looked at her for a brief moment.

She backed towards the car with Ruby. "I'm sorry, Daddy. I'm sorry."

Then it was just me and him.

"I was against this idea, her coming to see you," he said. "I know what you are and I know what you did."

He paused, keeping his eyes on mine. "You weren't here for her," he continued. "I was. We've got a nice little family going on here and there's no place for a man like you. You've seen them. Good. But don't contact us again."

He pointed at me.

"Maybe it's not up to you. Maybe that's up to Tina," I said.

He stepped up to me. Looked me in the face. Pointed his finger.

"We're a Christian family. I am the head of the household. I say what we do. Not Tina. Not you! Me! Do you hear me!" he shouted in my face. Tina was half out of the car, looking on. Ruby was watching, a few people, Sarge and Travis, gawked.

"You understand me?"he said again, sticking his finger in my face.

I tried to breathe and quiet my rage. My chest heaved once. With my left hand I grabbed his pointer finger and twisted. With my right hand I grabbed him by the collar and pulled him to the ground. I let go of his pointer finger and stuck my knee on his chest. He was smaller than me and I had him in a position where he couldn't move. It was the instinct for self-preservation, something that had protected me in the past, in prison. If I would've stopped for a second and thought. Listened. Let him say his piece, maybe things would've turned out differently.

Tyler Keith

Tina ran towards us, yelling, "No daddy. Don't hurt him. Don't hurt him!"

Ruby started crying inside the white Mustang. Tina pushed me off of him. I backed away. I swallowed. Straightened up into a fighting stance. Tina tried to help David up, but he pushed her away.

"See Tina, I told you this man can not be around our daughter." He pushed himself up. Held his left hand out by his side. "Get back in the car, Tina."

He backed away towards the driver's side door.

"Don't you ever try and contact us again. You hear me?" he said, pointing with his good hand.

"Tina, I'm sorry," I said, looking at her, trying to let her know that I really was.

"Sorry, Daddy," she said. She knew, but it didn't matter.

David cranked the Mustang. Revved it up and backed through the gate, and fishtailed around. I saw Ruby fall into the backseat, Tina yelling at him. He peeled out in a cloud of dust and off onto 98.

I stared in shock watching the car drive away. A sweeping emptiness flushed through me. Travis walked up behind me. Put his hand on my shoulder. I didn't notice for a moment.

"You okay, Ronnie?" he asked.

I shrugged his hand off my shoulder and walked away from him. I walked past Sarge. He stood there with his arms crossed. He might've had a slight look of sympathy in his eyes. But his head was cocked, and he said, "Nice going, Harrison."

I don't know why he said that. Maybe it was as close as he could get to a sympathetic phrase, but the under-lying sarcasm came through more than the sympathy. I turned towards him and made a dash to tackle him, in a fit of rage, and a flash of red. No thoughts but destroy. But Sarge saw me coming. As I tackled him around the waist, he grabbed me under my arms and around my chest. He rolled backwards and flipped me onto my back and he

crouched in a defensive stance. I rolled over and charged
back towards him. He swung with a big left hook and
busted me between the eyes. I fell back on my ass. Dazed.
I tried to get up. Travis came over and grabbed my shoulders. Pushed me to the ground.

"Stay down, Ronnie," he said.

I picked up a handful of sand but threw it back down.

"You fucked up, Harrison," Sarge said. "If this didn't
involve family matters, you'd be gone right now. Get it
together. You do one more stupid thing, any more bullshit, and you're going back to prison for the rest of your
twenty years."

Sarge took a deep breath. Looked at me, with his
hands on his hips.

"You hear me?" he asked. "Next time I'll break your
back"

I just looked at him. Wobbled, about to pass out.
Wiping my eyes, trying to get them to clear.

"Campbell, can you get him out of my face?"

"Yes sir, Sarge. I'll take care of him."

He helped me up. I staggered. Looked around the
camp. I could make out blurry figures standing in door-
ways. Looking at me. I felt silly for a half a second.

"What are you looking at, you bastards?" I screamed.
Then I laughed, a good, hearty, true laugh.

Travis took me to his cabin. It was closer to the
Fellowship Hall. It had just two beds. An older man sat on
one bed, drinking coffee.

"Mr. James, beat it for a minute, would you mind? My
friend's hurt." Travis looked at Mr. James and shrugged.

"I'm fine," I said.

Mr. James got up, nodded, and walked out the door.

"Have a seat, Ronnie." He pointed to Mr. James'
neatly made bed. "Let me get you something to drink."

"Water," I said.

Travis went to the bathroom and filled a glass of
water from the tap. Brought it back to me. I drank it down.

"Man, old Sarge has a nice left hook. Wow. You all right, Ronnie?" he asked with a stifled grin.

"Yeah. I'm fine."

I reached up and touched my face between my eyes. I tried to rub out the fuzziness.

"Here, let me get you a real drink," Travis said and went to the side of his bed and picked up a red-and-black checkered thermos. Took the lid off and poured some dark liquid into the cap.

"This will fix you right up, Hoss. Just drink it," he said.

I smelled the dark liquid, and took a cautious sip. The bitter flavor made me wince. Warmth flowed through my body. Moonshine and coffee. I sipped the dark liquid. Thought about what had happened. That little piece of shit husband of hers. Maybe I don't blame him. Then again, he has no right. I wondered what was going on in Tina's mind. If I could talk to her alone, maybe I could smooth things out. But I wouldn't be moving in with them. I have to get out of Camp Eden. I felt like I could lose it right then. Run off. Maybe hurt someone. Sarge. Anyone who mouthed off. Travis. What Travis said about my uncle came to my mind. I could work for him ... I didn't want to. Maybe I did now. I'd have money. They'd put me up with family. Maybe the P.O. would buy it.

I set down the cup. I thought about Holmes County, and my piece of shit uncle. Travis took a small glass, wiped the rim with his shirt and poured himself a drink from the red and black plaid thermos.

"This stuff's pretty good, huh?" He looked at me.

"It's not bad. Brings back some memories," I said, raised my glass for a toast.

"Holmes County," I said. I took a drink then set it back down on the floor.

"I hated to see what happened out there. A husband ought not get in the way of a daddy and daughter like that."

"Yeah," I said. I doubted if he really believed that. "I don't want to talk about it."

"I hear ya, Hoss."

I didn't look at him. I didn't give a shit.

"You look kind of cross-eyed," Campbell said with a big grin.

"Fuck you."

"Oh come on, have some more Indian coffee."

"What?"

"Indian coffee. This is my Creek friend's favorite drink."

He refilled my plastic cap with more coffee and moonshine.

"I don't think he's a real Creek. I think he just likes the artifacts. Might be part Cherokee. Then again who ain't?"

I took a long sip.

"It's pretty fucking good, whatever you call it."

I paused for a moment. You could hear the wind rising outside the cabin. The sky outside the window had darkened a little.

"Speaking of Holmes County, what's up with that shit-weasel uncle of mine?"

"I'm glad you asked about that old bastard. He's running things almost strictly from his new house now. It's off Highway 24, right before you cross the Choctawhatchee. There's a dirt road that follows the river. You know, right before you get to East Pittman. It's about a half mile down, on the bluffs. You know where I'm talking about?"

"Yeah, at the bend of the river?"

"Yeah. It's on stilts. He's got one of those escalators that cripples use to take him up the stairs. Just stays up there on the porch. His son, Charles, runs everything with his word."

"I worked for Charles those years," I said. "He's not the friendliest man. Better than Albert, I guess."

"They need men down there. The money is rolling in, too. There's just not enough trustworthy men that aren't

Tyler Keith

dip-shits or junkies. They want you to come back. You ought to. Make some money. Then you can get out. Get your daughter back."

I sat there.

Maybe I could get some payback for my time, I thought. *Payback for everything.*

But I wasn't feeling like planning for my future just then. I seethed with rage and disappointment at myself, at this place, Camp Eden, at this man, Travis, pretending to be my friend. I drank down the last of my Indian coffee and handed Travis the cup.

"Gotta get a shower. See you at prayer meeting, Travis," I said as I walked out the door and headed to my cabin.

Tyler Keith

MY UNCLE KILLED his first man at nineteen, his broth-
er-n-law, Ralph Hill. I first heard about this killing as a
child in Bonifay. Me and Junior waited outside the True
Value Hardware on Main Street while Uncle Albert went
inside. Must've been six years old. We played on the
mechanical horse out front even though there was no
money in it. We were dressed in our cowboy outfits, little
red hats and toy guns. We crawled around on the horse,
taking turns.

A woman and her daughter walked by. Uncle Albert
stood inside at the counter, paying for his things. He was
a big man with a tattered denim work coat and a straw
cowboy hat tilted sideways on his head. The woman
stopped and pointed at him through the glass window.
She said to her daughter, about twelve, "That's the man
that killed your Uncle Ralph."

He looked at the woman with a blank expression. She
scuttled off, grabbing her daughter by the hand. I didn't
know exactly what that little scene meant at that age, but
I never forgot it. I'd hear stories about that murder, and
others, over the years. I'd think about that woman and
little girl.

It seems Albert had a particularly protective rela-
tionship with his sister, Ivy. Hadn't cared for any of the
men who'd come around. She was a dark haired beauty.
Strong-willed. She met a boy from over in East Pitman,
just around the bend from where the Harrisons all lived.

They'd met at a church event. She'd come over to
his church with a girlfriend. Ralph Hill was there. He
was a hard boy. Handsome and mean. Defiant. More so
than most of his kin. They were pious dirt farmers. They
avoided trouble. Not like the Harrison clan, my bunch,
who lived for trouble, and travelled in the safety of
numbers.

Ivy's father and brothers didn't like Ralph. Forbade
Ivy to see him. Warned him not to come around. Neither
of them listened. They ran off to the Justice of the Peace
and got hitched. Neither family took much happiness in it.

The Hill clan feared and looked down on the
Harrisons as outlaws and heathens. The Harrisons saw
the Hills as a self-righteous bunch of truck farmers that
thought too much of themselves. They were stuck-up.
Getting hitched didn't stop the infighting. Ralph fought
a few of the brothers. This would lead to fights between
Ralph and Ivy. She'd go back and forth between families.
Ralph did a little time on the work gang for fighting. Hit
one of the brothers over the head with a lighter knot.

Albert hatched a plan to take out Ralph once and for
all. One Sunday morning, when Ivy and Ralph were separated, Albert had someone slip Ralph a note supposedly
from Ivy. She said she wanted to see him and to walk over
to the Harrison house after church. She'd talked it through
with the family. She desperately wanted to see him.

After the church service at East Pitman Baptist,
Ralph made the several mile walk around the bend and
over the hill to the Harrison place. Albert waited for
Ralph around the side of the porch. As soon as Ralph
stepped onto the Harrison property, Albert stepped from
around the side of the house and nearly cut him in half
with both barrels of a shotgun.

Some stories claimed Ralph had bent down to get a
drink from a pitcher pump in the front yard, and when he
stood up Albert blew him away.

A Harrison relation was the local judge. Declared it

justifiable homicide since he'd come onto the Harrison property. Ivy never forgave Albert. She moved off to the next county and married a widower who owned a store in Caryville. She died in childbirth a few years later. Everybody knew the story. People feared Albert. Feared the whole clan. They stayed to themselves living on a dogleg dirt road that backed up to the river. Had their own church down there. Occasionally some of the men would venture out to local honky-tonks and the women would come to town to shop. They still live there, although there's not as many of them. Best not to go down that dogleg if you've got no business being there.

There were casualties on the Harrison side, too. Albert's younger brother was shot and killed in a firefight with the notorious revenuer Pistol Pete, who'd come down to Holmes County with his federal badge and his shotgun, killing and breaking up stills all over the county. Pistol Pete got in a firefight with the Harrison clan. Killed Albert's brother. He'd been Albert's old man's favorite son. The old man never got over it. Turned to the bottle. Wandered around drunk for a few years. Albert took over the family whisky business in the meantime. When the old man sobered up and wanted back in, Albert ran him off. Albert built the business. Built the fear. It was Prohibition. He made a killing, but never showed the wealth. I often wondered where all the money went.

The Harrison clan took on all comers with ruth-lessness. Kept it in the family. Made the highest quality whisky and diversified to running marijuana and later methamphetamines. Bodies floated in the Choctawhatchee River. People disappeared. Sometimes the innocent. But to take revenge or seek out justice you'd have the whole clan, all the Harrisons coming down on you. They fought like a pack of wolves. As a child, I couldn't feel the fear of the regular people. Not 'til later when I came back over to work for my uncle. People in the county would cross the street to avoid us. To avoid some provocation that would prove they were cowards. And there were a lot of cousins and nephews, mean and stupid kids who started fights if you looked at them wrong.

"What did you say to me?" one would ask an innocent passing stranger.

"What? Nothing. I didn't say anything!" The stranger would almost be crying. "You said something. I heard you," he would say back. Staring straight into their eyes.

"No, sir," shaking.

"You calling me a liar?"

You know the drill. I stood by and watched these ridiculous games play out endlessly, sometimes in backwoods honky-tonks, and sometimes right on the streets. Occasionally the Harrison family member would pick on the wrong person and suffer an ass whipping. But sooner or later, the victorious party would be alone somewhere. They'd pay with a beating by a whole group of family members. Maybe wind up in the river.

The law turned a blind eye for years. The amount of money coming in made sure things went their way. Payoffs and threats were made. Albert ran kin in local elections. He had judges in the family. No one got busted. But, by the mid-seventies, things started to change. The federal government got involved. Cocaine came in. People came in who couldn't be paid off. People started making so much money they couldn't hide it all. But Uncle Albert still had the bloodline. His secret was family loyalty. And the whole family knew that you didn't say anything. Family didn't mean you couldn't be killed, for suspicion, disloyalty, or disobedience.

But Albert had other sons, loyal yard dogs ready to tear anyone apart who entered the yard uninvited. His son, Charles, was particularly vicious. He was the face of the family for years. Albert retired from the public eye, not that he was ever that visible. For the last twenty years he never left his house. He was rarely seen. But he called the shots, and Charles took them. Who knows the

                                          Tyler Keith

body count? There are people missing. Some were said to have run off. Some were found in shallow graves. Some made an example of. Then there were the suicides and reckless ones who self-destructed. Burned shit up before burning out.

I really only knew of two murders that came at Albert's own hand, Ralph Hill and Junior. But I knew he was behind several others. I knew he wouldn't hesitate to end my life if he felt he had to. But the murder of his own son always weighed on me. I felt the guilt of association, working for him. Many times on the long truck drives, I'd think about Junior. I'd tell myself that maybe he just drowned in that pound. Maybe it was an accident. But I knew better. Eventually I had to stop thinking about him and just take the money. I was just like the rest of Holmes County, the others. I let it pass. I'd let everything pass ... until I killed a man and they put me away.

Tyler Keith

10

I HALF-KICKED THE door open. Stood in the doorway. Lit a smoke. Beasley and Davis were sitting at the little table by the window playing dominoes. I just glanced at them. They were looking at me with something like pity.

I didn't look back. I stumbled to my bunk, and sat looking over at Davis' empty bunk, dragging hard on my cigarette, silent for a full minute. In the room you could hear the outside, the constant breeze, and little spurts of rain.

"You all right, Harrison?" Beasley spoke up. "That Sarge had no right to say anything."

My mind raced between thoughts. *Should've kept my mouth shut...Never should've touched that fucking squid husband ... Sarge should've kept his mouth shut ... Tina, I'm sorry.*

"What the fuck are you two still doing here?" I asked. Looked at them. "Really? I get why you're here, Beasley. Davis? I can't wait to get the fuck out of here."

There was another pause.

"As soon as I get my pay for this week," I said, staring back at the wall.

"Shit, Harrison, I hope you're not expecting to get paid this week," Davis said.

"The fuck you talking about? I'll have a 50 hour week by Friday afternoon."

"Did you hear the man when you got here? Expenses. Room and board. Cigarettes. Gas money. Clothes. Various fees and taxes. Comes out of your pay first."

"You can still make a few bucks, Harrison. Put some

back. Sarge'll keep the cash for you. Got a safe on the office. The Reverend will put it in the bank for you when you need it," Beasley said.

"What the fuck," I muttered.

"You know what's going on here, Harrison?" Davis asked.

I shook my head slowly.

"Eden ministries has these men working: you, me, Beasley, these other men out here. The federal government subsidizes most of our pay. These people get cheap labor. Eden gets paid. No taxes. Donations. Shit, there's eight or ten of these places across the South, just like Eden. Memphis. Birmingham. Jacksonville. Atlanta. The big city Edens operate more like homeless shelters. They let everybody in, not just ex-cons. But just like here, you got to work for that room and board. You add it up, if Eden has a thousand men that's a thousand paychecks. They have thrift stores. Collect charitable donations. Shit, they even help a few people. They just …"

He stopped. My head hurt with thought and questions, and the Indian coffee.

"Let me put it this way, Harrison," Davis gestured slowly, reaching out his hand towards me like a Sunday school teacher. "You want to know why I'm here? It ain't the money. I was seventeen years old. I killed a boy. I did twenty years. While I did that time, my mother died, two brothers were killed, sister moved to California. I had nobody. After my mother died, I had no visitors. No letters. Just prison. The routine. I grew up there. When I found out I got paroled, I couldn't wait. They sent me here first. I could see things. I could see the world, how things had changed. Last time I was out there was 1966. This place here is fucked up, Harrison. I know that. But I can breath the air. I can look round. I come back to my bunk and sleep like a fucking baby."

Beasley broke the silence after the speech. "The

                                                      Tyler Keith

food at this place beats the shit out of prison!" he said. "Tonight's spaghetti night! Time to hit the mess hall."

I noticed that Beasley always tried to change the subject when things got too intense.

"I thought that was Saturday?" I asked.

"Wednesday *and* Saturday, Praise the Lord. It's like the Israelites in the wilderness. Manna from heaven."

Beasley did a little dance and raised his hands towards the sky like Walter Huston in "Treasure of Sierra Madre."

"Praise the Lord!"

Davis stood up and they moved towards the door.

"We got prayer meeting after," he said.

"I'm going to grab a shower, then I'll meet you boys there," I said. "Go on without me."

I started unbuttoning my blue work shirt. It felt damp with sweat and smelled half-rotten.

"Better make it quick, Harrison. That bastard Sarge will lock the door on your ass," Beasley warned.

"God forbid," I said.

11

RIGHT BEFORE I went to prison I bought a '69 Skylark,
dark metallic blue. Four door. 350-horsepower V8 engine.
Four-speed transmission. Fast. Almost invisible in traffic.
It looked like half the cars on the road. The trunk could
fit four bodies. I gave up the big rig runs. Claimed a bad
back. The long drives made it worse, I said. Picked up
the Skylark at a used car lot in Panama City. Truth was I
wanted out altogether. I had some money stashed away.
Tammy knew what I was doing. She hadn't said anything
yet. Everybody was on edge: the family, the bosses, the
cops. I thought if I stopped driving the truck I might be
able to just ease out of everything before I wound up dead
or caught.

I started driving the Skylark to places: Fort Walton,
Tallahassee, Gainesville. They'd fill up the trunk. I'd park
it somewhere. Leave the key on a back tire. Take a walk.
Come back and take off. I had nothing with my name on it
in the car. No title. The tag was not traceable to me. I could
ditch the car anywhere and the cops couldn't trace it back
to me or anyone connected to my uncle. They couldn't
open the trunk without a warrant. Not likely to get one.
The less I knew about what I was carrying, the better. But
I knew. In the past, driving the truck. I never worried. As
Tina grew and I had a few close calls with the police, I
began to think about getting out. My nerves were shot.

The day it happened they sent Jimmy McElwain
with me, a kid, maybe twenty-two. He was high strung.

Albert's son, Charles, had taken over the day-to-day stuff on Albert's orders. I think he could tell my mind was drifting. He wanted someone to watch me. Jimmy volunteered.

Something felt off that day. They were sending me to Fort Walton Beach, a club called the Corral, part beach bar / part Urban Cowboy bar. We didn't go over there much. The Dixie Mafia controlled a lot of the shit over there, from the Mississippi Gulf Coast to Panama City, and they didn't like competition. But Spring Break had come to the beach. The phenomenon, "Spring Break." College kids from all over the country were heading there for weeks of reckless partying, and there was lots of money to be made. The people I worked for wanted in on the action. Specifically, they wanted a foot in the college bars and the strip clubs. Selling weed and coke to the kids.

We took Highway 79 south. Passed through Bonifay. Through Vernon and New Hope. Took 20 west through Freeport. Down to 98 through Destin and over the bridge into Ft. Walton Beach. We passed the Gulfarium and the Green Frog strip club. Past the Blue Horizon Motel. The Corral was a giant dark brown barn-looking place. These big country bars seemed to be all the rage just then. I couldn't see anybody wanting to ride a mechanical bull in a swimsuit, but what the hell did I know about college kids.

Jimmy chain-smoked the whole ride. He was jumpy. I'd seen his hand shaking when he lit his last cigarette. The parking lot was lined with small palms. Shady. As I slowly pulled into the parking lot, I noticed a car parked at the back of the lot by the green dumpster. Late model Ford maybe. Looked like two men in the front seat.

I pulled the Skylark in to a parking space by the front door, and kept it running. Jimmy mashed out his cigarette in the ashtray and reached to open the car door. He looked at me, waiting for me to turn off the car. I put the car in reverse. Looked at Jimmy.

"Not today," I said.

I backed the car up.

"What the fuck are you talking about," he said. "They're waiting for us."

"We'll come back tomorrow, then. This doesn't feel right," I said, spinning the car backwards and slamming it into drive.

I didn't speed out of the lot, but I didn't crawl out either. As I made the turn back onto 98, I looked in the rearview mirror. The sedan slowly moved from the back of the lot. Jimmy watched me. I watched him, and then checked the rearview. The two men in the sedan wore sunglasses. Sports coats. They were either cops or thugs.

"Who are they, Jimmy?" I asked.

"What do you mean? I don't know," he said.

He looked back. They hadn't made the turn from the parking lot yet.

"We better just go back to the club," he said. "Your uncle's gonna be pissed."

The sedan made the turn.

Jimmy looked back. "Shit. Everything's gonna be cool," he said.

I picked up the pace but stayed on the edge of the speed limit. The dark sedan kept back but kept up.

I'm just going to drive back to Holmes County, I thought. If I could get there, I could find a place to pull off. Hide. Or ditch the car. If I got busted in Holmes County, I'd have a sympathetic judge. I cruised through Destin. The sedan pulled closer.

"Everything's alright, man," Jimmy said again.

"What's going on, Jimmy?" I asked.

He didn't say anything; just lit another cigarette and looked back. As we turned onto 79 past Freeport, almost to Ebro, I picked up speed. It was a two-lane highway with some curves. The sedan matched my speed, and even moved a little closer. There's a little curve into a straight-away right at New Hope. I made my move. Hit about 95 and made space. When the dark sedan made the corner a blue light was flashing on the dashboard.

"Shit," I said, looking in the rearview mirror. Then I looked at Jimmy hard in the eyes. He started to say something a few times before he came out with it.

"Ronnie, they don't want us. They want your uncle." He looked at me then looked away. Then back at the cops. They made up ground on the straightaway.

"I didn't..." he stammered.

"Just shut the fuck up," I said. I stepped on the gas.

There's a dirt road when you get into Vernon, right after a sharp curve, and a little white church past that. If I could make the dirt road I might could get behind the church, and maybe not be seen. Or I could make a run for the woods.

The dark sedan moved up close. Gave the Skylark a warning bump. The back end of the Skylark did a quick fishtail, but I pulled it back in line and came down hard on the gas. In the rearview, I could see the passenger in the dark sedan motion for me to pull over.

"Ronnie, pull over, man. Please! You're gonna get us killed," Jimmy said, almost weeping. He made a motion like he was going to grab the wheel. I slapped his hand away.

We passed under Interstate 10. Passed a gas station doing about 95. A sheriff's deputy pulled in behind the sedan and turned on his lights. I hit about 110 as we entered Vernon. I'd pulled away a bit but I'd have to slow it down to make the turn onto the dirt road. Jimmy dug his finger into the dashboard, then as if he'd had an epiphany he reached to put on his seat belt. As we rounded the corner, and I could see the dirt road in front of me on the left, I stomped on the brake and turned the wheel to make the cut. The Skylark felt like a boat in the Gulf, half of the car seemed to sink into invisible water. Leaned lower to the ground. The tires shrieked and a grinding sound came up from under the wheels. I had the turn. I was going to make it until we hit the gravel and rocks. Things happened in an instant until it slowed to a near stop as we skidded towards the woods on the side of the old road. A giant yellow pine appeared like a monolith. We knew we were going to hit the pine. I saw the terror on Jimmy's face, the realization. He screamed like an animal just as the Skylark made contact. The scream joined the crunching sound of metal. The tree impacted the center of the Skylark, Jimmy's eyes wide as his head smashed the side window. Then his body and head flung back the other direction as the car slipped around the giant tree. My head crashed my window and it shattered. Just before everything went dark, I saw the lights go out in Jimmy's eyes.

I know now that Jimmy was an informant. He'd gotten busted for weed. They put the fear in him. He'd set me up to get himself off the hook. I could take his place and he'd be free. Jimmy was free now forever. I wasn't going to be free for twenty years. They offered me deals. Talk and walk. But I knew I couldn't do it, even if I'd wanted to. I had a family. My uncle and his people knew where they lived. I knew Albert would do anything to stay out of prison. Keep his kingdom. I never even thought about it. I got lucky with a sympathetic judge and a decent lawyer. Maybe some payoff. But I'd still killed somebody. A kid. It made the papers. I had to pay. I could've gotten life, but they gave me twenty years.

I thought about the kid every day for the first few years. All the while constructing a defense for myself. Justification. *He was a rat. It was an accident. It was the cops' fault for making him do what he did. They'd chased me. He'd distracted me by reaching for the wheel.* I recreated the final seconds while laying in my cell. But then I just took it. Admitted it. I'd killed the kid. After all the denial, I just took it. Then I just put it away with all my other guilt and regret. Hell, I had to live.

But I was a killer. I was like Cain. I killed my brother. Tried to kill myself. But God wouldn't allow it. I had to wander and live with it. Bear the mark. After awhile, the guilt and regret turned into something like hate. Anger. A big ball of resentment. Something I couldn't explain but I felt it with me at all times. It gave me the capacity to do things. To not care. It lived there with the guilt I felt about what I'd done to my family and to my own life. That seemed to be the biggest sin. Hate or despair were two sides of a coin tossed into the air and randomly landing on either side. But most of the time I felt nothing. Like I was frozen. Empty. But now that I was out of prison, everything started to melt. The coin tossed into the air. I was waiting for it to come down. Hate or despair.

Tyler Keith

12

THE HOT WATER rolled down my face and body. I just
stood there with closed eyes trying to make sense of the
last hour. *Maybe I could patch things up with Tina? Maybe.
It'd take time.* I could see it in her eyes that she loved me.
Wanted me to be her daddy again. Wanted the family
together. But she needed the security of her own new
family. Needed to protect that at all costs. Her husband
would come first. No matter what type of asshole he
might be. Even before Ruby, and probably because of me.
My being gone when she needed me, when she needed
someone. I thought about Davis. I understood more now
why he stayed here. The routine in prison can be sort of
a comfort. I'd felt that. But I was adult when I went in, a
grown man. I knew what I had and I knew what I'd lost.
But the outside world didn't stop. It kept spinning. And I
wanted out of the cage that I'd built around my own feelings. Now. I could feel the coffee and liquor still — just a
touch. I wanted more to quench the rage. Or fuel it.

By the time I got dressed and made it to the fellowship hall, the doors were locked. I didn't care. I didn't
want food anyway. I strolled around to the back door.
Stood under the awning. It was raining. The door stood
open. I could see the men eating in there. I could smell
the same old spaghetti and the French bread, and I could
see Beasley getting an extra piece of bread. Sadness crept
up on me, seeing all these men together. They had no one
else but each other. Even though, if it came down to it,

they'd stick a kitchen knife in each other's back for $200, there seemed to be a bond between them, a bond of failure and, for some, remorse. I could hear waves of laughter. Hear the talk swell and ebb. I thought about the sermon on Sunday, about Cain, and about these men. What they had to offer God didn't want. So out of anger and resentment and selfishness they killed and stole and whored and raged. For that they were sent out of Eden. They bore the mark. There was no salvation or forgiveness for Cain, just exile and humiliation for his great sin.

Travis gathered dishes in the bus tubs and silverware trough, taking them to the dish station in the corner by the back door. He saw me lurking in the doorway. He disappeared for a second then hurried towards me carrying a Styrofoam cup.

"You look thirsty. Here's some tea," he said, handing me the cup.

I raised my hands in protest.

"Trust me, Harrison, you want some tea."

He forced the cup towards me until I grabbed it. I looked at him, then at the cup. Took a sip, and then raised the cup for a long swallow. It was sweet tea and moonshine, the over-sweet flavor of over-steeped Baptist church or service station tea with the wallop of almost pure grain alcohol coming up the backstretch.

"Goddam! What'd you call that?" a little smile crept up on my face.

"I don't know, the Backslider?" he asked.

"Goddamn right."

"I noticed you missed dinner. You want a plate?" he asked.

"Fuck food." I pulled out a smoke.

He smiled and went back to collecting the dishes.

The rest of the men turned their chairs towards the serving tables or turned sideways on the benches to face the front. The old man who always sat in front of his door strumming his guitar made his way to the front. Sarge

                                    Tyler Keith

looked my way. Caught my eye. Jerked his head like he wanted me to come in and sit down. I nodded. Just saying hello. I looked towards the front at the man with the guitar. I stayed in the doorway.

The man raised his hand to quiet the talking and then started in on "I Saw the Light."

Some of the men tried to follow along on the verses, but almost everybody came in on the choruses. Even me. I couldn't help it. The song was part of my soul. My unconscious. Songs like this. "Will the Circle Be Unbroken," "The Old Rugged Cross," "This Train," "How Great Thou Art." If I heard people singing these songs, I joined in without a thought. As I sang *Straight is the gate and narrow the way*, a wave of nostalgia and longing swelled up inside me. The songs had lost whatever religious importance they'd once had, but they remained part of me. The language in the songs were some of the first words I'd ever sung, the first words I'd ever heard. My eyes filled with tears. I thought about my father. I could almost hear his deep tenor reverberate around my brain.

I wondered where he was. I hadn't wondered in years. These songs brought back thoughts of him.

I surveyed the crowd of men again. I could see the earnestness in many of their eyes, a craving for the unconditional love of Jesus, or something or someone that might forgive them. Not judge. Not a vengeful god, but the everlasting arms of forgiveness and peace.

Beasley sang out with a smile. Davis sang along, barely opening his mouth. Maybe this answered my question of why they stayed here: a little peace, another reason why I didn't belong here and had no desire to stay. Although I wanted some type of forgiveness, some type of peace, and these songs felt comforting, I'd given up my faith long ago. And I did it with such fury and anger that I knew it could never come back. My break with my faith came after my father left. After one last attempt at the Christian life. Witnessing to strangers on the beach. Handing out gospel tracts downtown. Trying to "win souls." Praying. Praying at night to a deaf god. No answered prayers. No father coming home. No sober mother. No comforting spirit. No comfort in the word. Just nothing … and I accepted it. Accepted nothing into my life. I prayed, "Dear nothing, come into my life. Fill me with your infinite space. No one knows the size of your great nothingness. In nobody's name, Amen."

That was my prayer.

After that, after I gave it up, living felt good. Living for the day. Drinking. Gambling. Women. Joy is real. Love is real. When I settled down with Tammy, things made a little more sense. Love between two people, that made sense. When we had Tina. Holding a child in your arms. Holding life in your hands. That's real.

"I Saw the Light" turned into "Will the Circle Be Unbroken" and back into "I Saw the Light." When the medley ended, the man sat down. Jessie came to the front with a new Bible. It had pieces of paper sticking out and he held it in his left hand, by his side. He stood in front of the men in silence for about thirty seconds, looking back and forth like a kid preacher does, mimicking the old guys.

"Sarge said I could read a few verses tonight before we collect the prayer requests and have final prayer."

He reached out his right hand and pointed to the sky.

"I think some of you might know, I've been trying to read the Bible through. It's hard, especially for someone who never finished school. I don't always know what it means, but I sometimes do. I'm just about halfway. Ecclesiastes. I found some things that made sense to me somehow. Maybe you too will know."

He lifted his Bible in front of him. Opened to the middle, took out the felt marker. Looked at the pages. Looked up and then back down.

"Ecclesiastes 9," he said a bit louder. "I'm just going to jump around in this chapter. Ecclesiastes 9:1. King James

                                    Tyler Keith

version. 'For all this I consider in my heart even to declare all this, that the righteous, and their works are in the hand of God: no man knoweth either love or hatred by all that is before them.' Now verse three. 'This is an evil among all things that are done under the sun, that there is one event unto all: yea also the heart of the sons of men is full of evil, and madness is in their heart while they live, and after they go to the dead.' Four: 'For him that is joined to all the living there is hope. For a living dog is better than a dead lion.' Amen. Five: 'For the living know that they shall die: but the dead know not anything, neither have they any more rewards; for the memory of them is forgotten.' Six: 'Also their love, and their hatred, and their envy, is now perished; neither have they any more a portion for ever in anything that is done under the sun.' Now verses ten and twelve: 'Whatsoever thy hand findeth to do, do it with thy might; for there is no work, nor device, nor knowledge, nor wisdom in the grave, wither thou goest.' Amen. Twelve: 'For man also knoweth not his time: as the fishes that are taken in an evil net, and as the birds that are caught in the snare; so are the sons of men snared in an evil time, when it falleth suddenly upon them.'"

Many men said, "Amen." A few said, "Praise Jesus." Jessie closed his Bible and held up a little box.

"Here's the prayer requests from last week. We won't read them out loud but just pray on them. If you have more for next week, bring them up after and put them in this box. Who wants to lead the prayer tonight?"

A few hands shot up, but an old man stood. He looked towards Jessie in a cold stillness. "Mr. Reeves, how about you?" Jessie pointed to the old man.

As the old man began to pray, "Dear heavenly father, our precious lord and savior…" I turned around and stepped back outside and hit out another smoke. The rain fell harder on the tin awning. The Gulf breeze picked up and moved through the pines in a whooshing sound. Almost like words.

I mumbled to myself, "A living dog is better than a dead lion."

I got a tap on the shoulder.

"Glad you could join us for dinner," Sarge said.

"Didn't know we were required to eat." I looked him in the eyes. No emotions.

"You know you were lucky earlier," he said. "Just due to the circumstances, I didn't stomp you into the dirt. Usually, any time a man takes a swing at me they wind up in the hospital."

He paused for a second, and looked at me. Maybe he detected my ambivalence.

Or maybe he had a heart in there somewhere. Or felt bad. "But under the circumstances, I'll let it slide."

Maybe he wanted to say, "I shouldn't have made that wise-crack right at that time, but you see, I fucked up my family life, too, so I figured I'd fuck with you. My bad, Harrison."

But he couldn't say it. All he could say was, "Way to go, dumbass."

We looked at each other for a moment.

"Why don't you stick around the fellowship hall and help Campbell clean these dishes," he said.

As Sarge turned and walked away, I said, "Sir, yes, sir." Gave him a salute.

I thought, *If I ever get a chance to swing at him again I'd better make it count, because I had no doubt he'd beat me to near death and call my parole officer to my hospital bed.*

I walked over to the dish sink next to Travis.

"Give me another Backslider, and I'll help you out with these dishes," I said.

He took my cup and scooped some ice from a metal bowl, pulled out a half-pint bottle with no label and a cork in it from his back pocket. Poured some into my cup and tipped the tea urn forward to get some of the last bit of tea. He saw me watching Sarge leave through the front doors.

"Don't sweat that clown," Campbell said. "They just keep that guy around to keep order. He can't do anything."

"Why doesn't he fuck with you? Drinking, whatever. Fucking off. Missing work."

"That's what I'm saying, he can't. I know more people than he does. If I fucked up, the most he could do is send me to another one of these places."

"You know people?" I asked.

"Yeah. I know people," he said. He stopped scrubbing a pot. Looked at me.

"Ronnie, you know people."

I assumed he meant my uncle. I looked at him. Took another drink of my Backslider.

"People that come from around here, the Panhandle, people that's been around, that's got these kinds of businesses, this kind of money, they know each other.

"You get me, Hoss?"

I didn't want to know the details just then. Just the question at hand. "What the fuck are you doing here again?"

He smiled a quick smile, "I told you, I'm supposed to see if you want to come see your uncle. Come back and talk to him ... or."

He paused.

"Or what?" I asked.

"Or nothing." He stopped smiling.

I looked at him. Looked away. Shook out a smoke from my pack. Grabbed it with my mouth. Stuck the pack back in my shirt pocket. Pulled out a lighter. Lit the cigarette. Put the lighter back in my pocket. Took a long drag. Blew out the smoke through my mouth and nose. Looked back at him.

"I need some air," I said. Walked back out the back door. The rain fell on the tin.

"Look, all I'm saying is if I can't get you to come back to Holmes County, I'm not sticking around here. Lighten up, Ronnie."

He patted me on the back.

I looked at him sideways. I couldn't figure this guy out. I knew for sure this man was dangerous. I'd heard stories. Brutal beatings. People disappearing. Arson. Never seen it with my own eyes, but I still knew he was dangerous. Only a minute earlier he'd given me a subtle look, a flash. *Maybe I'm here to kill you if you don't come back,* it seemed to say. Maybe I was paranoid. But I liked the guy. He was the one person at Camp Eden that didn't seem broken or defeated. The guy could never walk the straight and narrow, but he wouldn't pretend to. He never bowed his head when someone prayed. He never sang along with the hymns.

After a moment, he said, "We need some fucking women."

He put his arm on my shoulder. "Don't you know any women down here, Hoss?"

I thought, *Darleen.* Her number ran through my head.

"Yeah. Yeah, I do." I turned and faced him.

"I'm calling someone," I said and backed towards the direction of the office out from under the tin roof and into the rain.

"Wait, Ronnie. She has a friend. Right? A friend for me? Right, Ronnie?"

"Let me see. Let me set this up."

The booze set my veins on fire. The rain cooled me off. I turned around and hurried to the pay phone by the office.

"Wait a second, Hoss." He pulled out a quarter and flicked it towards me. It seemed to hang in the air forever. It fell in the mud. I picked it up. Showed it to him and hurried towards the pay phone.

I put the quarter in the pay phone, and thought for a second. Dialed the number. It rang five or six times. I almost hung up and then she answered.

"Hello," a soft, smoky voice said.

"Hello, Darleen?"

"Yes, this is Darleen."

"Hello, Darleen. This is Ronnie. I met you the other night. The Fire and Fiddle, I believe it was," I said tentatively.

"Ronnie. I didn't think you were going to call me."

"Well, I haven't had a chance 'til now. Had some stuff to take care of."

"Yeah, it seemed like you might. I'm glad you did though."

"Yeah? Me too. I had a good time. Maybe too good."

There was a short pause.

"Yeah, I had a good time, too."

"Hope I wasn't too much of a handful."

"You were pretty sweet. Mostly."

I heard her light a cigarette and the tinkling of ice in a glass.

"I'd like to see you again." I paused. "Soon."

"I'd like that," she said.

It hit me how crazy this was. *Why would she? Maybe she's older than I thought. Maybe she's desperate. Maybe crazy. She must be nuts to wind up with me in the first place. Maybe she doesn't like to drink alone. Hell, maybe she likes my looks. Couldn't have been my prowess in the bedroom. Maybe she could tell I wasn't the type of man to push a woman around. Maybe she felt sorry for me. Maybe she liked ex-cons. Who the fuck knows?*

"Ronnie, are you still there?" she asked.

"Yeah. Can we meet tomorrow night?" I asked, thinking she'd probably say "no."

"Tomorrow night? I can't tomorrow night, hun," she said. "I can't meet 'til Sunday."

"Not 'til Sunday? Okay. The only trouble is I don't have a car right now."

"I figured as much."

I tried to explain my situation as nonchalantly as I could. Like it was no big deal. There was silence. Then she said, "I know what it's like, Ronnie. Let's just say I've had trouble of my own. Two ex-husbands. Two ex-cons."

She paused and added, "But I can read people pretty well, Ronnie. I like you."

"I'm glad you said that. I like you, too, Darleen. Been thinking about you since I woke up Saturday morning and you were gone."

"Oh, boy. I had to work in the morning. Not a fun day let me tell you."

"Sunday at nine?" I asked.

"Okay, Ronnie," she said.

I gave her directions. Told her to park at the end of the street with the lights out. We'd meet her there. She went for it.

"Oh yeah, one more thing, do you have a friend?" I asked. "See, I've got this friend."

"Do I have a friend?" she asked. She laughed, then coughed. "Yeah, I got a friend. Let me see if Debbie is free. She probably is. Me and her usually drink and run around together." She paused. Took a drag. "See you Sunday, Ronnie. If you need to call me, if you need to talk to someone before Sunday, feel free."

"See you Sunday, Darleen." She hung up.

I ran back through the mud to the back of the fellowship hall. Travis put away the last of the dishes.

"What the fuck's the deal, Ronnie?" he asked

"Looks like we're in business. Let's have a drink," I said. "Only thing is they can't do it 'til Sunday."

He came out back under the awning.

"Damn, Sunday? I hope I can wait that long. I don't plan that far ahead. Hell, I may not make it through the weekend," he said. "You're full of surprises, Ronnie."

He pulled out the half-pint and handed it to me. I took a long pull. Made an uncontrollable "aahh" sound. Handed it back. Travis took a long drink. Finished it off and threw the empty bottle into the mud behind the building.

Just then the red New Yorker turned the corner and made its trek down the dead-end street.

"Right on time," said Travis.

Tyler Keith

"Shit, we're gonna have to deal with Jessie if we're gonna get out of here."

"You let me worry about Jessie."

"Nine o'clock Sunday." I stumbled back towards my cabin, the first bit of good news in my head. *Darleen.*

"You're alright, Ronnie. No matter what your uncle says about you," Travis said. That remark took the smile off my face.

13

SOMETIME IN THE night, I woke up from a nightmare. My arm was under my body and had gone numb. When I woke up, it was limp and useless. Panic set in as I slung it around to try and get some feeling back. Get the blood flowing again. By the time I got a tingle of feeling back, I was wide-awake. I guess I'd passed out. I was still wearing my clothes and my shoes. I crept outside as quiet as I could, and smoked on the corner of the porch. A light rain fell on the tin overhang, but I could still smell the bay water on the wind. I closed my eyes and rubbed my face with my free hand. The door creaked open. The old man poked his head out and smiled at me, then he came on out, and just looked at me with a wicked smile, like Gabby Hayes eyeballing John Wayne.

"You want a cigarette?" I finally asked.

"Well, since you're offering," Bailey said.

He took the smoke and put it in his mouth. I handed him a lighter. He lit the cigarette, took a long drag, and stared out into the yard.

"Did I hear something about you being from over to Holmes County?" he asked, not looking at me.

"Let's just say I have some deep roots over there," I said. "Why do you ask?"

"I thought I heard that, and it reminded me of a story a friend of mine from over there told me."

He smiled and looked over at me. "You know Jimmy Foxworths over there?" he asked.

"I know a few Foxworths. Don't recall a Jimmy," I said.

"He may be dead now. Well, he told me this story. Seems there was another fella over there that kept chickens. He had this neighbor that had a dog. The dog kept coming over to the man's yard and killing his chickens. The man with the chickens had seen the neighbor's dog over there. So he goes to the man and says, 'Your dog is coming over to my yard and killing my chickens. You need to tie your dog, or kill your dog, or somehow keep him from killing my chickens.' Well, the man with the dog tells him, 'It's not my dog.' The next week, the dog comes back over and kills a couple more of the man's chickens. Again, the man goes over to the dog owner's house and says, 'Tie your dog. He's killed some more of my chickens.' 'It's not my dog,' the man says. Well the man knows it's his dog 'cause he's seen the dog. So the man with the chickens goes to the hardware store and buys some strychnine, you could buy it back then for varmints and whatnot. Then the man goes to the butcher shop and buys some hamburger meat. He mixes the strychnine with the hamburger meat. He goes to his house and gets his 12 gauge shotgun. Goes to the man's house and throws the poison meat to the dog, and when the dog owner comes out of the house, the man holds the shotgun on him and makes the man watch his dog eat the poison meat."

The old man grinned.

"That sounds like Holmes County," I said.

"The dog didn't kill any more of the man's chickens," the old man said, satisfied with the completion of a good story.

"I think I've heard that one before," I mumbled.

"You must know Jimmy then," he said.

"Shit, he's probably my kin."

"See, I went back over there to Holmes County a few times back in them old days. Never did like it all that much. Always felt a little bit on edge over there," he

                                    Tyler Keith

laughed. "But, you know, back in them days I used to go over to Peppertown.

"You know where that is?"

"Yeah. Right over there by Bonifay. Nothing over there now but some empty buildings," I said.

"You know why they called it Peppertown, don't you?" he asked.

"No. Why?"

His take on Holmes County interested me. The stories. Even though I planned to never go back, the place haunted me. The strangeness. The tall tales. Even the bad times meant something.

"They called it Peppertown 'cause it was hot!" He let out a hardy laugh and coughed. "They had some boarding houses down there, two or three honky-tonks, a few houses-of-ill-repute. When I was down there, there was still some logging being done. I guess I was fifteen, nearly sixteen. I worked a couple weeks. Damn hard labor. Come payday, Peppertown would be hopping. Most of the men would start drinking on Friday and stop on Sunday evening if they hadn't fallen out before then. And they had that good, clean, corn liquor. Anyhow, second weekend, I got my pay and got me a little bottle and headed to my rooming house. I was gonna clean up. Rest a bit. Hit that bottle and then hit one of them honky-tonks. I laid down on my bed. Took a few drinks. I hear a commotion outside my back window. These two men are fighting. There's a big man and a smaller man. The big man has the smaller one in some kind of bear hug. The smaller fella is scratching the bigger fellas face. The big man leans in and bites off a piece of the man's cheek and spits it on the ground. The littler man goes wild and starts grabbing at his own face with a kind of pitiful scream. The big man kicks him to the ground and pulls out a Bowie knife out of his boot and just stabs the man in the back. The man falls over dead."

As Beasley's telling the story, a look of fear comes over his face. He looked at me and then back out into the rain.

"The big man looks around to see if anybody saw anything. He catches me looking from the second story window. He tucks the knife back in his boot and starts walking real fast towards the boarding house. I realize, real quick-like, that he's coming for me. Hell, I took off out the front door. Left all my things. My bottle. As I'm coming out the front door, he's coming around the side. He sees me. He wasn't running. Just walking real fast towards me. He yells out, 'Boy, you better run. You better not come back here. I know who you are, boy.' Kept walking towards me. Peppertown was really close to the tracks back then, and I got down there right as a log train was passing. I jumped on there and stayed on 'til past Mobile. Never did go back to Peppertown, or Holmes County. I wouldn't recommend anybody going back there. Know what I mean, Ronnie?"

"Yeah, I hear ya," I said, startled by the story.

"You got another smoke, hoss?" he asked.

I tossed him a smoke. He laughed and put it behind his ear.

"Thanks, buddy. Now get some sleep. You're gonna need it."

He smiled and quietly slipped inside.

Was that some kind of warning? I'd heard other stories like that. Some about men I knew. Or I knew their sons and nephews. When I worked over there, I'd stay three or four days, sometimes a week. We'd haunt some honky-tonks and juke joints. We'd see a good deal of violence. But I got the feeling that just a few generations before me there was some real trouble. The men that had been there since Prohibition and the Depression had a look about them, something around the eyes, and a roughness in the hands, missing fingers from mill work, and scars on their faces.

You'd see some of these men in churches with their families. You knew they'd been through hell. But

they had a sweetness to them, a gentleness. They were
thankful for surviving, for their families, and the comfort
of the church pew.

You'd also see some of the other men, the mean ones,
men like my Uncle Albert. They seemed to have bitterness,
and a dangerous anger that showed in their faces, like the
markings on a poisonous snake you know you should
steer clear of. Their families would cower behind them,
whipped into submission by corporal violence, nobody on
the outside willing or able to help them.

It seemed like the whole community fought a pitched
battle between the flesh and the spirit. And as the battle
for the town raged on, the battle raged in each and every
person in the town. I could almost hear my daddy from
the pulpit, preaching a sermon.

*The flesh and the spirit are in a constant battle, Matthew
6:24. 'No man can serve two masters: for either he will hate the
one, and love the other; or else he will hold to the one and despise
the other. Ye cannot serve God and mammon.*

I could picture him in the pulpit with his black suit
and black tie and horn-rimmed glasses, sweating and
shouting. The congregation shouting 'Amen!' Some
chanting a prayer. My mother raising her hands towards
the heavens with her eyes closed.

*You must choose between God and man! The Bible says
in Revelations 3:16 'So then, because thou art lukewarm and
neither cold nor hot, I will spew thee out of my mouth.' You've
got to choose, people!*

As a child I was afraid. *Was I good or bad?* My father
told me I wasn't old enough yet to decide, but he was sure
that I was good. The Lord loved me. I felt nothing but fear.

After he was gone, I wasn't convinced that anyone
could ever be just one thing. Could just love God and not
the flesh. I had both in me. Good and evil or whatever
you call it. The war would never end. No side would
win. I felt like this war might just kill me, and then there
would be nothing. It wouldn't matter anyway. It'd just be

darkness. And if that was the case maybe the things in me fighting each other weren't God and the Devil, but just destruction and creation. The desire to let the wild side take its course with the violence, sex, and the drugs, or the peacefulness of family and the comfort and security of a home. I'd been able to put the fight on hold while I was in prison, but now the hostilities had begun again. It was almost like each side was making its case to me through circumstances and through fate and through my reactions to them. There was a third part of me that almost longed for prison again, for the quiet. The walking death of being locked up. But then I thought of Tina and I cried. And out of the tears came a rage, all in a split second. Then, tiredness hit all at once. I tossed my cigarette into the rain and quietly returned to my bunk and somehow I drifted off to sleep, my last thought, *Fuck it...who gives a shit anyway.*

14

THAT NIGHT I had another dream, almost like a memory. It was summer in Holmes County. I was a kid. Me and Junior took my dad's old green canoe. Took it down the Choctawhatchee. We must've been about ten years old. We'd stop and fish at a few of our secret spots. Pull out sparkling blue gill and bream. Had a good stringer full. Our destination and favorite spot was a crystal clear deep well-spring, called the Washington Blue Spring that jutted right off the river. Holmes County is full of natural springs. One in Ponce De Leon was thought to be the fountain of youth the explorer supposedly found. Vortex Springs. Others. The springs fed the river. Made the moonshine pure. This place was our favorite. We followed a small stream off the river that ended in a deep blue hole. Crystal clear and year round temperature of 68. We pulled the canoe to the bank then dove into the center of the springs. No one I knew had ever touched the bottom. You could see clearly 30 or 40 feet 'till the light disappeared. Someone said that it led all the way out to the Gulf of Mexico. There were vast caves that twisted and turned for miles. People would go missing from time to time. Divers. Treasure hunters. Kids. Some people thought the waters had healing powers. There was something mystical about the place, the clear water and the canopy of cypress, and the Spanish moss that hung from the scrub oak. The deep woods' earthy smell, and the sandy soil. It did seem magical. Healing. The water felt electrifying. We took turns diving, timing each other to see

who could dive down the farthest. We'd get nearly two
and a half minutes. The panic set in as I stretched towards
the light, the last few strokes seemingly like I might not
make it, exhaling the very last of my air just before breaking
the surface. In my dream, Junior dove in and sank deep.
Two minutes. Three minutes. I panicked. Ran around the
big hole. Screamed his name. Finally I saw a dark figure
rising slowly with his hands outstretched. When the figure
breached the water it wasn't Junior. It was my father. He
treaded water and looked at me in silence. Then he dove
back down the deep blue hole. I stood for a moment then
dove in after him. I swam down as far as I could, just able
to see his feet in front of me. But the figure pulled away
into the darkness. Then I was in darkness. I panicked and
stopped swimming down. I looked above and could barely
see a pinhole of light. Fear rushed through me. With a fury,
I pushed and kicked my feet back towards the light above. I
couldn't breath. The light began receding. I pushed harder.
Outside the dream, my body began to tense and shake. I
tried to wake myself. Tried to scream. To move my arms
and legs. "Wake Up!" I screamed inside myself. In the
dream, my eyes bulged. I knew I couldn't make it to the
top, but I made one last push towards the light. Finally, my
body moved, my actual body, and I woke up with a strange
mumbling speech. Some gurgling half-mumble, half moan.
I sat up in bed drenched in a cold sweat.

On the morning ride to work, I thought about the
dream, and the events of the week. The cliffs on the Scenic
Highway inspired a longing and the eternal question,
"Where was my father?" Could be dead. He'd be in his
seventies now. Maybe he's been dead for years. I could
never understand why he never even called. Just disappeared without a trace. In the back of my mind, I'd always
thought something bad happened to him. If that was
the case, that something probably happened in Holmes
County. My dreams thought so too.

I thought about Darleen. I tried to get a clear picture

                                    Tyler Keith

of her face. I could almost touch her body. Pale white. Soft curves. Soft lips. Mouth tasting of liquor and cigarettes. But I couldn't bring up any details, just a soft glowing face with her hair light brown, almost red, turning grey, and crows feet that gave her a softer, sympathetic look. I knew I was lonely. Hope gone. Hungover. Sarge and Travis had their windows rolled up due to the rain. Sweat formed on my forehead and down my back. It smelled like mildew in the van. Almost all the men had hand-me-down work clothes. Clothes others had worked in and discarded for new ones. You could smell their bodies on the old clothes. The radio played, "Just My Imagination" by the Temptations. My thoughts jumped around, from Darleen to Tina and even to my mother.

Everybody was quiet in the van. I looked at Beasley. He gave me a sly smile. Raised his eyebrows. Davis didn't look at me. They both had had it with me already, since I'd spent the last few nights drinking with Travis. I didn't blame them.

When the first break horn blew, I spent a good long while at the water fountain. I went into the break room and got a cup of coffee. It was strong and bitter. Because of the rain, one of the big doors to the factory floor had to be shut. It felt like a steam room. My clothes were damp, but I felt better. The poisons trickled out.

Travis sat across from me on the green picnic table style benches. "You gonna make it, Hoss?" he asked with that shit-eating grin.

"Yeah. If I don't die before the end of this shift."

"Shit, you're sweating out all the poison. Get back; get a shower. Drink a few Backsliders, and you'll be a hopping frog."

"Like I said, if I make it."

"Tell me about your gal's friend. What's her name?" He squirmed around in his seat, almost standing up.

"Her name is Debbie. I don't know nothing about her. Darleen said they like to drink and run around together."

"Hot damn," he said. Rubbed his hands together.

"What are we going to do about getting out of there without catching shit from Jessie and Sarge?" I asked.

"I told you, there's a hole in the back gate. As far as Jessie goes, you leave that to me."

"Right. You'll take care of it."

"That reminds me, I gotta make a call." He stood up, fumbled in his pants, looking for a quarter. I watched him walk out to the factory floor and use the pay phone. I caught Davis' eyes. He just shook his head and downed the last of his coffee.

15

NOT LONG BEFORE the first afternoon break, Sarge showed up with the prison preacher, Ricky Wilkins. I was surprised to see him. I guessed once I left that place, I'd never see him again. Didn't want to. I wanted to leave those six years locked up. As they walked towards me Sarge waved at me, calling me over. Reverend Ricky just smiled, hands on his hips. He was about average height, maybe a little shorter, dark hair parted on the side. Beard. He wore starched bellbottom jeans, running shoes, and a tight blue Izod shirt.

I set down my buffer, pulled my goggles down around my neck, and walked over, wiping my hands on my apron. Sarge reached out his hand to shake mine, but quickly pulled it back when he realized I wasn't going to shake his.

"Harrison, I believe you know Reverend Ricky," he said, gesturing from me to him.

"Yeah, hey Rev." I moved to shake his hand, but he pulled me in for a hug.

"Hey Ronnie, it's so good to see you," he said. He kept a hand on my shoulder for a moment.

"I'll let you two catch up," Sarge said. He walked off towards the office.

"How's Camp Eden treating you?" Ricky asked. "Sarge says you've been having trouble adjusting."

"Things are fine," I said, forcing a smile. I had an urge to slap his face for some reason unknown to me.

Just seeing him brought up feelings of resentment. Even though Reverend Ricky had been a bright spot, a distraction from the boredom and depression, the memory of prison, maybe the fear of going back, made me angry. I wasn't even a week out and it felt like years ago. Waking up all my sleeping emotions pushed everything else back in time, like some dark ages. Seeing him brought it all back: the loneliness, the static mind. I could smell the penitentiary on him, the bleach and misery. Maybe that was the trigger.

"Things can be hard, getting back into the swing of the real world, Ronnie. Even in a place like Camp Eden," he said. "Everybody wants the best for you."

"Oh, I know it. I'll be back in society before long," I said.

A little over a year ago, I'd met this man. My last two years, the time had started to crawl … after I'd given up everything else. After my mother died, I had nothing left. I'd let go of everything. A fellow inmate suggested I look into the church services. Several times a week you could get out of your cell. Set up chairs. Sing some hymns. Wasn't much, but it helped. There was talk of future field trips, and a few more privileges. It looked good on paper, too. A few of the men were good men, just trying to get by. The sermons provided some mental exercise. There were discussions. Nobody knew I was a preacher's kid; that I wasn't ripe for saving. The Rev put the hard press on me for salvation a few times. I finally told him that I was already saved. "Once saved always saved."

He finally left me alone about it.

The Reverend had seemed legit, but then again he was an ex-con grifter before becoming a preacher, so I never really trusted his shtick. Something about him seemed *too* perfect. His calm demeanor and his ability to have an answer for everything. But the man gave me a good recommendation when early parole came up, so I figured I owed him the benefit of the doubt. And when he suggested that I go to Camp Eden, I went for it.

I had to go somewhere ...

"I know you had some trouble with your family, your daughter. We talked about her. I know she's important to you," he said.

I'd forgotten I'd ever mentioned her to him. I wanted to strangle myself for letting him know about her. It must have been a moment of weakness.

"Sometimes our loved ones are not ready for us yet. They haven't learned to forgive," he said.

I nodded.

"The best way to deal with this, Ronnie, is through two things: prayer, and patience. I know that can be a heavy burden, but anger is never the right answer," he said, squeezing my shoulder.

"You're right about that, Rev Ricky," I said, slightly raising my shoulder to get him to move his hand. "I've been praying a lot lately. I can feel it working. Everything's going to be fine now," I smiled.

Was he here to get me back in line? I thought. *What the fuck? He just shows up out of nowhere?*

He looked at me like he wasn't sure if I was being sarcastic.

"Well, you feel free to call me anytime you need help," he said.

He took out a business card and handed it to me.

"Anytime. Call me collect," he said. "Camp Eden really is the best place. It's done wonders for Davis and Beasley." He looked over towards the two men working on the line.

I nodded my head and eased back to my position on the assembly line.

He knows them, too? What the fuck?

Reverend Ricky walked over to Davis and they hugged. Davis seemed genuinely happy to see him. They kept holding each other's hands while they talked. *I guess*

Davis and Beasley got out before I met the Rev. Kind of strange we're all at Camp Eden, and all in the same cabin. The Rev. had a similar reunion with Beasley, although Beasley seemed like his usual excitable self.

Before the Rev left the factory, he went over to the office and shook hands with Sarge. With his back to me, I could see an envelope in his back pocket. I blinked and my head pounded. I clinched my jaw. *This guy's on the payroll, too?*

When the afternoon whistle blew for our break, I hurried to the break room and waited by the open door for Davis to come by. I grabbed him by the sleeve and pulled him over towards the men's room. He jerked his arm away.

"Hey, you know Rev Ricky?" I asked.

"Yeah, I know him," he said.

"And he knows Beasley?"

"Yeah, he's a prison minister."

"Don't you think that's weird?" I asked. "I think that's weird."

Davis grabbed me by the wrist and pushed me into the bathroom, slamming me up against the wall.

"I don't give a fuck what you think, Harrison," he said. "That man saved my life. I was in the penitentiary a long time, and I learned a lot of ways to hurt people."

His face was close to mine. "But Rev Ricky taught me how to forgive. So I'm going to forgive you for talking about my friend. But I'm not going to forget. Just keep your fucking head down and your mouth shut around me, punk."

The bathroom door kicked open and Travis stood in the doorway. Davis looked at him while still holding me against the wall.

"Well what's going on in here, boys? Getting a little action on break?" Travis asked with a smirk.

Davis let go of me and turned to walk out. "Fuck you," he said as he walked past Travis.

                                                          Tyler Keith

The work whistle blew.

"Shit, Davis, I can't right now, I've got to get back to work," Travis said. "Maybe later."

"You all right, Hoss?" he asked.

"Yep," I said. I pushed past Travis and headed to my station.

As I worked the final hours of the shift I couldn't stop thinking about why the Rev came by. Was he trying to keep me in check? Make sure I didn't lose it? How could he really know how close I was to cracking up? Sarge called him. The thought of him mentioning my daughter made me angry. The ache in my heart started again, a real physical pain. I'm going to call her again when I get back to Camp Eden. We can fix things. Maybe her husband would listen to reason. Tammy could talk to her. What happened to her while I was away? Could I have done anything? I needed to know. Maybe I could do something now. If someone hurt her, maybe I could hurt them.

16

WHEN WE GOT back to Camp Eden, I jumped out of the van before it came to a complete stop, and I hurried to the pay phone. Took the scrap of paper with the phone numbers on it out of my wallet and stared at Tina's number. Seeing her face again nearly broke me. Her skin was so pale and clear. Tender. But her eyes looked so pained and the slight dark circles made her look older than her years. The worry. I could see it. But physically she still seemed so awkward, and lanky, and thin like she did when she was fourteen, the last time I saw her outside of prison.

Before I slipped into a tunnel of memory and despair, I dialed the number. He answered. I thought maybe I made it in time to miss him.

"Hello," he said.

I stayed silent. I couldn't speak to him. He just breathed into the phone for a long moment. Then he spoke again.

"Mr. Harrison, is that you?" he asked. "Tina is not going to talk to you. I thought I made myself clear. We don't need someone like you in our family. Do you understand me?"

I heard a muffled voice in the background. I thought I heard the voice say, "Who is that?"

"It's nobody," he said. "Wrong number."

"Tina!" I yelled as if she could hear me.

The man hung up the phone

"Hello? Hello?"

I called right back. Busy signal. I called back three

more times. I was desperate. I called Tammy's work number. It rang about ten times. Just when I was about to hang up, Tammy answered.

"Dolphin Realty, this is Tammy. How can I help you?" she said.

"Hey it's me, Ronnie," I said, trying to sound calm.

"Ronnie," she said with exasperation and sympathy. "I'm just leaving. I can't talk right now."

"Tammy, I've got to talk to Tina. I can't get through. The fucking guy won't let me talk to her."

"The guy you beat up? Ronnie, the guy is her husband, okay?" she said.

"I didn't beat him up. I just pushed him. It was a fucking accident. Look, if I can just talk to her, I can explain everything," I said.

"You're just going to have to give it some time. Despite everything that's happened to her, and everything you did, she still loves you. But she need him more than she needs you right now," she said.

"I don't understand," I said. "I don't know what happened when I was gone. I need to know what happened."

There was a long pause, like she was thinking whether she should tell me or not.

"Why, Ronnie?" she asked. "What could you do about it now anyway?"

"Please, Tammy. I need to know. If I know maybe I can figure out a way to make things right," I pleaded.

"Okay, Ronnie, you want to know?" The touch of sympathy had disappeared and pure anger replaced it. "You really want to know? Okay, I'll tell you what happened. After you stopped answering her letters, she had a few months where she ran wild. She stayed out all night. Got in trouble for drinking. But after she got in trouble, she gave it up. It scared her. She started going to church. I thought it was a good thing. I was working two jobs, and she had a place to go and a few friends there. Well, she met

                                    Tyler Keith

a boy there. He was a Navy guy. He was twenty years old. At first I forbid her to see him, but she would anyway. She would sneak around and meet him, so I allowed them to date. I thought it was okay. He seemed so nice and polite. And they met in church, for Christ's sakes."

"Twenty years old?" I asked.

"Don't fucking say anything, Ronnie. You have no right!" she said. "You just shut up."

"I'm sorry, Tammy," I said. "Go on."

"They had a few dates. I made sure she was home early. She kept up with her schoolwork. The day before the guy was shipping out for eight months, they went out. She came home crying and ran straight up to her room. I banged on the door and tried to talk to her. I thought maybe he's broken things off because he was shipping out. She wouldn't talk to me, and I had to go to work that night. For the next few days, she wouldn't leave her room or talk to me. I thought she must've just been heartbroken. She wouldn't talk about it. This all happened at a time when we were very distant. She hardly talked to me at all. So I left it. A month later Tina's pregnant … then she tells me what happened. That night she came home crying, the boy had wanted to go all the way with her. He told her he was leaving, and he loved her, and all that bullshit. She said 'no.' She wasn't even that crazy about the guy. She was sort of relieved the guy was leaving. But he didn't take 'no' for an answer. You know what I mean, Ronnie?" she asked.

"What the fuck? Please no."

"Yes, Ronnie."

"Why didn't you tell me?"

"I hadn't talked to you in two years. You hadn't talked to Tina in over a year. And she didn't want me to tell you. She was ashamed, Ronnie. Do you even believe that?" she asked. "She was ashamed. I went to the police. They wouldn't do anything. They said it had been too long. I went to the Navy, and they wouldn't do anything either. But she met her husband there. David was an MP or whatever they call it. He helped her. He was kind, and made her feel safe. She needed someone. Yes, a father figure. Because her father was in *prison!*"

Tammy paused for a moment. I didn't say anything. I couldn't. I was crying tears of rage and regret and sympathy.

Tammy went on, "She clung to David. Not long after the baby was born, he married her. He's treated that baby like it was his own."

She paused again. "That's the story. You won't get in-between them. He's not going to let you. But Tina still loves you. You're just going to have to give it some time."

I couldn't speak.

"I'm sorry, Ronnie, but I have to go now. Just give it some time," she said and then hung up.

I didn't feel like I had much time. I put my face in my hands and cried; raked my hands back and forth across my face. I had such a deep feeling of regret, I wanted to take off running towards the bay and just run straight into the water with my eyes closed and sink to the bottom. I took a deep breath and exhaled, and it was almost like I exhaled all the regret. When I took another breath, I inhaled anger and rage. The kind of rage I could put just below the surface. I could put it away just enough so I could walk around and not show it. Maybe I could smile and laugh. Ball up a fist behind my back maybe. There it was again, something in my mind, a terrible thing that had happened, that I could do nothing about. The back of my neck felt like a twisting rope. My jaw tightened. My temples throbbed. I wanted a drink. I wanted to forget again.

                                        Tyler Keith

17

I TOOK A long hot shower, and I felt almost like a man.
A little weary, but eager to forget. I combed my hair back
in a slight pompadour. Looked at myself in the foggy
mirror. I hadn't recognized myself in years. In prison, my
skin became a sickly yellow. Under the fluorescent lights
nobody looks well. I avoided mirrors other than to shave.
It was like taking LSD, stay away from mirrors.

I got dressed in my one set of street clothes: jeans,
black shirt, and jean jacket. I laid down on my bunk for a
quick rest. The radio played "Radar Love." It ended and a
weather forecast came on.

*Hurricane Elena is strengthening in the Gulf, moving
closer to land fall possibly Sunday or Monday morning. It is,
at this time, expected to hit land near Gulf Shores area; possibly
Biloxi, but could move southeast towards Perdido Key, Fort
Pickens, or possibly Pensacola Beach. Please stay tuned to this
station for later updates.*

"Shit, maybe they'll move us out of here," Davis said.

"Maybe they'll close work," Beasley said.

"It's moving towards Gulf Shores and Biloxi. We'll be
fine. Might have some high winds. Maybe high water," I
said. "I've been through a bunch of these."

"Man, you don't ever know where these things are
gonna end up," Davis said.

"Hey Davis, give me a shake before you go to eat, will
ya?" I asked. "I'm going early. I need some coffee."

"Beasley, you got me?"

"Yeah, I gotcha covered."

"What's for dinner tonight? Beasley?" I asked.

"It's meatloaf night, Harrison. You ain't never had any meatloaf like this."

"I bet I haven't." I said before I shut my eyes and fell asleep.

Later, I sat at a table in the Fellowship Hall, looking at the meatloaf. It was crisp around the edges with a layer of this ketchup shit along the top. Served with instant mashed potatoes and canned Italian cut green beans. The meatloaf tasted like something left in the Econoline van all day. It was just ground beef with the sticky thick stuff on top. Beasley watched me eat it. Smile on his face.

"See," he said. "You ain't never had anything like that, huh, Harrison?"

He took a bite of his.

"No. No I haven't, Beasley." I answered, chewing slowly.

Travis came by and set a Styrofoam cup in front of me. "I think you left your tea up by the green beans," he said and looked me in the eye.

"Thanks," I said. I was already holding a cup, but I picked up the one he left me and gave him a smile. Took a long drink. The Backslider. It sent that familiar warmth pulsing through my body. All the way down to my toes.

"Maybe you can help me with these dishes later."

"Sure, no problem. Let me finish this," I said, not looking at him. Trying to play it off. Beasley and Davis ignored the whole charade. They weren't stupid. Travis didn't care. He liked to rub it in. He liked people to know that he did what he wanted.

I finished half of my food. Took my tray and dumped it, and picked up a few random pieces of silverware and put them in the bus tub. Brought the bus tub over to the dish station.

"Need another Backslider, Hoss?" Travis slapped me on the back.

"Yeah, I'll take one," I said. Forced a smile. Travis'

                                    Tyler Keith

friendly facade started to make me leery. I knew this guy
wasn't my friend. Didn't have my best interest at heart.
But I went along. See how things played out. I wished I'd
never told Darleen to bring a friend. The idea of a double
date with two ex-cons and a couple of barflies seemed
absurd. Never been on a double date in my life. In fact,
I'd never been on a date. When I started seeing Tina, we
just started doing things together. Then we were a couple.
Then she got pregnant … then we were married.

After we finished the dishes, we stood under
the awning and smoked. We didn't talk much. Travis
refreshed our drinks. Each time he made them a little
stronger. I felt a little drunk. Felt good, but in the back
of my mind I worried. Back in my younger days I had
a drinking buddy named Wallace who used to tell me,
"Remember, Ronnie, it's a marathon not a sprint."

I still had questions about how all this shit worked.
About Travis and my Uncle Albert. How they were
connected. Reverend Ricky. Dr. James Millford.

"I still don't get it, Travis. How do you just come
and go and do what the hell you want to around here
and not catch hell?" I asked. "I know there's a connection
between whatever it is you do over in Holmes County for
my uncle, and this fucking place, but what the hell is it? It
don't make no sense."

"Well let me tell ya, Ronnie, the man who owns this
place, and many others like it, the great Dr. Millford, he
comes from the Geneva, Alabama, Samson area, right up
the Choctawhatchee from Holmes County. His father and
your uncle go way back. They did business together for
years. Shit, they may be kin," he said.

"In the last number of years, since you been locked
up, we had a cash problem. The good kind of cash
problem, *too much!* We had so much cash up there, we
didn't know what to do with it. I mean barns full. Can't
put it no bank. But you can run it through charities.
Offerings. Donations. Church building projects. Invisible

mission trips. They've got all kinds of ways of laundering the money. For instance, Albert's got some contracting businesses, big building companies that get these big church projects. Well they don't build shit. He just puts some money in the bank and pays himself with it through Eden Ministries or whatever they call it. He's got several contracting companies all in his kids' names."

"But what about this place?" I asked. "Camp Eden?"

"Of course the mighty Dr. Millford gets his cut. Millford's got an insane spread down by Naples. Don Pedro Island or somewhere. Calls it a spiritual retreat. But anytime Albert needs some info about someone in prison, or needs a place for someone to hide out, maybe get somebody out on early release, he can run 'em through here. A few months back, I had a little trouble with an aggravated assault charge. Managed to get it down to simple assault, but I had to do a few months in the county lockup, then they'd let me come down here. Once I get here, I can take the weekends, and really, given the circumstances, I could leave for longer. They like me to do a little of this work, too. The parole or probation officer can sign off without much worry about anybody else checking on the details.

"Know what I mean, Ronnie?" he asked with a little smile.

"Yeah, I see what you mean," I said. "Looks like a pretty good deal all the way around."

"It works okay. Sometimes the Reverend Doctor will assert some of his authority and make me attend church. And due to their long-time connection, Mr. Albert makes me do what he says. It's kind of an arms-length deal. Neither would admit the other is in charge."

"That's fucked up," I said, trying to make sense of it all.

"Yeah it is," Ronnie agreed. "All this shit is fucked up. The best thing you could do is just come back to Holmes County. Just come for the weekend. Hell, you might even enjoy yourself for a change."

"I don't know. I want to stay out of trouble," I said.

"You're doing a great job at that. How long you going to last in here? You got a temper, Ronnie. You could be making money every weekend. Lots of money. Get out of this place a lot quicker. Trust me. Come on, just for the weekend," he said, nudging me with his elbow and looking at me with that bullshit grin.

"Fuck, man, let me think about it," I said, looking away. "Give me another drink of that shit."

"That's what I'm talking about, Hoss," he said, slapping me on the back as he handed me the bottle.

I was sick of this place — Camp Eden. *Fuck this place. My daughter was out of reach, for the moment anyway. What did I have to look forward to around here this weekend? A game of horseshoes in the rain. "Extra work" on Saturday. Sarge giving me shit. Some stories from Beasley. And it would just be for the weekend, right? I could just test the waters.*

I took another drink and handed the jug back to Travis. There was something about the land, too. I wanted to see the river and walk around on the dirt. So many of my early childhood memories live there. My family history lurked there in the old broken down shacks and handmade cabins. I was related to half the county in some way, from my father's or mother's side, one. I dreamed about the place for god's sakes. I always had. The river always flowed through my dreams, ever since I was kid. Sometimes I'd have dreams of drowning and sometimes the water was a source of peace.

"Why don't you just sleep on it, Ronnie," Travis said and walked back towards his cabin. He turned around just before he entered his cabin and shot me with his fingers in the shape of a gun.

I stood there and smoked. Drunk. Vaguely angry. Sad. Closed my eyes and leaned against the metal building, mulling over the idea of heading back to Holmes County. But my thoughts weren't clear. I couldn't weigh anything out. I started humming a song, "Branded Man" by Merle Haggard, remembered the words that tell a story of a man who leaves prison branded with a number he can't shake, a name no one uses. I laughed out loud. The song made so much sense it struck me funny.

"I know you two are drinking," a voice said.

I opened my eyes and Jesse stood there shining the flashlight in my face.

"Get that damn light out of my face," I said, covering my eyes with my hand.

Jesse pointed the light to the ground.

"I know y'all are drinking," he said again.

"I was just helping with the dishes, Jesse," I said.

"I know y'all were because I use to drink. That's why I'm in here."

He put a hand on his hip and loosened his stance to appear more relaxed.

"You don't have to, though," Jesse continued. "I don't no more. I just got right with the Lord."

"Is that so?"

"It is so. You know what else got me in trouble?" he asked.

I didn't answer.

"Being friends with the wrong crowd. They'll lead you astray."

"You're right about that, Jesse."

He turned and walked back towards the cabins. Just like clockwork, the red New Yorker made the turn into the cul de sac.

"Jesse, your friends are here," I said.

He didn't turn around. Just walked faster towards his cabin.

I shuffled back to my own cabin, humming Merle Haggard. I tried my best to be quiet getting into my bed, but Davis and Beasley had already gone to sleep and the lights were off. I stumbled over some shit on the floor and collapsed on my bed, making a racket.

"Sorry," I said to the figures in the bunk next to me. Beasley just kept on snoring, but I thought I heard Davis

                                        Tyler Keith

whisper, "fuck you." I was drunk enough to say something back, but I didn't. I knew Davis had had about
enough of me. Something told me not to push my luck.
I closed my eyes and little white lines swam across the
blackness.

*That Jesse is just a poor stupid kid. At least he has some
sort of plan. Or he knows enough to stay away from assholes.
Then again, he has his past driving by every night.*

18

I WOKE UP the next morning with Davis sitting on the edge of my bed, looming over me. He held an open pocketknife by my neck.

"If you keep coming in drunk, waking me up, I'm going to cut your fucking throat," he said quietly, with a slight smile.

I smiled back.

"Now get up. You already missed breakfast."

I'd slept in my clothes again. I sat up and patted my coat for a cigarette. Beasley walked over with a coffee and a biscuit.

"Don't worry about Davis," he said. "He's not a morning person. He needs his eight hours. You missed breakfast."

He handed me the coffee and the biscuit.

"Thanks, Beasley."

"If you're gonna get a shower, you better get in there. Sarge is in a hell-of-a mood today," Beasley said.

The shower was short and sweet. The cold water didn't have time to turn warm. It gave me a bit of life. But I was still drunk. It was false good feeling. I put on my work clothes and headed to the van. Everybody was already loaded up and the van idled in front of the office. The front passenger seat was the only one open. I got in and stared straight ahead.

"Nice of you to join us, Mr. Harrison," Sarge said. "I was about to leave you."

"It's okay by me," I muttered.

"What was that?" he asked, staring at the side of my head.

"Sorry I'm late, sir," I said.

He paused, about to speak, but turned up the radio instead, then backed out and spun out in the mud. The radio played some god-awful contemporary gospel. "Satan is a liar/And he will try to make you think." Possibly the worst music to hear when you're developing the beginnings of a wicked hangover. "That was 'Praise the Lord' by Russ Taft. Now we're going to get into some prayer requests," the DJ said.

I rubbed my head and moaned. Sarge laughed out loud and turned the radio up a touch more. Travis, sitting behind me on the bench seat, patted me on the shoulder and said, "Praise the Lord." Everybody could tell I was hurting. The whole van started laughing, first a little titter then everybody was howling with laughter. I tried not to laugh, but even I couldn't stop myself.

The work that day felt even more tedious and futile than usual. I worked slow, just doing enough to not be standing completely still. Why not go to Holmes County? You've got nothing to lose. Look at these men. They're just doing this pointless bullshit. Polishing fucking marble sink tops. Useless. This is the kind of thinking that got me into Holmes County in the first place. I could never get my mind around doing a stupid meaningless job for nothing but money. Especially for little money. Seemed like such a sucker's game. I guess you wouldn't wind up in jail with some kid's blood on your hands though.

Sarge came in and out. Really did nothing. I watched Beasley work. It seemed like he was just here to have something to do. Without prison or Camp Eden, he'd probably be on the street. Davis had lost his life in prison and didn't know how to live without structure. Travis may end up dead in a ditch somewhere, someday, but he'd get some kicks first. The man was dangerous. I knew it from the stories I'd heard about him. I could feel it lurking there underneath his calm, joking surface. But I could keep my distance. Stay aware and alert. I knew he was here to get me to come back or else. And I wasn't sure I was ready to deal with the "or else" at this point. If I went back to Holmes County, I could hoard some cash. Get enough to start over. I certainly didn't want to continue with this charade. Working here. Going to church. Rehabilitating.

The morning break whistle blew. I waited by the break room door for Travis. When he came by I pulled him aside.

"I'm in," I said. "I can't take this shit no more."

Travis patted me on the back. "Goddamn right!" he said. "Let me make a phone call."

He walked over to the pay phone. I saw him leaning over the phone, cackling like a crazy man. He strutted back over to me and said, "I got us a pick up at 6:30 tonight."

"Sarge is just going to let me go?" I asked.

"He's going to get a phone call. He'll want us back by Sunday," he said. "He's not going to like it, but fuck him."

We went into the break room and he sat down. I got a cup of coffee and sat down across from him.

"What are we going to do all weekend?" I asked. I was nervous already. Excited to get away from Eden, to get away from these other men for a few days. But I was afraid of what could happen. What could go wrong?

"Your cousin Charles wants to see you tonight. Then I imagine we'll drink a shitload of beer," he said with a smile. "Who knows, maybe you might even make some money."

"What are you talking about?" I asked. "I just got out a week ago."

"They may want to see if you're serious or not," he said. "Don't worry about it, Hoss. You won't have to do anything you don't want to do."

"I haven't driven a car in six years," I said. I'd missed it, too. I'd dreamed about driving through those back roads in Holmes County.

"We'll fix that," he said.

After the horn blew for the end of the first break, I walked back towards the floor past Davis. He looked at me and shook his head and smiled. Yeah, this was a dumb idea but, with what had already happened, I didn't really care. The rest of the day I continued to work at a snail's pace. Just enough. But now it was because my mind rumbled with visions of Holmes County, and the thought of driving a car through the whole county two or three times without seeing many other cars. Two lane roads. You could really open things up. Flat terrain. Nice curves.

When we got back to camp, everybody headed to their cabins.

"Harrison!" Sarge yelled. "I need to speak with you in my office."

I followed him to the office. He sat down behind his desk. He rustled around some papers. Then he just stared at me.

"I guess you want a weekend pass?" he asked.

I nodded.

"I don't think it's a good idea," he said. "First off, you don't deserve it. Some of the shit you've pulled this week. Second, you're not ready for it."

"I'll be alright," I said.

"You got old in prison," Sarge said. "It doesn't make you sharper or smarter. And do you think things have just stayed the same since you were locked up?

"There's younger, harder people coming up. More money. More competition. More police."

"I'm just going to see some relatives and some old friends," I replied.

"You think I'm stupid? I know you don't like me, Harrison, and to be quite honest, I don't like you. I think you're just a weak puppet. You let everybody else do your thinking for you," he said, then paused. "But I do this job to help men like you. You can believe that or not. And my

Tyler Keith

advice to you is to keep your nose down and stay out of trouble. That's your best chance to fix your shit."

"I appreciate that, Sarge. I really do, but I'm just going to see some friends and family."

"Well, if I can't change your mind, you're going to need to be back here by two on Sunday. If you're any later than that, then I'm cutting you loose. I'll be informing you parole officer that you are M.I.A. Do you hear me?" he asked.

"Yes sir," I said.

He reached into his desk drawer and pulled out an envelope. He tossed it towards me.

"You might need some spending money," he said. "Here's your week's pay."

"Thanks," I said. I was starting to think Sarge was okay. I opened the envelope and there was two twenties and a five. "What the fuck? Forty-five bucks? I worked a fifty-hour week."

"I told you at the first of the week that some expenses would come out of your check."

"What the fuck, though?"

"This is just the first week. You had a lot of expenses this first week. It'll be more next week.

"Remember you got that carton of cigarettes too," he added.

"Goddamn, though," I said. "You know what, forget it. Thanks."

"Two o'clock Sunday. Don't be late," he yelled as I walked out slamming the door behind me.

Forty-five bucks! I knew I was going to get screwed, but fuck … I'd never save enough money to get out of this place with this kind of deal. It's like sharecropping. Soon enough I'd just accept my fate like Beasley and Davis. I'd be waiting every week for fucking spaghetti day.

I took another shower, and it helped to wash off the sluggish feeling I'd had all day. Helped me feel almost human. I put on my jeans, shirt, and jacket — not too fresh from the other night. Shaved. Combed my hair. I put my

toothbrush and disposable razor in my jacket pocket. I sat
on the edge of the bed and smoked a cigarette, waiting for
6:30 to roll around.

Davis and Beasley sat at the table, playing a game
of dominoes. "You getting out of here or something?"
Davis asked.

"I got a weekend pass," I said.

"I bet you're headed to Holmes County with
Campbell," Beasley said. I didn't respond. "Maybe you
can bring me some of that white lightning if you run
across some?"

"Okay, Beasley," I said.

"You're even dumber than you look," Davis said.

"Look at it this way, Davis, at least I won't wake you
up when I come in tonight," I said.

"Praise the Lord," he said.

I got up and walked out to the porch. It was raining
lightly but it was still hot and the sun still shown through
in certain spots in the sky.

19

ME AND TRAVIS waited outside the gates of Eden in the rain. An '85 Chevy Monte Carlo, black with red piping and maroon leather interior, glided up to the gate and stopped in front of us. The passenger door opened.

"Ronnie, why don't you climb in the back seat," Travis said.

I got in. The driver wore a red bandana that held his hair back and he had a light mustache. Travis sat in the passenger seat and gave the driver a sort of handshake.

"Hey, Marty, this is Ronnie. Ronnie, this is Marty. He likes to drive too."

We nodded at each other. "Hey, Ronnie," Marty said, checking me out in the rearview mirror. He slammed the car into gear, fishtailing in the mud then catching on the wet asphalt. He turned up the radio. "I'll Wait 'Till Your Love Comes Down" by Van Halen filled the car with pulsing sound. We made Highway 98 doing fifty and quickly hit somewhere near eighty. I got a sinking feeling. *Fuck … what am I doing?* I felt an urge to just get out and walk back to the camp, but it was too late for that.

Travis turned around sporting that grin of his and handed me a Busch. The beer was ice-cold and tasted like the greatest beer I'd ever had, next to the one I'd had one week earlier at the Fire and Fiddle. I closed my eyes, leaned back, and took another long drink.

Travis nudged me again. This time he handed me a joint. I took the joint, gave it the once-over, then took a long hit and handed it back to Travis. I tried to exhale slowly, keeping the smoke in my lungs, but my slow exhale turned into a coughing fit.

Travis broke into a little laugh. "That's it," he said.

I closed my eyes, leaned back, and took another drink. When I opened my eyes again, I was stoned. A mild panic set in. I took a few deep stuttering breaths. We turned off 98 towards Holmes County. There was no more sun, but it wasn't completely dark yet. Everything slowed down. The music seemed to warp. The drum fills pounded across the contours of my skull. I laughed but nothing was funny. I pictured Tina in my mind's eye, just like I'd seen her a few days ago. She was looking at me with those sad eyes, her little daughter hiked up on her hip holding on. I stared out the window at the rain and the green pine forest, not really knowing where I was but knowing where I was going. The car jolted to the right sprawling me on the back seat as we hit a turn too fast.

"What the fuck," I shouted. I'd spilt half a beer on my lap.

Travis turned down the radio and turned towards me. "Sorry, Hoss. We gotta meet Mister Charles at the farm. We're running late. Marty's just trying to make up some time," he said.

Fuck! Charles... I'd almost forgotten about meeting him.

"Well give me another beer then," I said.

This is what you signed up for, dumb ass. Your cousin Charles. The family business. The farm...

The "farm" was a kind of headquarters for the Harrison clan. The whole county was set up around different clans, many going back one hundred years or more. Families staked out an area and settled on it like pioneers in the West. They cleared the timber. Put up houses. A chapel. A road running through it. Over the hill or around the bend there'd be another clan with all their people, their church, and their road running through it. Mostly you stayed with your own people. Not every clan

Tyler Keith

wanted to visit with the neighbor folks. Some clans could
be what you might call "war-like."

The Harrison clan lived on a three-mile dirt road half-
circle following along the Choctawhatchee river, twenty
or thirty homes, some old dog trots built a hundred years
ago, dilapidated but still occupied. Behind those there
may be a trailer or two, or an old Airstream from the
fifties fixed up with a window unit. People'd be sitting on
their porches all day, watching who's driving by, making
sure whoever it was was supposed to be. There'd be a
few newer ranch-style houses with fairly nice lawns, and
usually a fence with a few horses, maybe a couple of cows,
grazing. Some folks lived off of the road, down gullies
closer to the Choctawhatchee. They were river people.
They fished all year around. Made some moonshine, either
to sell or just drink and give to friends. Probably grew
a little weed for the same purposes. Most weren't real
criminals, but they kept their eyes open anyhow. Your kin
meant more than country. Didn't like cops or strangers just
cruising by. At the beginning of the dirt road there was a
chapel and at the end there was a general store, and everybody on that loop, most all Harrisons or relations, knew
who was running up and down that road. If you had no
business cruising that road, you were noticed.

Halfway down that dirt road, almost in the exact
middle, was the farm. The front of the property was
heavily wooded so you couldn't see anything from the
road. There was a cattle gate at the entrance and beyond
that, down the gravel drive, was a ranch style house, a
large wooden barn, and two doublewide trailers with
small built-on porches. The property backed up to the
river. They had a johnboat and an old green canoe, and
an old fish cabin that was just a screened-in porch with a
kitchen and a bathroom.

The farm acted as a sort of headquarters for the
Harrison criminal clan. Back when I was a kid, it was more
of a family place where kin from out of the county could

stay and fish. They'd have family reunions and the like. But sometime in the last ten or fifteen years, it became the headquarters for the criminal side of the family. For the shit they did — weed, whiskey, whatever — headed by my Uncle Albert, the day-to-day shit handled by Charles.

"Motherfucker," I said quietly.

I don't know why I didn't think I'd be going to this place. I hadn't thought things through. The place held some dark memories. I'd been present for some acts of violence. The Harrisons were diligent about keeping competition out of the county. Usually it was just some dude selling some weed or pills, but if they got caught them they'd hurt them and send them off as a lesson for others who might think about selling something down there, or they'd make a deal for half of their profits. Half the profits is a better deal than losing a finger or winding up floating in the river. That kind of shit was why I liked driving. I didn't have to be there much. I'd pull my rig in and hook up or pull my car into the barn, go have a beer and come back and drive. The place also held some good memories from my time working here, the kind of memories that you don't really remember, just vague flashes of drinking beer all day by the river, long afternoons fishing and swimming, nights of loud music, girls, and partying.

The idea of seeing my cousin, Charles, didn't thrill me. He was Albert's oldest son, the one who did his bidding without question, however ruthless the request. Always the obedient son. And he was hand picked to take the mantle when Albert's days were done. Charles always put on this air of congeniality, and an "aw shucks" face of a stupid man, like he was just a country bumpkin. But he was anything but stupid. And he was brutal. Even as kids, we would run when we saw him coming. He was the kind of kid who would tie a bottle rocket to a cat's tail for kicks. At the same time he was a family man with four or five kids and a wife he kept in a nice house in Defuniak Springs, across the county line. Owned a few convenience stores over there, sitting right where people would turn off I-10 headed towards Fort Walton Beach.

I didn't want to see him, especially in the state I was in. I didn't know if I could keep it together. Just a little weed and four or five beers and I was already in a haze, my head cloudy and my emotions a dangerous mess. Somehow I knew I wasn't cut out for this shit anymore, even if I was just driving again. I'd forgotten the hanging around, and the being a witness to the off-handed violence. I just didn't want to see it or be around it, to see the folks that participated in the game … but I didn't know that's how I felt yet. It was just an idea forming in the numbness of my brain to the thumping sounds of Van Halen in the back of an '85 Monte Carlo on the way to the farm. One thing I did know is that I shouldn't have gotten in this car, and I was on the ride until Sunday.

We pulled up to the farm. Travis got out and opened the gate. The rain fell lightly on the gravel drive. A couple of cars and a pickup were parked at the house. It was pitch black except for the porch light and the headlights of the Monte Carlo.

When we entered the house, a group of four men were standing at the breakfast bar at the edge of the kitchen. Three young girls sat on the couch. Somebody handed me a mason jar of blackberry moonshine. I recognized Charles, salt and pepper curly hair, neatly trimmed beard, tall and heavy-set, wearing crisp blue jeans, dress shirt, and a dark blazer. I recognized two of the men, but couldn't recall their names, and the third guy was a stranger. Charles stepped out from behind the bar holding his drink in the air.

"Here's a toast to my cousin, Ronnie. Too dumb to live; too smart to die. Welcome home," he said and swallowed his drink. The rest of the guys, including Marty and Travis, raised their glasses and gave a little hoot.

"All right guys, I need a word with Ronnie alone for a minute. Go keep the girls company," Charles said, pointing over to the couch. He poured himself a finger of Wild Turkey from a bottle on the counter. He drank a sip and walked over and shook my hand.

"I'm really glad you're back," he said, putting his hands on his hips.

"I'm glad to be out," I said. "It was a bit of a surprise."

"Yeah, it was. I sure wasn't expecting it. You could've called and let us know, Ronnie," he said.

"I know, Charles, I'm sorry," I said. "I didn't even have a chance to tell my family."

"How is your family?" he asked.

"Oh, they're good. Tina, my daughter, is married and has a kid," I said.

"Well, I'll be damned," he said. "They grow up so quick. You see that guy there?"

He pointed to the man I didn't know.

"That's my oldest boy, Bob," Charles said. "He's all grown up. At least he thinks he is."

He leaned in towards me like he was telling an important secret.

"Dumb as a rock. And will not listen. Kind of reminds me of Junior."

"Yeah, he favors him a little bit, too," I said.

"You think so?" he asked, then answered his own question, "Maybe so."

I nodded and shrugged.

"Things have changed a little around here since you've been away," Charles said. "Gotten a little more complicated. There are more eyes on everything. More money around, too. More outsiders want a piece. There's a diversified product list. But in the end, things are just the same as they always have been. We've got the same problem we've always had. We need good men. Always. People we can trust. Skilled labor, too. That being said, we may have some work for you here. You fit the bill. You're reliable and you're family. We can help you get back on your feet. Or should I say behind the wheel.

                                    Tyler Keith

"What do you think, Ronnie?"

"I just got out, Charles," I said. "I'm still trying to get my feet under me."

He studied me with a displeased eye.

"But I feel like I'm back home here," I said. "It feels good."

That was a lie. I felt tense and my mind muddled at the same time. I felt like he wanted me to say that. He had a way of looking at me, through me, a way that melted my resolve, and made me just go along with things.

"I'm glad to hear you say that," he said. "Although Daddy's very much in charge," he leaned forward again, "he's not going to live forever. I've got my own ideas for the future. Daddy's old school. Stuck in his ways. Hell, he's been doing this for sixty years. One thing he's taught me is to keep good people around you. Relations are best. But times have changed."

"How's your Momma?" I asked, trying to change the subject.

"Momma's real good. Just looking after Daddy. He's still sharp. Mean as ever. He just doesn't get around as easily as he did. He still tells me I'm not too old for him to whip me if I need it," he said.

"Tell her I said hello," I said.

"I'll do that. She always was partial to you. Maybe because you were so close to Junior."

He put his left hand on my shoulder, and gave me a penetrating look, shaking my hand.

"All right, fellas, let's get the fuck out a Dodge," he yelled to the men on the couch. "Just think about what I said, Ronnie. Travis is going to talk to you tonight. Give you some more details."

Charles pulled two tickets out of his coat pocket and handed them to me.

"We've got the big rodeo tomorrow night over in Bonifay. I want you and Travis to meet me there. We'll talk more. See what you decide to do. I think it would be good for your all-around well-being to come back over to the family."

He squeezed my hand and cracked a smile.

As the men walked by, Charles stopped his son and made him shake my hand.

"Bob, this is your cousin, Ronnie," he said.

"Hey, Bob," I said and shook his hand.

His hair was shoulder length, parted in the middle, and he had a pathetic mustache and wore a shell necklace. He gave me a weak handshake and said, "Hey, Ronnie." He stared blankly at me, just held my hand looking stoned. Charles pushed him towards the door.

"All right, let's get the fuck out of here. It's a good thing you can't die of a reefer overdose," Charles said.

The group, including one of the girls, left the house and got into a blue Cadillac Deville with Charles driving and the girl in the passenger seat, they took off out of the gate and down the dirt road.

Tyler Keith

20

"SEE, RONNIE, MR. Charles ain't so bad," Travis said after closing the door behind his boss. "Just don't piss him off or he'll throw you down the well back there."

He laughed and patted me on the back.

"He's been threatening to throw me down that well since we were kids," I said.

"Ronnie, I want you to come over here and meet some lady-friends," Travis said, ignoring my remark.

I followed Travis into the living room where Marty and the two girls were sitting on the couch. The two girls stood up. The first girl looked to be in her late twenties, but somehow she seemed older. Something about the way she carried herself, a confidence, an ease. She was tall and thin, wearing suede moccasins, blue jeans, and a tight black Motorhead t- shirt. She held a Busch can and a ciga-rette in one hand.

"This is Heather," Travis said.

We shook hands. The other girl was a little rounder. Her dirty blonde hair was slightly teased. Her skin was pale and she looked young, maybe eighteen. She wore flip- flops, faded jeans, a tight black tank top, and a Levis' jean jacket with the sleeves rolled up. She was drinking a wine cooler.

"This is Britney," Travis said.

"Hey Ronnie, Travis had told me about you," the girl said.

We exchanged pleasantries and shook hands. She had a rosy glow about her face, and through her pale skin you

could see little blue veins, even in the shadowy darkness
of the living room. *How old is this girl?* For a split second, I
thought about Tina. I thought about the places she might
have been when I wasn't around. I felt a bit of comfort
knowing she was safe with her asshole Navy man. At least
she wasn't out here like some girls her age.

The girls sat back down on the couch. I sat on the
arm by Britney. Travis picked up a half of a joint from the
ashtray, lit it, and handed it to me. I took a hit and handed
it to Britney. The joint went around the room. Travis took
the last hit and put it out in the ashtray. He exhaled the
smoke and slammed the last of his Busch, crushed the can,
and said, "Let's hit the bar."

The rain had stopped and the windows of the Monte
Carlo were rolled down. I could smell the mud and the river
in the air, and there was a thickness to the night. It kind of
hung on you. I took my jacket off, and folded it up and put
it on the floorboard. Rolled up my sleeves. The Monte Carlo
rumbled down the dirt road. Marty was a good driver. He
had an easy grip on the wheel and he paid attention to the
road, and didn't talk much or look around the car. He, Travis,
and Heather sat in the front seat, and me and Britney sat
in the back. She sat on the hump in the middle of the back
seat smoking a cigarette, clutching her wine cooler. I leaned
forward, smoking and ashing out the window, mild paranoia
and drunkenness on me. I kept stealing looks at Britney. She
was always looking at me with a nonchalant smile, her face
half invisible in the darkness. I tapped Travis on the shoulder.

"Where are we going?" I asked.

He half-turned his head, yelled, "Honky's," and let
out a holler. It seemed like Marty stepped on the gas. I fell
back in my seat. Looked out the window and ashed my
cigarette, just catching the ash on the wind. I looked over
at Britney. She gazed at me with a little smile. Her eyes
seemed to catch a passing flash of light. She put her hand
on my thigh, ever so lightly. She gave it a gentle rub. I
dropped my cigarette out the window, then I leaned over

                                    Tyler Keith

and we kissed. The Van Halen cassette must have flipped over a few times without anybody changing it because, I swear, "I'll Wait" played again.

Honky's had once been called something else with Honky Tonk in the name. The rest of the sign, except Honky, had fallen away and they just kept it and used it for a name. It was close to the Alabama line, north of East Pitman right past Smith Crossroads, just south of Black, Alabama, not too far from Geneva where my mother's folks came from. Honky's was a fitting name, too. It was the bar one might find if they died and went to redneck heaven.

We pulled off the main road onto a long dirt drive. The old place shimmered in the misty night, the neon beer sign flashing like a beacon in a raging sea. If you saw this place in the daylight, with no lights and no people, you'd be sure it was abandoned. Despite the rain and the mist, the parking lot was full of cars, trucks, and a few motorcycles.

The five of us got a spot at the end of the bar by the cigarette machine. The place had a pool table, jukebox, six or seven tables, and a little stage in the corner. A three-piece band played the song about being an old chunk of coal. That song brought a smile to my face. In prison, one of the few pleasures was my little transistor radio. I didn't care too much for the newer country, but this song, sung by John Anderson had really hit home, and had become a favorite of mine. We all got drinks, and I leaned on the bar, looking around. Travis ran off outside with a little redneck man. He left me alone with Heather and Britney.

Out of sheer awkwardness I asked Heather, "So how do you know Travis?"

"I sell weed," She said, looking at me like I was an idiot.

I looked at Britney. She nodded and said, "Among other things."

They both laughed. The band sang "I'm Still Crazy," the singer sounding like a parody of Vern Gosdin. They finished the song and took a break.

"Thank God. I hate that shit," Heather said.

She walked over to the jukebox and seconds later "Ace of Spades" by Motorhead blasted through the bar. I felt a little shaky, tiredness weighed on me, a kind of heaviness in my body, but I still felt half-sharp. The drive had helped clear my head. But I had no idea what to say to Britney.

"You know Travis long?" I asked.

"He used to hang out with my mom," she replied. "He would give me joints. Sometimes my mom would be gone for a few days and Travis would come over. Sometimes he'd bring some friends. We'd party. That's how I met Heather."

She leaned a little closer to me.

Heather banged her head to the music, singing in Marty's face. He drank his beer and ignored her, keeping his eyes on two bikers at the opposite end of the bar. They were checking him out too.

Travis hustled back into the bar with the man he went out with. The man was a little wiry guy wearing a dark blue snap-buttoned western shirt, and a beat up straw cowboy hat pulled down low. Travis sidled up to me and Britney at the bar.

"Three shots of Crown," he said, pounding on the bar.

We took the shots and Travis pulled out a small baggy under the bar. He motioned from me to the bag with his head. It was a little bag of white powder. I shook my head. I wasn't quite ready for that yet. He gave me a little smile and a look that asked, "Are you sure?" and put it back in his pocket.

Travis, Marty, and the skinny guy all leaned on the bar staring at the two bikers.

"The problem we're having over here in Holmes County is a little unhealthy competition," Travis said, not looking at me, but still giving the bikers the slow eye.

"The two bikers?" I asked.

"There's a bunch more of 'em. They set up shop down here. Growing weed, but mostly cooking up speed. Things started getting out of hand. Some rival gangs came over. The cops pulled a few bodies out of the river. This tweaker kid shot his parents and took the cops on a chase through the woods. They had a big standoff. He killed a few cops. Made the papers outside the county. Got people's attention in Tallahassee," he said, all of this while skull-fucking the two bikers and casually drinking his beer.

"Bad for the family business," I said.

"Goddam right."

The two bikers whispered to each other, still looking our way. Maybe they decided four against two might not be the best odds. They finished their drinks and made for the door. Travis tossed some cash on the bar, gave me a look and a nod towards the door and headed for the exit.

"Heather!" Travis yelled.

"I just put some money in here," she yelled back, but she followed him anyway. As we exited Honky's, the two men revved up their bikes and pulled out onto the main two-lane.

"Dirty Love" by Motorhead started up as the door to Honkey's closed.

The windows were down in the Chevy and as we picked up speed the wind gave a little relief from the stifling heat. It helped me keep the softness out for a few more minutes, the fuckedupness. They'd passed around another joint and a half pint of moonshine in a Seagram's Gin bottle. It was all threatening to shut me down. The edges were getting blurry. I'd leaned back in my seat and put my arm around Britney as we caught up to the two bikers. Before we got too close Marty cut the lights and we eased up behind them. The music pounded from the back speakers. Travis leaned out of the car window and then I heard a gun shot. Marty cut the lights on the bikers. One of them swerved into the other lane, almost laying down his bike, and then they took off. Marty stepped on the gas to keep up.

"What the fuck!" I yelled.

Travis fell back into the car laughing.

"I just shot up in the air, Ronnie. Don't worry," he said, leaning over the back seat, holding a 9mm and smiling.

Marty followed the bikers from about fifty yards back. We followed them for a few miles until they turned off into a dirt drive.

"That's their place," Travis said and pointed.

I leaned up so I could get a look. Marty slowed. I could see a big bonfire with a bunch of bikes and a crowd of people standing around. Then it was like a hive of pissed off hornets, people getting on their bikes, cranking up their engines, all of which were made for the sole purpose of making a roar. Marty punched it. Looking out the back window of the car, I could see them pouring out onto the black top, a whole procession of bikes. It reminded me of angry villagers with torches coming after some strangers to burn them alive.

I sunk down in the back seat so I could barely see out the back window. They were catching up fast. I got a look at the first bike in the line. There was a guy on the back with, looked like he was carrying a sawed off shotgun. I panicked. I pulled Britney down. I peeked out again and noticed we were passing the Harrison Chapel. I knew we were close to the dirt road. We'd be safe if we could make it there. I saw a flash come from the shotgun and saw the bike wobble and almost go down before I heard the blast. A few pellets hit the window.

I stayed down now. I heard a few more pistol shots and then I felt Marty make a big turn. A memory and a fear shot through me, a muscle memory from the day I killed Jimmy. I thought about the kid I'd killed. It was like the bottom dropped out of my gut, a sickening feeling. Then the dirt road moved under us and the wheels caught. Through a cloud of dust, I could see the bikers ride off down the main road. We'd made it to the Harrison's loop, and something like safety.

21

THE BUZZ OF the little combat with the bikers carried
me through about an hour of partying back at the farm.
Bob, Charles' son, showed up with a couple of girls. They
laid out some lines and cranked up the music. Bob seemed
much less like the stoned-out loser than he did earlier. He
had everybody laughing. Seemed to be real close to Travis.
Travis slapped him on the back and laughed the loudest.
They seemed to be in competition to see who could do
the most blow. I did a line, partially to avoid the peer
pressure, partly because I wanted one. I thought it might
keep the fog away. Maybe keep me alert. Britney took a
few turns. The closeness we'd had in back of the car had
waned a little. I think she wanted to enjoy the party.

The coke only kept me alert for a fleeting moment.
The smoke and the music and the voices brought back
the fog. I stepped out onto the porch to grab some air and
a cigarette. I walked out into the drive so I could barely
hear the music coming from the house. A different sound
surrounded me, a roar in the night, a noise that made me
feel a moment of peace and comfort. The sound of crickets,
maybe millions of them, was like the brilliant static you'd
hear if you turned on an old Philco radio. It was a sound
I'd forgotten, a sound of the real, natural world. The
elements. The sound of real things that make the world of
men and machines seem fleeting and impermanent. None
of the dumb shit I did or the people in the house mattered
in the least. That house, the barn, the trailers would all

rot away into the mud, but the sound would continue.
The fucking insects would sing. The river would run.
Goddamn, I'm fucked up ...

"What the fuck are you doing out here, Ronnie?" a
voice called from the porch. It was Travis.

"Getting some air," I said.

He walked over to me and put his arm around me.

"Air is kind of thick out here," he said. "Let me show
you something. You're going to like this."

Travis walked towards the big barn. I followed him.
He slid the barn door open, and in the darkness I could
see the outline of an automobile. He walked around to the
passenger's side of the car and flicked on an overhead,
florescent light. The light flashed on and off a few times
before catching.

"What do you say about that?" Travis asked.

It was a 1973 Camaro Z28, with dark green paint,
black sport stripes, and black vinyl top.

"1973. The last year before they put all that pollution
shit on 'em," he said. "This machine will purr. It will run
the roads."

The car seemed like a vision glowing in the florescent
light. I ran my hand along the hood, and then bent down
and looked into the driver's side window. Black leather
interior. Clean.

"Why don't you crank her up?" Travis tossed me
the keys.

When I sat in the car, the black leather felt so soft,
like my granddaddy's old leather chair. I put both hands
on the wheel and it sat just right. I almost felt like I was
already driving. I stuck the key in the ignition and gave
it a soft fluid turn, and the engine fired up like an explosion, rumbling to a steady shake. I lightly pressed the
gas, then pushed a little heavier. It roared out a warning.
Travis hooted and hollered and motioned for me to pop
the hood. I popped the hood and revved the engine a few
more times. I got out and checked out the engine. It looked

                                        Tyler Keith

all original. The thing shuttered and shook with perfection. *Maybe I could get back on the road in something like this.* It was a dream car.

"Maybe tomorrow you can take it for a spin," Travis said, closing the hood. I cut the engine and got out and shut the door. Travis cut the lights and shut the barn door. I stumbled but caught myself, trying to light a cigarette.

"You're fucked up," he said.

"No," I said, not looking at him, still trying to light my cigarette.

"You see that old Airstream back behind the house? They keep it pretty clean. There's a bed in the back. You just go get comfortable and I'll send Britney over," he said.

"Ok," I said. "I mean, no. You don't have to send her."

"She likes you, Ronnie. Trust me."

"I'm fucked up," I said.

I stumbled to the trailer and opened the door and made my way inside. It smelled like mildew, Pine-Sol, and cigarettes, but it was clean and well taken care of. I flashed on a memory of being in this trailer with Tammy and Tina in happier days. This same trailer used to be closer to the river then, back before the farm became the headquarters for the shit. It was a weekend getaway, back when the days seemed to glow in the sun, and nothing was complicated, and the light reflected off the river like a flashcube exploding. There was a half-empty bottle of Old Charter on the counter. I took the bottle and made my way to the back, banging into shit like a pinball.

I fell on my face on the bed. Rolled over and put the bottle on the mahogany side table next to the lamp and a ceramic ashtray. An old metal fan (we used to call them finger choppers) spun and cycled around the room. When it made it around to my face the air felt good. It was hot back there. I sat up a little on the bed and lit a cigarette. Took a long hit off the Old Charter. I had my eyes closed. Beyond the sound of the spinning fan, I could hear the crickets hum. Lying back on the bed with my eyes closed,

listening to the sounds, must have been something like
meditation because I felt a calm and a quiet I hadn't felt in
some time. If I was a little less drunk, I'd be crying about
my child and losing my wife. If I was a little more drunk,
I'd be asleep.

I heard the door spring creek slowly open, like
someone trying to be quiet. Then it slammed shut. I heard
Britney say, "Shit."

"It's alright," I said. "I'm back here."

Britney made her way to the back, bumping into
things, too. She stood in the doorway, and seemed to glow,
her hair soft and golden at the edges.

"You want some company?" she asked, siting sideways on the bed.

"Yeah," I said.

She climbed onto the bed and crawled back to me
on her hands and knees, and sort of collapsed onto my
chest. I held her there close to me. My eyes closed again,
and I was unable to have a real conversation with her, but
we had one in my head. *I'm old enough to be your father. Is
Travis making you do this?* Don't remember giving myself
any answers. The heat, booze and the events of the day
brought me to a point of perfect exhaustion. I drifted off
slowly; it was like a preacher baptizing me, dipping me
into the Choctawhatchee River, like closing my eyes and
being covered in water like sleep.

                                        Tyler Keith

22

I WOKE UP with the sunrise. The birds were singing already but it wasn't all the way bright yet. People talk about the peace and quiet of the country. It's never quiet. At that moment I hated birds. I was still in my clothes with my shirt unbuttoned and my shoes off. Britney slept beside me with her back to me, a thin, tattered quilt covering the lower half of her body. I peaked over her shoulder to look at her face. She slept so soundly that I thought if I could even get one hour of sleep that sound I could conquer the world. The sleep of a child. As a little girl, Tina would just collapse in her toy box and be sound asleep when minutes earlier she was a live wire.

I crept out of bed, picked up my boots and my cigarettes, and made my way to the kitchen. I turned on the faucet, cupped my hands, and bent down and drank like a man who'd been lost in the desert, the water tasting cool and pure. I went outside and sat on the porch. I put on my boots and smoked a cigarette. The sun wasn't all the way up yet, but it was already getting hot. A mist rose from the overgrown field out beside the trailer.

The land here is so alive and green. In the still of the morning I could just hear the river, running high from all the rain. This country was apt to flood during a rainy year. The big flood here came in 1929. It wiped out a lot of folks. After the flood, some people just left for good. All the big timber was gone by then. A couple of the wealthier families raised some cattle. Some folks raised some cotton or corn. Just enough to barely live. They were mostly the religious type, accepting their lot as God's will. Some seemed to relish it, or wear their suffering like God's badge of honor. This life was not meant to be enjoyed. That came when you died and went to heaven. These kinds of folks didn't allow laughing at the dinner table. And they kept to their own kind. You didn't worry about your neighbor, or the clan in the next settlement. You didn't care what they did, and you didn't care about their souls. They were already lost, not among the chosen.

The folks who didn't leave and didn't go all in for the Lord, a lot of them made whiskey. Made it and sold it. And it was hard work. The stills were hidden back up in the woods around the creeks. You carried the shit you needed to make the whiskey into the woods on your back. You couldn't get a car back there. And then after it was made, you carried it out on your back.

In some sense those two competing ways of life had the same philosophy, or the same conviction in their mission. The difference was the moonshiners and their people had made the whiskey for generations, and it was their birthright to make it, and they had the perfect God-given land in which to make it. The more religious ones believed they were given this little stretch of land, their own Holy Land, to build their kingdom here, each man thinking he could become his own family's Abraham.

Many of the families from both sides went as far back as the 1820s, back when the Creek Indians and the Scottish settlers lived and traded amongst each other. But for the past sixty years people have been slowly leaving. It's one of the few counties in Florida to steadily lose population. There was a beauty here, though. It was something those that stayed cherished, a greenness. And the life that the river gave — there was always fish and things to do on the river, and something to gaze on. At one time, the river had a lively steamboat era, taking lumber and goods all the way out to the Gulf.

                                              Tyler Keith

Holmes County had been my home for a time as a child. My earliest memories take shape in the landscape of Holmes County, on the river with Junior, long days running free, my whole family together. The memories shimmered in my mind like the first faded color photographs every family has. Maybe that was the real reason I came back with Travis ... I wanted to see the land again. Maybe I could touch that old freedom when I touched the land. Catch a glimpse of something from the pure days. Maybe I'd see a vision of Junior, or my dad and mom.

I fumbled in my pocket for a lighter and I found I still had the keys to Travis' '73 Camaro. I laughed out loud at a thought. *I'm going for a ride. Hadn't he said last night I could take it for a ride?* Not exactly, but fuck it, I could convince him of it when I got back. I just wanted a leisurely drive through the county. *Was that wrong?* Last night was the first time behind the wheel of a car in a mighty long time. And this wasn't just any car either...*to hell with it. What's the worse thing that can happen? I could wind up back in prison?* But somewhere in my head, I knew the odds of that happening where already pretty good so, *who gives a shit?*

I walked over to the barn and open the door as quietly as I could. I got in the car and I just sat there and caressed the wheel for a moment. I put the key in the ignition and turned it. It thundered up like a dream. I put it in drive and drove out towards the dirt road, The Camaro was loud and I tried to ease it past the house without waking anyone.

Just as I hit the dirt road, I saw the front door of the house swing open and someone come running out, waving their hands in the air. I didn't wait around to see what they wanted. I roared off laughing like a lunatic, rolling down the windows to feel the wind on my face. By the time I hit the asphalt I was doing nearly 60. I felt as good as I'd had in many years.

I just drove south on the two lane towards Gritney and Westville. Past those towns, the road would take me to Highway 90. I could go right and ride past Ponce De Leon and cut up towards Vortex Springs and up to Highway 2 and make a whole loop through Bonifay and back to the farm. When you got off 90 (which ran west to Pensacola and east to Tallahassee) and hit the county roads there were hardly any cops: maybe a sheriff or deputy in Ponce De Leon or Bonifay.

After I turned off towards 2, I gave it some gas, and switched on the radio to an AM radio station out of Bagdad playing old country. The Mel Tillis song, "Life Turned Her That Way," played.

I passed Vortex Springs and thought about going in for a swim; sixty-eight degrees year-round temperature and the cleanest water in the world. And caves. But this time of year, even though it was early in the day, there'd be a bunch of people there. This was a big place for scuba diving. People got certified here. They explored the caves, and there was a campground and a big slide for kids.

I rolled on. The radio played, the DJ saying, *We're playing hit songs from 1967 today. That was Mel Tillis with "Life Turned Her This Way." Before that we had Webb Pierce with "Fool." Right now here's Connie Smith with "I'll Come Running." We'll be back with some weather soon. We're keeping an eye on that storm out there. It looks to be headed further west but you can't never tell.*

The pedal steel guitar on the Connie Smith number, a fast one, just made you want to drive fast. I hit Highway 2 and really opened it up. The Camaro simply floated on air. It was fast out of the gate but from 35 to 70 mph, it was like jumping into orbit. As I turned off of 2, a trooper passed me going the opposite way. I'd slowed down before the turn but I thought maybe he'd turn around. I could make a run for Highway 90 and probably make it, but he'd call for more cars. I knew a few friends on this road and had some kin that lived down here. My great Aunt Iris lived down here. I could just pull in and be welcome. Or just pull in and try and hide behind a tree or something.

                                          Tyler Keith

Her trailer stood under a couple of old oaks draped
with Spanish moss. I pulled around the side of the trailer
behind one of the trees to hide from the road, but realized
the trooper hadn't followed me. Before I saw the law, I
hadn't had a too much of a thought about being pulled
over. As soon as I got a load of that trooper, a wave of paranoia swept over me. My breathing stopped. Everything
tensed up. I wasn't quite ready to go back to jail.

I sat in the car collecting my nerves for a moment,
finishing my cigarette. Then I noticed Aunt Iris peaking
out of the screened-in porch door looking at my car,
squinting to see who the stranger was sitting in her
driveway. I got out and waved at her.

"Aunt Iris, It's Ronnie," I said.

She opened the door a little more and stood looking
at me.

"Ronnie Harrison," she said, finally figuring out who
I was. "Haven't seen you in years, Ronnie."

"It's good to see you," I said, walking up to her trailer.

"You're looking more and more like your daddy," she
said.

We hugged each other, and she invited me in. She
poured me a cup of coffee without asking me if I wanted
any. I sat at a yellow linoleum table in her kitchen. She
looked at me for a long moment. I knew I looked rough. I
probably smelled like a homeless bum.

"Let me fix you some breakfast, son," she said.

Some other day I would've said, "no thank you," but I
was so hungry I couldn't.

"You don't have to go to any trouble," I said. That
was like saying yes.

She got some fresh eggs and thick-cut bacon from the
fridge, and some frozen biscuits from the freezer. She put
the biscuits in the oven, and peeled off three big pieces of
bacon from the package and placed them in a large iron
skillet on the stove. Her home was clean and almost all of
the space on the walls were filled with old photographs.

I asked her if I could use her restroom. She pointed me down the hall.

The lights in the tiny bathroom made my face look drawn and gaunt. I scrubbed my hands and face with her yellow Dial soap. I wet my comb and pulled it through my hair. I looked under the sink and found a bottle of Listerine. I took big mouthful, swished it around and spit it out. I stared at my face in the mirror and barely recognized my reflection. It seemed like in the days since my release, I'd aged a few years. My hair seemed thinner and more graying on the sides. My five o'clock shadow poked out like the grey wire on a scrub brush. A hardness had formed around my eyes. I could see the early traces of an old man's face trying to bust out. If I got my shit together and lived healthy, the old man might wait a few more years to come out. But with the road I was on, he'd be here for Halloween.

When I came out of the bathroom, the smell of frying eggs and bacon made me take a deep breath. Aunt Iris had poured a glass of orange juice from a decanter with little slices of oranges on the side, and she'd refilled my coffee.

As I ate, we talked about various people and relatives I hadn't seen in years. Most of the old people I'd know had died in the last few years. Her two children were dead.

She was alone at 92. She'd outlived everybody. She was glad to have someone to talk to. After I finished breakfast, we went out onto the porch so I could smoke, and we sat on the swing. She talked and I listened.

"I used to help my daddy make moonshine," she said. "Back when I was a little girl. It was the Wild West down here then. When I was about four years old, Daddy took the back seats out of his car, and he'd load up. Momma and Daddy would be sitting in the front and I would sit on the keg of whiskey in the back. Daddy would tell me, 'Now, if you see any lights coming, you tell me.' So every time I seen a car lights coming I'd say, 'Daddy, here they come! Daddy, here they come!' He would do it on moonlit

Tyler Keith

nights so he wouldn't have to use his lights. That was the chase that went on here in Holmes County. It wasn't just daddy. It was a bunch of them."

"What about my daddy? Do you know where he went to?" I asked. I hadn't thought of asking that question before it came out, but being here and listening her talk about her daddy, just brought it up and out of my mouth. She knew my dad. They'd always been close.

"I don't know what happened to your daddy," she said. "But I do know he's dead, son. I'm so sorry, too."

"I figured he's probably dead by now," I said.

Tears appeared in my eyes, about to break loose, but I kept them back. I guess I'd never heard anyone say it before. I'd never heard myself say it: "My dad is dead."

Iris patted me on the back and gave me a hug.

"Your Daddy was a very complicated man," she said. "A very proud man. I think that pride was bad for him. It's liable to have gotten him killed."

"What do you mean?" I asked. "What happened to him?"

"I don't know, son. I really don't.

Iris got up, took our coffee cups, and went back inside. I followed her.

"You don't know what happened?" I asked again.

There was a picture of a young man and a women standing together in the snow. She walked over to the picture and looked at it.

"This is me and my husband," she said. "We were in Alaska. This was about the last time I heard from your dad. We'd moved up Alaska. We had to. My husband had done something. You could disappear back then and start a new life. My husband died up there. I had to come back here. I never saw or heard from your dad again."

"What did people say about him? Where he went?" I asked.

"I don't remember, son. Down here you learn to mind your own business," she said and changed the subject. "I do know your Daddy could preach when the spirit got on him."

"Yeah, he could," I said, still thinking about what might have happened to him.

"For all the outlaws and bad people here, there's lots of good people," Irene mused. "It all kind of comes down to whose blood you had."

"You're right about that," I agreed.

"If you're around in the morning, why don't you go to church with me?" she asked.

"I don't know. I'm not too much for church these days," I said.

"It's not one of those Holy Ghost churches," she said. "Just a plain old Baptist church. I don't really believe in that stuff. I think when you die, you're just dead. I've passed a lot of coffins in my life and it just don't seem like there's anything after. But I like seeing the people. At my age, it's just about the only time to see anybody."

"I'll try and make it," I said. *Maybe it'll give me an excuse to get away tomorrow if I need it.*

23

DRIVING TOWARDS BONIFAY, I passed Peppertown. I
could see a crumbling house in the distance. It could've
been the old boarding house that Beasley talked about.
Maybe Beasley and Davis knew what they were doing,
keeping themselves together, staying in Eden, keeping
alive and out of prison. If I got busted for even a misde-
meanor, I'd likely be headed back to finish the rest of my
sentence. Fourteen years. Just being down here was probably enough to send me back. Fear began to creep in. This
whole week had been like opening a release valve with
everything pouring out. The rage and anger and the regret
had the run of my life. Things had started settling down
in my mind just this morning, like I was coming out of a
blind rage and I realized where I was and what I'd done.
What I was doing.

As I got close to Bonifay, the little bit of traffic backed
up, and there was a detour from downtown. Then I
remembered that, on the day of the rodeo, they always
had a parade through town. People rode their horses,
some hitched up their wagons, some saddled the mule.
Growing up here, I had a roan mule named Lady. She had
a face just like a horse. Junior had an old quarter horse. We
rode all over the county at six years old.

I pulled over and parked on a side street off Main.
I walked the block past a dress shop that specialized in
prom dresses and tux rentals, past the Western Auto, and
stood on the corner and watched the parade go by. An

old wagon with truck tires on it pulled by a few horses and had a sign that said "Strawberry Hill Furriers" on the side rode by followed by Miss Holmes County sitting in the back of a new red Corvette convertible. Some of the people on floats threw candy to kids who scuttled around, filling their pillowcases with loot. Bull riding champs from the past few years sat on hay bales, bored on a flatbed trailer, waving to no one in particular. Florida is a horse state. Always has been. Down in the central part they raise race horses, and it has more cows than any other state but Texas. Everybody rides here.

Across the street I saw Ralph's Western Wear, a place owned by a third cousin back in the day. I smelled the shirt I was wearing and it smelled like cigarettes and sweat. When there was a break in the parade, I jogged across the street and went in to see if I could find a shirt and maybe see somebody, some kin. It was cool inside and smelled like new boot leather. I walked around the store checking out some of the boots. I found a sale rack of western snap shirts. There was a white short sleeve with gold thread and pearl snap buttons on sale for twelve bucks. I took the shirt to the counter, looking around for anyone I may know. The girl at the counter was a teenager, and I thought about asking her about some of my relatives but passed on it. Just bought the shirt and left the store.

As the last few people rode through the parade route, a handsome older couple rode through on two good-looking horses. They looked so at ease on their mounts. They had a pride in the way they rode. I didn't know them, but I'm sure they knew my kin. They knew my family's reputation. *What makes whole families go bad? Fuck it.* I needed a drink. There was one bar on Main Street. I headed there.

The place was an in-town honky tonk. Not too wild, they played the latest country hits on the jukebox, served Heineken. I went straight to the men's room. I took the shirt out of the package and took out the pins, took off my

                                          Tyler Keith

old shirt and put the new one on. I rolled up my sleeves once and tucked in my shirttails. I splashed water in my face and ran a comb through my hair.

Sat down at the bar and ordered a Bud longneck. The first beer of the day tasted like heaven. Cooled me off. With my new shirt and a cold beer, I felt pretty good. Parade goers came in and out, buying one or using the facilities. No one took notice of me. A few bikers came in and sat at the bar. I wasn't sure if they were the ones causing trouble or just weekend warriors riding through town, stopping off for a drink. But more and more came in. Some played pool and horsed around. I knew I was safe in town, and it was the middle of the day. They gave me the once over, staring me down. I thought one of them might have been one of the two guys from last night. I couldn't be sure. I decided to have one more and go. I paid for my beers and sat drinking my last one when Marty appeared in the doorway, waving at me. I took one last slug, almost finishing it, set it down and headed outside where Marty had gone.

The bikers all stopped and watched me walking towards the door. They knew Marty and they now knew who I ran with. Almost at the door, one of the bikers made a fake motion towards me. I didn't blink or flinch but just continued outside. But my breath skipped a beat. I'd flinched on the inside. The fear of trouble, what that could mean, I felt it swelling like a wasp sting. Oddly enough, it felt like the same fear I had entering prison, the fear of violence, and conflict that might go on indefinitely. The paranoia. I thought of the saying, "If you're not paranoid, you're not paying attention."

Marty stood just outside, leaning against the wall. I lit a cigarette and said, "Hey Marty. Nice parade, huh?"

"Yeah, man. Lucky I saw your car ...or Travis' car," he said.

"Is he pissed?" I asked. "I thought he said I could take it for a ride."

"Yeah, he's pissed, but he'll get over it if we get back soon," he said.

I took the road back the same way I came, really opening up the Camaro. Marty came up behind me and we locked in together all the way to the farm.

"Like a dream, Travis," I said, holding out the key to the Camaro. He took the keys with his left hand, still smiling, and gave me a quick, hard punch in the gut. It caught me off guard. I fell to my knees, grasping my stomach, and vomited my breakfast in the dirt at Travis' feet, wheezing and struggling to catch my breath, but laughing a little in the middle of it. It came out sounding like an old mule. I sat there on my knees for a moment, spitting and laughing. I figured I'd had that coming for taking the car without his consent, but Travis sucker-punched me.

That's what killed Houdini, I thought.

Travis reached his hand down and helped me up. When I got to my feet, I kicked dirt over the vomit to cover it up.

"Sorry I had to do that, but there's some shit in the trunk that would send both of us back to prison for the rest of our natural life," Travis said.

"I guess I had it coming, taking a man's car," I said. "I gotta say, hell, it was worth it."

"She does run the roads like a show boat, don't she," he said with a grin.

Travis told me to go inside and clean myself up. The house felt cold and dank. I took a shower, and afterwards I found an empty room with an unmade bed. I felt clean but worn out. My brain churned slowly, and my stomach felt like there was a bruise inside my body somewhere. I collapsed on the bed, pulled the blanket around me and shut my eyes.

24

I WOKE TO the sounds of a party, Nazareth blaring from the stereo. I could hear Travis and Bob yelling jokes at each other, laughing. I could smell fish frying even from inside. Despite the earlier punch in the gut, or because of it, I was hungry. And thirsty. I sat on the edge of the bed and smoked a cigarette. Ran a comb through my hair, that urge to walk to the main road and hitch a ride out of here played right on the edge of my brain. The money may be good over here, and it may help me take care of important things, like a place to live, and Charles could give me a cover job in one of his legit businesses. I could start giving money to Tina. I know the Navy don't pay much. Money would help ease the tension. It usually did. But if I stayed down here …

But I wasn't ready to take off yet. I had to give it the day. Travis couldn't be trusted for anything but as a partner in a good knock-down-drag-out bar fight. Despite the loyal soldier act, he looked out for number one. He seemed real chummy with Bob. Bob was young. He'd picked Travis as his hell-raising father figure instead of his hard-assed dad. They could party together. Travis could match anybody drink for drink and line for line. Just his size and his performance last night told me that. What I'd seen of Marty was a blank slate. Young, but a good driver, and he didn't talk much. I liked that, but it made me nervous. In my growing paranoia, the kid gave off a cop vibe. Or somebody that may take off on an errand and just never come back. Never be seen again.

Charles wanted me around to mediate all of this. I could see why, dealing with all these personalities had to be a challenge. There were other characters to deal with: the people who grew stuff and the people who made the whisky. It wasn't just the bikers and the other folks from down south he wanted me to look out for. And, in the end, if something happened, I'd proven that I could keep my mouth shut, and if some violence came to me, I was expendable if he needed a sacrifice. He certainly wouldn't cry over my casket when the lowered me in the dirt. He had too much of his daddy in him. Even with his own family, and his respectable business cover, he was a sadist at heart. I'd seen it as a kid. He had no qualms to kick a dog, or punch his little brother in the head without provocation.

I stumbled out into the hazy afternoon; the heat felt like someone draped a warm, wet jacket over my shoulders. Three or four people stood around two gas cookers, one with a large pot filled with sizzling blue gill, crappie, and largemouth bass, and the other with a cast-iron skillet filled with hushpuppies. I got a plate with some bream, hushpuppies, slaw, and cheese grits. I grabbed a cold beer from a cooler under a large oak. I sat on the cooler and ate a few whole fish trying to be careful of the bones. In the Panhandle, the fish fry is the go-to event. The rivers, lakes, and the Gulf gave an almost endless bounty, and the Choctawhatchee is a rare gift. I can recall fishing on the river where the end of the day came from sheer exhaustion from pulling them in. You were too tired to catch more. Over two hundred fish in a day was not unheard of. And the holes they lived in were, many times, crystal clear, giving the fish a clean taste unmatched in my experience.

Maybe I could live down here and work at the feed store or something. Not be involved in all this other shit? Yeah right. I knew better.

                                        Tyler Keith

Marty came up to the tree looking for a beer. He motioned for me to get off the cooler. I stood up with my plate of fish, and he kicked open the top and grabbed a Busch, popped the trop and took long drink. He was still dressed the same with the bandana and the dark glasses. I couldn't see his eyes, but he stared a hole in my head. I could feel it. He stood square to me, and I just blankly stared back still chewing some hushpuppies.

"So Travis tells me you killed a guy in car wreck. That's what sent you to jail," he said.

The question made me a little defensive and I just smiled and looked at him for moment.

"Yeah, I killed a guy," I said.

"Fuck, man, these roads down here are a trip. It's like the fucking Dukes of Hazzard shit," he said.

"What?" I asked. I gave him a look to remind him without saying it, that I'd been incarcerated for the last six years.

He realized that I had no idea what he was talking about but instead of explaining it a was a TV show, he just went on with his speech, almost like he'd practiced it or something.

"I've had some close calls myself," he said.

There was an awkward pause. We just looked at each other with blank faces, like playing a kid's staring game. Neither of us laughed.

"You just got out of jail, huh?" he asked.

"Prison. Yeah," I said.

"Just last week?"

"Yeah, what's it to you?"

"Nothing, man. You're just already back down here …"

He didn't finish his sentence.

"Fuck you, man," I said. "I don't see why you give a shit what I do."

I put down my plate of food and stepped towards him. He hit a nerve. Just like he planned.

"All I mean is, if I was you, I'm not sure I'd be over here so quick after just getting out," he said.

"You ain't me, Hoss." I'd picked up Travis' slang already.

"No offense, Ronnie, I just mean to say shit is real crazy over here right now," he said. "And it's about to get crazier."

I couldn't figure out if this was a warning from a rival or something else.

"What do you mean by that?" I asked.

He didn't answer for a moment, like he was mulling it over. Now, when I think about it, I know his purpose, but then I couldn't be sure.

"With this biker shit, and this shit between Charles and Travis, and just the general shit going down. There's a lot of eyes on shit." He seemed to think about what else to add to his speech. "Maybe you've lost a step since you been locked up."

"In prison," he added, "you definitely got old. And I got the driving covered down here anyway. You ought to think about your future."

I opened the cooler still looking at him, smiling. I pulled out a Busch, cracked it open, and took a long swallow.

"I'm just down here seeing some kin, Marty. Eatin' some fish," I said. "You ought to worry about your own self-interest instead of trifling in my life. You ought to know that people from Holmes County like to keep their business to themselves.

"You ain't from around here, are you? Where are you from anyhow?"

"I sincerely hope you're just visiting your kin," he said, ignoring my question.

From across the yard Travis yelled to Marty, waving him over. He had a smirk on his face, and he slowly ambled over to Travis after giving me an up-and-down look. Travis and Marty huddled together, Travis putting his hand on Marty's back, Marty shaking his head. After a few heated words, Marty got in his car and drove off. Either Marty wanted me out of the way so I didn't encroach on his place here, or he was being egged on by

Travis to fuck with me. But that didn't make sense because
Travis had been so adamant about getting me over here.
The third option, and the most dangerous, was that Marty
was some form of law enforcement. He was trying to warn
me off; genuinely trying to get me out of here. I might
mess up his set-up. More people meant more complica-
tions. Maybe he was just a good Samaritan and wanted
me to succeed in life; he could see my potential and didn't
want me to waste my talent down here. *Hah!* Whatever
it was, something didn't sit right about Marty. One more
thing to worry about.

"You get you a plate?" It was Travis. "You must be
hungry after throwing up that breakfast."

I just nodded.

"Hey, Hoss, no hard feelings. I just get a little sentimental about my car," he said.

"I can see why. I guess I had it coming."

"You getting to know Marty?" he asked. "He's quite a
character. He seems so quiet but he's always listening. He
don't miss much."

"He's a real charmer. Where'd you meet that guy?"
I asked.

"Don't worry about Marty. He's just a little protective
of his job," he said.

We made small talk and then he told me we'd be
going to Bonifay to meet Charles shortly.

"That old gal's looking for you," he said.

I finished my fish and grabbed a fresh beer. Britney
was standing on the edge of the group in cut-off blue
jeans and a Rolling Stones t-shirt with the sleeves cut off,
drinking a wine cooler. I sidled up to her like I didn't see
her. She tapped me on the shoulder.

"Hey, Ronnie," she said.

"Hey," I said, knocking out a cigarette.

We talked about nothing, and I told her I had to go to
this rodeo in town. She said she'd be at the farm all night
and make sure and find her when I get back.

"Okay," I said.

Marty was out on a run, so Travis drove the Camaro with Bob ridding shotgun and me in the back again. Travis was more of a country music fan so he has Allen Jackson on the tape deck at full volume. He passed around a half pint of Holmes County's finest, and we had cold beer in a cooler in the back. Travis and Bob yelled back and forth to each other, laughing and carrying on.

"Ain't that right," Travis yelled at me, half turning.

"I can't hear you," I yelled back.

Travis turned down the stereo.

"That Charles is a card," he said looking at me in the rearview mirror.

"That's an understatement," I said.

"What's he want to talk to you about?" Travis asked. "Did he say?"

"No, not really," I said.

"He's probably going to ask you to spy on me and Bob here," he said.

"Yeah? Well, I'm really not the narc type."

"That's right," Travis replied. "You're true blue, Ronnie. Charles is a little too stuck in his ways. He's too old school. We're missing out on a lot of money-making opportunities. Me and Bob got some ideas but he don't listen much."

I didn't respond. Bob looked back at me and smiled. Handed me the half pint.

"Just take everything with a grain of salt," Travis said.

He turned up the radio as we rode into Bonifay, the sun setting in the August sky. Outside the rodeo, vendors sold rebel flags, t-shirts, cowboy hats. There was a midway rifle shooting game where you shot a pellet gun at a tiny target. You could win everything from a roach clip with a turkey feather on it to a giant Pink Panther stuffed toy. There were pony rides for the kids and a petting zoo with some goats and a llama. The smell of cotton candy and funnel cakes drifted through the early evening air. The town set up giant makeshift stables so folks could ride into town from the surrounding areas and park their horses. On the street in front of the arena (the high school football stadium), townsfolk rode back and forth on their finest saddles.

I followed Travis and Bob through the crowd to the entrance. Travis handed our tickets off, and we followed him down to the far side of the field. The stands were packed with folks, families and couples decked out in their best western wear. Charles stood with his hands folded, staring into the empty ring. He saw us and came down from the bleachers with his wife to greet us. He wore creased Wrangler's, a purple polo shirt, and a new straw Stetson with a rattlesnake band. His wife wore new blue jeans tucked into red cowboy boots, and a plaid western shirt with pearl buttons and golden thread throughout. She hugged me and commented on the fact that we'd all gotten old since we'd seen each other last. I must've looked like hell. She hugged Bob and ignored Travis.

"Why don't y'all sit down and enjoy the show. Me and Ronnie are going to chat," Charles said.

We walked to the edge of the bleaches and both looked out onto the empty field. The intercom crackled and a voice said, "Please stand for the singing of the national anthem, sung by the Missionary Baptist Church Men's Quartet."

Afterwards, a lone girl on horse back rode to the center of the ring.

"That's my daughter, Elizabeth," Charles said, pointing to the girl. "She's just graduated. She'll be going to Florida State this fall. Look at her."

He gazed at her with sheer wonder as she rode to the center of the field and waved a giant American flag to the crowd, spinning her horse in a small circle.

"Ronnie, it's all about family. Elizabeth is so much better than us. She's going to get out of here. Get out of this mess," he said.

After she stopped, the gate opened and riders came

out of the chute at the other end of the field, galloping full speed around the track. They kept coming until there was upwards of a hundred riders circling the grounds. Elizabeth took off, joining the crowd in the wild merry-go-round.

"Bob's a problem child," Charles continued. "Always has been. And I've been hard on him."

"Not like Albert was with me. Or Junior," he said, glancing at me. "But he's resented it. Held it against me. He's always done whatever he wanted and taken the punishment. And he acts like a stoned-out surfer, but he's smart. And his mother's always coddled him. It almost broke up our marriage. She always takes his side. Protects him. I guess that's what mothers do."

The arena continued to fill and turned with riders. A few fell off and scrambled to the center of the field in an effort to avoid a trampling. Some security riders picked up the fallen and slung them on the backs of their horses.

Charles went on. "Bob's become enamored with Travis. He's become a father figure to him, a mentor. God knows I'm no role model, but Travis is a dangerous man, which I've needed and trusted, but let's just say he's up for anything. And Albert likes him. Despite the way it might look, Albert still has the last word. He still has all the contacts. Travis is nothing if not charming when he needs to be. He's played Albert enough so I can't get rid of him. But Travis has ideas."

"What kind of ideas?" I asked.

"You've heard of 'the three Ms' of Holmes County?" he asked.

"No," I said.

"Well, I guess, maybe you haven't. Moonshine, mari-juana, and methamphetamine. You might not have heard of the last, although you surely know what it is. Speed. We've steered clear of it, but the bikers are bringing it in. They're making it down here. The profit margin is insane, but it's trouble. We've seen that."

I nodded in agreement.

"Thing is, Ronnie, it's hard to find good help down here. We can find folks that will stab their grandmother in the back for a dollar, but they can't be trusted. And they're stupid. Travis is smart, but he's ambitious. Bob's at an age to make big mistakes. I want you to watch them. Keep me informed."

"I'm not much of an informant, Charles," I said.

"I know that," he said. "That's why you're here, why you're walking around at all, because you can keep your mouth shut. This isn't ratting. It's just keeping an eye on our own interests. And my son, for fuck's sake."

"To be honest, I'm not sure what I'll do. I just got out and I'm still getting my mind right."

"I get that. Take your time," he said. "It's about family. You're family. Despite what Albert's done to us in the past. I'm lucky to be standing here. You know what he's capable of. But we've made it despite that."

He looked at me. "Take a little time, but I don't see much choice for you now. At your age. Your situation. It's either here or the wilderness for you, Ronnie. Do you really want to be out there on your own right now?"

Rodeo clowns stood on the edge of the action, sometimes darting in to help a rider who'd fallen from his horse as the rest rode by at full speed.

"You know what I've learned in my time, Ronnie?" he asked, staring out at the action. "If you can stay on your horse and keep circling, then you're all right. Or like the bull riders, you just need to stay on for eight seconds. But as you know, those eight seconds can seem like a lifetime."

"Guess I've always felt like the clowns, standing on the sidelines," I said.

"Hell, everybody knows the clown is the most dangerous job on the rodeo," he said. "They take the full wrath of the bull."

I walked off to the concession stand to get a coke and a hotdog. I ate the dog and walked around the side of the building by the fence to have a smoke. In the darkness and shadows outside the fence, I could see Travis' silhouette. And I could see him talking to a man who looked like one of the bikers from the other night. He wasn't wearing his colors but it looked like him. I eased back into the shadows of the concession stand. They parted with a handshake, looking around to see if anyone noticed them.

I got back to the bleachers and sat next to Charles. He motioned for me to give him my cup. He took it and pulled a pint of Crown out of his pocket and poured a generous amount into my coke. The bull riding had started and a bull named Dillinger had thrown his rider, and the rodeo clown was out there waving at him and steering his attention away from the cowboy.

That's what I am. Goddamn rodeo clown. Between these two, Charles and Travis.

Between Camp Eden and Holmes County.

The anxiety just sat on me like Dillinger had his foot on my chest, looking down, just waiting to crush the life out of me. For a second, I almost longed for prison, and the blandness of my cell and bunk. Or even Camp Eden, someplace that had a simple routine.

Travis strolled up.

"Y'all finished your talk?" he said, looking at Charles and then at me.

"Oh yeah," Charles said. "Why don't you guys get out of here. This is a family place."

"Good call, Hoss. It smells like cow shit out here," Travis said.

They shook hands and both laughed, but you could feel the tension between them, like the stare-down before a prizefight, except they hadn't agreed to fight yet.

On the way back to Travis' car, I stopped to make a phone call at the pay phone. I felt an overwhelming urge to call Tina. Or Tammy. But instead I called Darleen. She answered after a few rings.

"It's Ronnie," I said, then going blank.

"Hey, Ronnie, what a surprise to hear from you," she

　　　　　　　　　　　　　　　Tyler Keith

said. Her voice had that slight growl and warm low timbre that gave immediate comfort.

"Just checking on tomorrow night," I said.

"Yeah, Ronnie, we'll be there," she said.

Travis walked up on me.

"Who the fuck are you talking to?" he asked, surprised to find me making a phone call.

"Darleen," I said, cupping the phone with my hand.

He got excited and did a little dance.

"Are we still on for tomorrow?" he asked.

I nodded. He patted me on the back and pointed to his car.

"Are you still there?" Darleen asked.

"Yeah, sorry," I said. We made small talk. I told her I was at a rodeo in Holmes County.

"Dear Lord," she said. "Are you hanging in there?"

"I think so," I said.

"The first few weeks after you get out are the hardest. You've got to set your direction right off. And stay away from your old friends. That's the only way," she said.

"That's good advice," I said. "I'm just seeing some family."

We shored up plans for the next night and I hung up.

Stay away from old friends...

<h1 style="text-align:center">25</h1>

THE BONFIRE AT the house would seem to be too much on a hot August night, but it kept the mosquitos at bay, and a pleasant breeze blew in from the gathering storm in the Gulf, There were people I didn't know, but I assumed they worked for Charles and Albert. Heather circled the fire with a jam box blasting Black Sabbath. The smell of burning pine and pot smoke wafted through the air. Travis eased up next to me with a Buck knife and a tiny bag of yellowish powder. He took a bit from the bag on the edge of the knife and put it to my nose. It startled me, and I looked sideways at the knife. It appeared to be a small amount so I leaned in and snorted the substance off the edge of the knife. It burned going down. The sting wasn't coke.

"What the fuck is that?" I asked. "Goddamn.

"Fucking magic powder, partner."

He laughed and stuck the knife back in the bag and came out with a bigger portion and snorted it. He threw the knife into the grass and it stuck. I could feel the speed rush to my head. He hadn't given me much, but it burned and slid down my throat. My brain lit up and I took a deep breath.

"Fuck you, Travis," I said.

"What? This shit's going to make us a lot of money, Hoss."

"I don't want any more of that," I said, looking away.

"Just trying to be neighborly," he said. He picked

up the knife and pointed it at me with a smile, and then wandered off towards the house.

I pounded the rest of my beer and walked over to the cooler. A Mason jar of moonshine with pieces of watermelon in the bottom sat on top of the ice. I took a long drink from the jar then got a fresh beer from the cooler. *I'll have to drink a lot to get to sleep tonight,* I thought.

The jam box played more Black Sabbath, some song about saving your soul before you end up in your grave.

I focused on the music from the jam box. Everything disappeared for a moment. I looked up into the black sky.

"Can I get a beer?" someone asked. It was Britney.

I handed her a beer.

"You all right?" she asked.

"I'm okay. Travis made me do some speed off the end of a knife," I said.

"No one *makes* anyone snort anything off the blade of a knife," she said. "You seen Travis?"

"I don't know where he went. In the house?" I pointed.

"Catch you later, Ronnie," she said. She walked towards the house with a slight wobble.

The wind switched direction and brought cooler air that hinted at a coming storm. The fire whipped and whistled, mimicking the music in a wicked symphony. It wrapped around my brain like someone spinning a microphone, feeding back, above my head, a warped, stinging sound. I noticed Heather standing beside me singing along to Sabbath into her beer can, sometimes her eyes closed, sometimes smiling at me. Just as she handed me a joint, the sky cracked and a hard, hot rain fell. The revelers around the fire let out a simultaneous scream and ran to the house. Heather just laughed, and I handed her back the joint.

Inside the house, the music played loud and people crammed into the living room and the open kitchen. Me and Heather made our way to the hall that led to the bedrooms looking for Travis and Britney. Heather opened

                                    Tyler Keith

the bathroom door and a female voice shouted, "Wait! I'm in here."

But Heather pushed forward, thinking the bathroom was vacant. Britney had her hands on the mirror and her jeans pulled down to her knees, Travis behind her, his hands on her hips sweating like a convict on a chain gang, his big buck knife and the bag of speed on the bathroom counter beside them.

At first, before it registered what was going on, Heather said, "Excuse me," but then said, "What the fuck? You piece of shit." She stood there looking at them in disgust. Then she kicked the door all the way open so they could be seen by the whole party. She laughed with her arms crossed, and then turned around and walked out the door.

Britney pushed Travis off of her, pulled up her jeans, her face a shining crimson, and ran after Heather out the front door. Travis pulled up his pants, a shit-eating grin on his face. He stuck the bag of dope in his front packet and grabbed the knife, his face flushed red and his hair sweaty and stuck to his head.

"It's supposed to be a party, right?" he said with a shrug.

There was a silent pause in the party. Everyone stood dead in their tracks. Then someone let out a yell and another followed. Bob came out of a back bedroom, shirt-less, brown corduroy jeans slung low and no shoes.

"What the fuck's going on?" he said.

Travis turned with the knife in his hand. He acciden-tally brought the knife down as he turned and sliced Bob's forearm in a deep two-inch long cut. Blood squirted like someone had stepped on a ketchup packet. Bob let out a high-pitched scream, just looking at his arm.

"Goddamn, Bob, I'm sorry! It was an accident!" Travis shouted.

He ran into the bathroom and grabbed an old dirty towel and wrapped it around Bob's arm. He told him to keep pressure on it. Bob was in near hysterics while one of his lady friends tried to calm him down. Travis took another peek at it and winced. He told one of the girls to take him to the emergency room in Bonifay. Blood pooled on the floor, and some had splattered on the walls.

Somehow this whole scene struck me funny. I covered my mouth and eased out the back door by the kitchen. Took a couple of beers with me. The rain fell hard on the house, and I stood just under the lip of the roof in the back yard. I could just barely hear the party, and there was a dank smell of mud, and a mosquito killer bounced off of the one floodlight at the corner of the house. I was always on the edge of the party. That's where I always seem to end up, my whole life; or in the kitchen by the back door, ready to make my escape.

I heard the sliding glass door open and I scooted around the side of the house. I peaked around the corner and saw Travis and Britney in a huddle.

"Heather's going to hate me now," she said.

"You don't worry about her," Travis said. "I'll smooth it out. She don't understand about us. I'll just make it a simple party foul."

Always on the edge of the party and not knowing what the hell is actually going on.

Tyler Keith

26

TRAVIS MUST HAVE gone back in through the pantry and come out the front door and around the side of the house. I didn't hear him come up behind me. Maybe it was the sound of the rain.

He grabbed me around the neck in a chokehold. "Hey, motherfucker," he said just loud enough so I could hear him. "You think I didn't see you out here?"

He let me go and pushed me away.

"You scared the shit out of me," I said.

He just looked at me and laughed.

"I need you to help me with something," he said.

"What do you need me to do?" I asked.

"We need to go meet Marty," he said. "We'll take the Camaro."

We ran through the wet grass in sheets of rain to the sound of a thunder crack.

Travis opened the barn door and we climbed in the car. It smelled like old leather and mildew. He cranked the engine. It rumbled and shuttered. We sat there in silence for a moment.

"You know how I got over here? How I got this particular job?" he asked.

"Selling a lot of weed?" I said.

"Shit, I sold a shitload of weed," he said. "But anybody can sell a lot of weed, especially in the Panhandle. It's because I was ready, willing, and able to do the dirty work. To do the things that needed doing without hesitation or backtalk. Your Uncle Albert needed such a man. After you do things that need to be done, hard things, there's a trust that's built up between people. It's a trust that can go deeper than kin. Sometimes that kin can develop some resentment. But you know as well as I do the only rule out here is, 'don't trust nobody.' "

He popped the car into drive and eased out of the barn into the rain. We drove out from the farm onto the dirt road, by the time we hit the blacktop the rain had stopped and a mist rose from the hot pavement. Travis picked up the earlier conversation like he'd been having it in his head since the topic first came up.

"Hell, I sold a lot of weed. Goddamn, that's how I met Britney," he said. "Her mother sold weed for me. They lived in a trailer park just north of Fort Walton towards Eglin Air force base. I had a trailer there, a crash pad. I met Britney's mom, Candace, over there. We ran around together. Partied. But she was wild. She'd be gone for days. Britney was only 13 or so. I'd have to look in on her, even though by then she was already like a grownup. She'd taken care of herself for a good while. Candace had problems with paying me too. She wasn't no good for herself or Britney."

"What happened to her?" I asked.

"Let me just say this, she had to go away for good. For everybody's sake," he said. "I helped Britney out, mainly with cash money. Give her some jobs now and then. Like I said, she could pretty well take care of herself. We developed a certain bond with each other. She's a real even-tempered girl. Not too emotional or dramatic.

"Not like Heather; that girl is high-strung. She's wild. That's what I like about her."

"You're going to have some explaining to do with that scene at the party," I said.

"Shit, I can handle that," he said. "I'll just have to spend some time with her. Maybe take her to the beach for the day. She's just hot headed."

                                          Tyler Keith

We turned down the road that led past the biker's place. I hadn't been thinking about where we were.

"What the fuck, Travis, shouldn't we be careful around here?" I asked.

Two bikes pulled in behind us as we passed their place. Travis drove at a leisurely pace.

"We don't need to worry about them too much. Charles has gotten everybody all riled up over nothing. Just between me and you, there ain't no reason to sweat them boys. I was thinking maybe it would be better if we could each help the other out instead of fighting with one another."

"What does Albert think about that?" I asked.

"Like I said, we've built a trust between each other," Travis said. "He don't know everything. Doesn't need to."

About a mile past the biker's place, the two bikes pulled off and did a U-turn. We drove about ten minutes, but I couldn't tell where we were through the fog. We eased onto a dirt road in a pine forest with signs from a timber company. We could see Marty's black car in the headlights. Travis pulled slowly behind and stopped.

"The keys should be under the mat," Travis said.

"Where's Marty?" I asked.

"We're going to meet him somewhere else. Drive his car and follow me," he said.

I followed him back past the turnoff to the farm, driving slowly but struggling to see the Camaro's tail-lights. We turned off on an old logging road, barely passable for one car, the ruts filled with muddy water. The road opened to a small clearing, and I pulled in and parked next to Travis. You could just see the river through some trees. I knew this place, a bend in the river that was the sight of the famous shootout between the despised revenuer, Pistol Pete, and some of my kin, Albert and my grandfather, and my ill-fated Uncle John. There was a little beach here for offloading booze from a boat and taking it out in a car back in the prohibition days. Now people came here to drink and party from time to time.

We got out of the cars and I stood looking around wondering why we were here.

"We're supposed to meet Marty here?" I asked.

"Yeah, he's already here," Travis said.

He pulled out a .22 pistol from his back waist band. "Go open the trunk." He motioned with the gun.

He's been in the trunk on the whole ride. Fear and questions rushed my brain.

What's he going to do to him? Or me. I stood still just looking over at the trunk.

"Open the trunk, Ronnie."

I fumbled with the keys as I walked over to the car. I could barely open it. My hands were starting to shake. My legs and arms felt heavy with an unknowable dread, like I wanted to stop doing what I was doing, but what my brain told me to do my body wouldn't obey. The trunk seemed to spring open when I unlocked it. Marty lay there in the spacious trunk, hog-tied and gagged. Travis pushed me out of the way, stuck the gun in his pants, pulled out a Buck knife, slung it open and cut some ropes freeing Marty's legs. He put the knife back in his pocket and pulled Marty out backwards and stood him up against the car, held him with one hand as he shut the trunk.

"Take him down to the river's edge," he said. He took the pistol back out of his pants and just held it by his side.

I guided him down to the edge of the water through a small path in the woods. The way was muddy and it smelled like earth and sulfur. Travis pushed me aside and pulled down Marty's blindfold.

"Cigarette," Marty said in a whisper.

I pulled out my pack and lit a cigarette and stuck it in Marty's mouth. He took a long drag and blew out a plume of smoke.

"That's right," Travis said. "Let's all have a smoke. You know where we are, Marty?"

He shook his head.

"Ronnie, you know where we are, right?" Travis asked.

                                              Tyler Keith

"Yeah. I've been here," I said.

"Why don't you tell Marty what happened here," Travis said.

"This is the spot of the famous shootout that killed Pistol Pete and my Uncle John," I said.

"Why don't you tell Marty the whole story," Travis said.

"My Granddaddy and his two sons, Albert and John, were bringing a load of whisky down the river on this barge they had. They had their car already loaded and on the barge. When they came around the bend there, to load off the shit here, Pistol Pete was waiting for them with his shotgun. He killed Uncle Johnny, who was just 14 years old. Wounded my granddaddy. When the smoke cleared, Pistol Pete was dead on the ground here. They took the bodies to town and put both of them on the bed of a buck-board and laid them out so the whole town could see."

"That's right," Travis said. "Two dead right here. Albert took me here himself. Told me the whole story. Although he lost his older brother, he said it was the most alive he ever felt. That night. He used to bring people here. Kind of like a place to interrogate a man."

Marty's cigarette ash had grown long so I took it out of his mouth, ashed it and stuck it back in. I caught his eye and he seemed to have a resignation about him. I looked away across the river.

"One thing I've learned about torturing people is that they just end up saying what you want them to. It's a pointless activity. It's best just to trust your gut feeling about people."

"Whatever you're thinking about doing, Travis, don't," I said.

"I think there's been a few suicides out here, too," he said.

In one fluid motion, Travis raised the gun to Marty's head and fired. I heard the crack of the .22. Marty fell at my feet, cigarette still clinched in his mouth. I stepped back and knelt next to the body. There was a small hole in the side of his temple with just a tiny, thick drip of blood oozing out.

"Why?" I asked, stupidly feeling for a pulse on his neck. Travis pushed me aside, cut the ropes on Marty's hands puts the gun in his left hand and shoots another bullet into the night sky, and dropped the gun next to the body.

Travis ignored my question. "You'd better wipe down the car," he said.

I thought about going for the gun, but I'd have to go through Travis to get it. He had the knife, and maybe another gun on him. Instead I just went back through the woods to Marty's car and started wiping the steering wheel down with the edge of my shirt, muttering under my breath, grinding my teeth. Travis came up behind me and dragged me out of the car by the scruff of the neck.

"That's good enough. Just leave the door open," he said and pointed at the Camaro. "Get in the car."

I rode in stunned silence as we drove back to the farm. The radio blasted some generic metal that just registered as white noise. Travis sang along to whatever it was, hitting a half pint of Dickel and looking at me, trying to get my attention.

"Look, Ronnie, like I told you, I'm the man to do things that no one else wants to do. I don't ask what the old man's motivations are. I just do it," he said.

I smoked in a slow controlled rhythm. The shot still seemed to ring in my ears, making a unreal warping sound.

"I will say this, nobody likes a snitch. You hear me?" he asked.

I didn't say anything, just smoked and stared at the dashboard. At the very least, I was guilty of accessory to murder, probably worse. And I was guilty of it, not just in the eyes of the law. There was a body at my feet. Blood on my hands. And now I'm stuck in the middle. Travis will hold this over me. I'll be doing his bidding forever. Worse than being a prisoner to Travis, I'd be a prisoner to that death. The image would play through my mind

                                    Tyler Keith

until the day I died. It was already starting. That image
of Travis pulling the trigger had connected in my mind
with the image of the man being executed in the streets of
Saigon. The repetition. The senselessness of it. The speed
of something happening that you know nothing about,
and you want to stop it but you can't. Somehow that image
appeared alongside the image of Marty tumbling down
on the rivers edge. I tried to shake it from my mind, both
images, but they repeated themselves with the flickering
light of a cheap Super 8 camera on a bare plaster wall, until
their faces merged. Then there was Jimmy, too, the boy
who'd died in the accident that sent me to prison. He was
with me. Sometimes I'd see him in the shadows of my jail
cell, staring at me. I dream about him some. Things can
haunt you without being a full ghost. The dreams and the
distorted images weren't as hard as the thoughts. The whys.
The gnashing of teeth. I'd learned to let it go a little, but you
lose some good things in the bargain. You lose your soul, a
little connection to the things you love and cherish. That's
the deal. But he'd be with me always, just like Marty would
now. I might catch them sitting in the back seat of the car in
my rearview, or see them on the highway by the side of the
road. That is if I ever got out of this. If I ever got back on the
road. If I lived through the weekend.

Rationalizations for Marty's death will come later. If I
found out why Travis killed Marty, it may help me. But the
truth was it didn't matter why. I began to feel an emptiness creeping in, a clearing-out of my emotions, the thing
I'd learned in prison, something to protect me from what
I'd done. I didn't want that. Not yet. But maybe I needed it
though. I needed to try and think of a way out of this.

27

WHEN WE GOT back to the farm, and parked the car in the barn, it was raining again. Past the Airstream, by the river's edge, I could see a light on in the fish house. I took a few beers from the refrigerator in the barn, and made a run for it. Travis yelled after me, but when he saw I was heading for the shack he let me go. I was soaked by the time I made it. A yellow mosquito bulb hung down in the room. It was just a porch with concrete floors, screened in and a tiny back room with a utility sink, a butcher table to clean fish, a deep freezer, and an old Frigidaire from the fifties. I sat down at the linoleum table and took a breath. The hard rain on the tin roof made an ambient noise that drowned out all other sounds, like the static on an old television if it were a living thing. The strange yellow glow of the light made me feel uneasy, a little sick. In the corner with some fishing tackle boxes sat an old Coleman lantern. I lit the lantern and set it to dim, then pulled the string turning off the overhead light. In the soft glow of the gas lamp and the impenetrable music of the falling rain, I felt a moment of peace, but not calm. I pushed the image of Marty out of head.

My mind drifted back to the days down on the river with my little family, Tina and Tammy. The simple days, the first few years when I just drove a truck, before I started working for Albert. I'd be gone for a while, and every time I came home it was like Christmas. I'd bring them presents, and we'd go to the beach or come down here to the river. Then, when I came down here to drive for Albert everything changed, slowly at first. Once I started working in Holmes County, doing what I was doing, I didn't want them over here. Didn't want them near it. And then, not only did not want them to come down here, but I wanted to stay away from home more and more. I'd rationalized what I was doing, but around them it was harder to fool myself. I just let the inertia take me away. Just let things take me in one direction until finally I had to act or fall off the face of the earth. Before I got a chance to act, I fell …

The few months before my release, I'd thought about all of this. I told myself I would take control of things when I got out. But somehow I was back to just floating along, but the difference was now I was angry and rudderless. I wasn't prepared for the anger. After all the years of rationalization and excuses, I'd let myself think that it was someone else's fault, what I'd done, the death of Jimmy. It was Albert's fault for making me take the kid on that run. It was the kid's fault for being a rat. Shirking the blame let me live with it. Let me forget as much as I could. It was all part of my hibernation and survival. But that little kernel of blame I put on others festered and turned into resentment that woke up the day I walked out of prison and it came out as a perfect pearl of hate. Now the hate seemed unearned because there was another dead body at my feet. There was blood on my hands again. Maybe inside I thought I'd need to get back my life, to get back the things I needed and wanted, my child.

The situation in Holmes County was a mess. Albert still held things together with his connections and his power and influence over Charles. Travis and Bob were a powder keg with the fuse already lit. And Bob was just a kid. If something happened to Bob, something would happen to Travis. He had to do something or something would be done to him. Maybe he knew it. Maybe that's why he wanted in on the speed, and why he had the connection with the bikers. I still didn't know why they wanted me here. Marty was still a mystery to me. Why did Albert want him dead? Was he a rat for Charles, or worse, law enforcement? If that later was the case, we were all in trouble. Was Travis that stupid? I was just a fucking driver. I'd been stable when I was around, and I'd done my time without a sound. I could make some real money quick down here, but it could all blow up in my face first. I was stuck in the middle. Charles thinking he had my loyalty because we were blood. Travis had me as an accomplice.

Since talking to my aunt Iris, I'd been thinking of another reason to hang around here. I wanted to find out about my father. Where'd he go? What happened to him? I'd always assumed he had he run off somewhere, but maybe he was buried down here in the Holmes County mud. Somebody knew … but the inertia. The lifestyle. The booze and the lines I'd never been able to say "no" to may just cancel out all the questions. It may just carry me along until something makes me decide. Or incarcerates me. Or kills me.

I'd found a six-pack of Schaefer in the old Frigidaire, drank it, and watched the rain. It stopped just before daylight and when the sun came up it was a clear and green morning with the songs of birds ringing in the trees. A mist rose from the river and the light made it silver and red and clear. I'd somehow drank myself sober. Maybe it was the speed or the absence of liquor, or the gravity of the situation, but I felt fine, and my mind was clear. My body felt dirty, and my nails were black. Mud hung on the edges of boots and the hem of my jeans.

I looked over at the house and it was still and quiet. I took off my clothes and left them on the table in the shack. The slowly moving water felt warm on top and a cool current flowed underneath. I entered the river to my knees at first to adjust to the temperature of the water, looking through the mist up-river, I could just make-out the frame of my Uncle's house, an A-frame on stilts on a rise on the other bank. Squinting, I thought I could see a figure sitting by the railing. It was only an outline.

These days, Albert never left his place and had few visitors. But he still ruled his family from up there. Everybody feared him like he was a vengeful god that you couldn't see but knew watched your every move. He'd been running things since Prohibition, and his connections went that far back. And he'd known all the people his daddy and granddaddy had known. They'd greased the wheels for almost a century. Some southern bootleggers never paid off the cops or worked with other big city organized crime folks, but that was shortsighted. Albert paid everybody from park rangers to state senators. He had real connections with cops and politicians in Tallahassee. And even though he'd let his family, especially Charles, run things, he had people outside the county, invisible allies, he'd use from time to time, people with no names or faces. He would play people off of each other, too. He would council with one person, and then, suddenly, he would stop calling them to his house, and start using someone else. It kept everybody off balance. It kept him untouchable. Everyone wanted to please him and be in good stead. Do his bidding. He probably had Travis around to fuck with Charles. Let him know that family didn't mean everything. Everybody was expendable.

I ducked my head underneath the water slowly, then stood like I'd baptized myself.

As I stood in the river, feeling the sun on my face, a vision came to me. I stood on the edge of the water with my mother. We wore our Sunday clothes. My father stood waist-deep in the water calling a young lady to come to him. A deacon led her out into the water. I could almost hear his voice as he pushed her underwater, "buried with Christ in Baptism unto death." Then he raised her from the water, "risen to walk in the newness of life."

The women headed back to the shore, crying and raising her hands to the sky. I wondered if the memory

Tyler Keith

might have happened in this exact spot. I think my father
would have loved to perform a baptism in a spot where
his wicked brother Albert could watch. He could show
him his righteousness. He could taunt him with the pride
of the Lord.

The image of my mother in a white gown, waist deep
in the crystal river, glowing in the morning sun, rocked
me to my core. *She was the real saint in my life.* She'd always
been, and I'd taken it for granted. Used her. Blamed her
for everything, for my father leaving, for my wasted
teenage years. I'd held it against her when she retreated
into alcohol. I'd seen it as a sort of neglect, but I'd never
thought it through. I never realized that she was just as
devastated as I was that my father was gone.

They'd met when she was fourteen. He was twenty.
He was already a powerful preacher by all accounts. Their
courtship was quick. Her parents were desperate to get
out of Holmes County, and when her dad found work in
Pensacola at the new Navy yard, they moved. Instead of
going with her parents she married my father and stayed
in Holmes County. The duties of a pastor's wife fit her
personality. She looked at my father with something more
than love; she worshiped him, and loved playing the role
of first lady of the church. After he was gone, it crashed
her whole world. It killed her faith. Nothing in the scrip-
tures made sense anymore.

We moved in with my grandparents for a time. That
was a happy time for me. My grandparents doted on me
and spoiled me. They drank some, but she really took
to the bottle, but on the sly at first. Then she got work
in a drugstore and we got a little place of our own. She
started seeing men, and they drank together. She'd stay
with them. She never brought them home, but she stayed
gone some nights. I was lonely and afraid at times, but
I never went without food. She always showed me love
and affection. But the older I got, the more I looked on her
with resentment. The more I used her behavior to do what

I wanted. Run wild. Skip school. Sell weed. Drink. When I got married and had a kid, she became grandma and gladly took care of Tina when I was gone for days driving a truck, and later when I stayed in Holmes County for days.

When I went to prison she always visited, even when I told Tammy to stop coming, and everyone else had stopped coming. Towards the end, I noticed she seemed thin and frail. She told me she was fine, but she wasn't. She had cancer. I only saw her twice after I first noticed she wasn't well. After she died, I really gave up. Reverend Wilkins broke the news. I didn't cry. I just laid down in my cell and just turned it all off. I stopped everything, all my emotions, so quickly and so finally that I'd hardly thought about her until this vision. I ducked under water again, and when I came up something felt different. Maybe I understood now. It almost felt like my father had baptized me, and my mother waited on the shore to dry me off and embrace me. They had forgiven me.

But it was all a dream I had. But, somehow, I felt cleansed this morning. A feeling of calm came over me. I knew it wouldn't last, but I sat in chair in the sun and felt its warmth and tried to capture this place, and this feeling in my head, this place where I felt some forgiveness. Maybe if I could keep it inside, I could go there when I needed a moment of peace. I could drop off my burden of sins, the bodies, long enough to make it out of this.

28

TRAVIS KICKED MY chair and woke me.

"We're late, Hoss," he said.

We took his Camaro. The ride was quiet, although Travis was in a good mood and would laugh for no reason and punch my shoulder like I was in on some unspoken joke. I was pretty sure he hadn't been to sleep. He made me nervous. This whole "date" tonight did too, although I wanted to see Darleen again, the thought of exposing Travis to anybody worried me. Travis was a little too close to crazy. Even in his right mind he was dangerous, but now he was on the edge of criminally insane. I knew what he was capable of.

Sarge flipped when we showed up with the Camaro.

"You can't have a car here, Travis," he said. "That's one of the main rules."

"Had to get here somehow, Sarge," he said. He laughed and walked towards his cabin. "I've got a buddy coming to get it tomorrow."

I didn't see him until after dinner. We met up behind the fellowship hall. The wind blew in strong and cool, but no rain came yet.

On the other side of the camp, I could see Jessie's flashlight bouncing around the office.

"Shit, man, it's Jessie. What are we gonna do about him?" I asked.

"I got it covered. You got any more cigarettes?" he asked.

"Yeah, I got another pack in my room. What are you going to do?"

"Go get them. I'll take care of it. I need to talk to him alone. Go get your smokes and come back when you see him coming my way."

"What are you going to do, Travis?" I looked at him. He looked back in the direction of the office. Jessie was coming towards the Fellowship Hall.

"Don't worry, Ronnie, I'm not going to hurt him. I'm just going to talk to him. Go. He's coming this way."

I walked slowly away at first. Then hurried to the cabin.

Beasley and Davis sat at the table playing dominoes. I didn't look at them. Just grabbed the small sack of goods from under my bunk. Got my last pack of smokes and headed for the door. They looked at me. I looked at them and smiled like I knew I was stupid. The radio played "Who Do You Love?"

"Storm's coming, Harrison." Davis said smiled, pointed to me like he was saying, "It's all you, buddy."

I chuckled and pointed back at him, "Right back at ya, champ," before I hurried out and slammed the door behind me.

As I got closer to the Fellowship Hall, I could see the maroon New Yorker parked with its lights on right by the break in the fence. Travis had Jessie in a bear hug from behind passing him through the gate to two men on the other side. Jessie kicked. The rain came down hard. I could see Jessie screaming but couldn't hear anything but the rain on the tin roofs of the cabins. The wind howled.

"Hey, What the fuck, Travis!" I shouted. But by the time I got there, the men were stuffing Jessie into the back of the New Yorker. One had a hand over his mouth and the other held his feet together forcing him into the car. When they got him in, the car sped off down the dead end street and turned and floored it down 98.

I pushed Travis. "What the fuck, man?"

He pushed back, laughing at first. Then he took notice

of my anger. He stopped smiling but still held his hands out in defense.

"They're not going to kill him or anything, Ronnie. Calm down."

"How do you know that?"

"Because I know them. They're going to give the kid a good beating. He's got it coming. He'll be back here tomorrow. He'll be fine. You know as well as I do that he had to deal with it someday. Might as well be now. Right?"

He smiled again.

"Bullshit, Travis."

"They're not going to hurt him too bad. Trust me."

"What about Sarge?"

"They'll leave Jesse by the gate in the morning. He gets fixed up. He'll be instructed to keep his fucking mouth shut. He'll spend a couple of days in bed. He'll be fine. The people will be happy they gave him a lesson. He won't have to worry anymore. He can continue reading the damn Bible through. He'll have the perfect end to his testimony. Believe me, we did the guy a favor."

"I don't know. Seems fucked up."

"Look, have a drink." He handed me the bottle from his back pocket. I took a long drink. "Comb your hair. We got ladies coming in ten minutes."

I handed him the bottle back. Took a comb out of my back pocket and combed my hair out of my face. Got a cigarette from my jacket and lit it up. I just watched the rain and then walked back under the back door awning. Leaned against the door and took a deep breath.

Travis came up beside me and put his hand on my back. "I should have told you about it." I shrugged his hand away. Turned around and looked down the street.

"Fuck it," I said. "The little bastard had it coming. Who gives a shit."

I only half believed it.

Ten minutes later, lights turned onto the dead end street.

"There they are."

Travis pointed. He seemed like a hyperactive kid. The violence earlier had his blood up.

"Come on, hoss," he said. We headed to the break in the fence. I threw my cigarette down and followed him. We stood by the road and waited for the car to pull up. The rain had picked up slightly.

Travis handed me the half pint bottle with the cork in it.

"Finish it off, hoss."

I knocked it back then threw the bottle over my shoulder and it landed in the mud.

The car pulled up to the curb, a '76 four-door, red Impala with the front window partially rolled down.

"You boys look like you could use a ride," Darleen said and smiled. Big red lipstick lips. Light red hair with a little bump in the back. A cigarette in one hand, the other on the wheel. She wore a black western shirt with white piping on the sleeves and the pockets. The girl in the passenger side got out holding a newspaper over her head with one hand. I hurried around the passenger's side. She pointed to Travis to get in the back seat of the driver's side.

When we got in. We all looked at each other and kind of laughed. I reached over and gave Darleen a little side hug. She turned her head so her lipstick wouldn't get messed up yet. She looked at me.

"You're better looking than I remember," she said.

"You're not so bad yourself," I said. "Last time you saw me, I was about passed out drunk."

She blushed. "That's right."

"Ronnie, this is Debbie. And who are you back there?" She looked in the rear-view mirror at Travis.

"Who me?" Travis asked jokingly. "I'm Travis, ex-con and genuine hell-raiser."

"Oh, Lord," Darleen said. "That's Debbie in the back. We run around together. We're like sisters."

"Shit, you like me better than your real sister," Debbie said. "Hey Travis. It's a pleasure to meet you."

                                              Tyler Keith

She stuck out her hand for Travis to shake. He took
her hand and gave it a little kiss.

"The pleasure's all mine, Miss Debbie," he said.

"Now let's have a drink," Darleen said. She pulled
a bottle from under her seat, a fifth of Wild Turkey. She
unscrewed the cap, took a long drink, and passed the
bottle to me.

"Goddamn, Ronnie, I like your taste in women,"
Travis said with a chuckle.

"We've got a six-pack back there, too," Darleen said.
"Ronnie, you want a beer?"

"Yes, ma'am."

"Debbie, would you hand Ronnie a beer?" Darleen
asked. Debbie cracked the beer can open and passed it
over the seat. I passed the Wild Turkey bottle back to her.

"Thank you, Debbie," I said.

She just smiled.

"So where to, boys?" Darleen asked.

I thought for a moment. No one else spoke up.

"Let's see what this storm looks like at the beach," I
said. "We got a bottle and some beers."

"Pensacola Beach, it is," Darleen said.

Darleen swung the big red Impala around and
headed down the dead end street, and took a left on 98
towards the Bob Sikes bridge. The radio played John
Anderson singing, "I'm Just an Old Chunk of Coal,"
Darleen turned it up. The wind blew the Impala all over
the road as we crested the bridge to Pensacola Beach.
We didn't see or pass another car. Maybe we should've
taken more notice. We passed the bottle back and forth.
Travis and Debbie seemed to be getting along in the back,
sitting close together and laughing. I had my hand on
Darleen's thigh. We drove by a few beach bars, but they
were all closed up. We pulled into a parking lot on the
Gulf side just west of the pier. The rain pounded the wind
shield. Darleen cut off the engine. Kept the radio on. She
cracked the window just a half inch. Smoke filled the car

anyway. We all smoked. Passed the bottle some more. The windows fogged up. Darleen slid across the seat next to me. She smelled clean. Light, flowery perfume. We looked at each other. We were both drunk. We laughed, then we kissed. Her lips were warm and smooth, loose and wet. I placed my hands on her hips and moved them up the side of her body. We checked each other out again. She was older than I thought at first. Her eyes were crystal green. The radio played, "The Girls All Look Better at Closing Time." You could hear the wind howling outside. Still hear the pounding of the waves. Then I heard a commotion in the back seat. A tussle.

"Stop it," Debbie said.

I didn't pay attention at first.

"Stop it. I mean it!" this time louder. "Get off. Get off of me! Godammit!"

I pushed Darleen away. Looked in the back seat. Travis had Debbie pinned down in the sprawling backseat. She was squirming under his bulk.

"Stop it!" she screamed.

Travis didn't seem to hear. Or care.

"Travis!" I yelled. "What the fuck are you doing?"

I grabbed his shoulder to pull him off. He looked at me. Slapped my hand away. Sat up looking at me, his eyes crazy, a meanness on his face.

"Turn around and mind your own business," he said, low and serious. No one said anything.

"Turn around and mind your own business," he said again. Silence again.

Darleen turned the radio down. Travis pointed his finger in my face.

Just then a police siren and blue lights came on behind us. Travis sat up. Debbie moved to the farthest side by her door, straightening her clothes. Looking straight ahead. Darleen scooted back behind the wheel just as the police knocked on her window. Darleen rolled down her window.

"You folks can't be out here. They're evacuating the beach. Hurricane Elena is moving this way. You need to vacate Pensacola Beach. Best get all the way back to Pensacola."

"Yes, sir, officer. We were just leaving," Darleen said.

"You'd better. If I see you out here again I'm going to take you in. Let's get moving."

Darleen started the car and pulled out of the lot and headed towards the bridge. The cop followed us to the bridge and turned off when he saw we were crossing over. No one said anything as we drove back to Camp Eden. Darleen pulled up to the same spot where she picked us up. I leaned over and gave Darleen a kiss.

"Why don't you call me again," she said. "Leave your friend at home next time. Me and you'll go out."

Before I got out, I took another long pull on the Wild Turkey.

As Travis got out, he said, "So long, Debbie."

"Fuck you," she said without looking at him.

We got out of the car. The wind and the rain had picked up. We ran to the fence and slipped through the hole and ran under the back door awning. I tried to clean my glasses off. Then I looked at Travis.

"What the fuck, man?" I grabbed his shoulder to turn him around.

He looked at me. No more good-time Travis.

"Don't you ever touch me."

He pointed at me again, his mouth tight. "You hear me?"

I didn't say anything. Just knocked out a cigarette and lit it up. I looked around the camp. The cabins had all the storm shutters closed. Two of the vans were gone. All of the lights were out. The whole camp was dark except for a light in the office.

"Let me have a cigarette," Travis said. "You know what, I'll get my own cigarettes."

"Everybody's gone," I said.

He looked around. "What the fuck?"

"They must've evacuated everybody while we were gone. There's a light on in the office."

"Sarge," he said. He started walking towards the office out in the rain. I took a long drag and threw the butt in the mud. As I was following him, I noticed a gun sticking out of the back of his pants. A little pearl-handled .25.

"Where'd you get the gun, Travis?" I jogged up beside him.

"I found it in Debbie's purse." He didn't look at me.

"You stole her gun from her purse?"

"Fuck her," he said.

When we got close to the office, he stopped and looked at me.

"When we go up in here, you stay behind me. We don't know what he might do."

"The fuck are you talking about?"

"Stay behind me."

He hurried up the stairs and pushed open the door just coming in far enough so I could see inside. Sarge rummaged though his desk, putting some papers in an open briefcase sitting on the desk. The safe stood partially open. Sarge stood up, trying to close the safe with the back of his leg. It didn't close all the way. He tried to keep his composure. We'd startled him. He tried to get into his drill sergeant authority figure role.

"Where the hell have you been?" he barked. "You know what, I'm so sick of you two. You're in serious trouble."

He looked at us. Looked at me. Looked at Travis. You could see him shrink when he locked eyes with Travis. He saw the danger. He quickly looked away.

"Where's Jessie?" Sarge asked in a quiet voice.

"I don't know, Sarge. Last time I saw him he was outside talking to some friends in a maroon Chrysler New Yorker. Looked like they were having a reunion. Catching up."

Travis slowly pulled the gun from the back of his

pants. He held it by his side for a few seconds. Sarge shrank a little more, although he tried to look calm.

"Harrison. What's going on?" Sarge thought maybe he could reach me. Talk some sense before things went too far.

"Harrison don't know shit," Travis said. "Move away from the safe."

He lifted the gun. Moved a little closer. I could see Sarge thinking. He made a dash for the back room. Travis caught him by the shirt collar and cracked him on the nose with the butt of the gun. His nose shattered. He made a groan as blood exploded out of his face. Travis pounded him again in the face. He let him fall hard on his back. When his body hit the floor, Sarge's head snapped against the concrete floor. Sarge went limp, blood spilling out of him in a dark red pool.

Travis let him stay there and pivoted around and pointed the gun at me.

"Get some fucking cigarettes out of the cage."

I thought about making a run for it myself but knew I'd never make it without taking a bullet in the back. I did what he said. Travis went around behind the desk. He dumped out the briefcase spilling all the papers onto the floor. I reached down to get the cage keys off of Sarge. His eyes were open. I could hear a gurgling sound. I checked his pulse. He wasn't breathing. I took a deep breath. Got the keys. Got two cartons of Marlboro Reds and brought them to Travis. I just stood there. I watched him put a few bundles of cash in the brief case. Maybe a few thousand bucks. I couldn't think of what to do. I froze, looking at Sarge's body, bleeding on the polished concrete floor.

Travis looked at me. "Stay with me, hoss. We'll get out of this."

He seemed to have calmed down a bit. "Toss me those cartons."

I did. He put them in the brief case and shut it. He sat there for about ten seconds, thinking.

"All right, let's get Sarge and move him out." He left the briefcase and moved around to Sarge's body. Straightened him out. Grabbed his hand. "Come on Ronnie, grab his feet. We're going to toss him in the bay. The storm will take him out to the Gulf. They might never find him."

I paused.

"I think he might still be alive," I said.

"I don't think he's gonna make it," Travis said. "You know at this point, hoss, we've both murdered a decorated veteran. 'A good man who helped people no one else would. And they killed him. Beat him to death.' That's what they'll say went on here. You were here, you're guilty. If they catch us, we'll get the chair. Now grab his legs."

I did what he said. I started to mutter to myself almost like repeating a prayer. Like a Pentecostal prayer, "Father God. Father God", but it was "holy shit, holy shit." Somehow it calmed me down. I took deep breaths as we dragged the body through the mud, around the fellowship hall, through the pines to the edge of the water. The bay churned like a washing machine. We set the body down close to the edge and both leaned over with our hands on our knees to catch our breath. I stood up first and tried to light a cigarette in the pouring rain. The wind howled and bent the trees like they were bowing to the camp. I gave up on lighting the cigarette and threw it on the ground. Travis stood up and pulled the gun out of the back of his pants.

"Damn, Ronnie, today is not your day, is it?"

"Fuck you," I said, looking him in the eyes.

"I wish I didn't have to do this, but dealing with this mess will just be easier with just one of us. Plus your uncle wanted me to kill your ass anyway. If you weren't coming back to Holmes County. Plus you know about Marty. That's not too good for me."

"I already did my time. Why would Albert want to kill me?"

　　　　　　　　　　　　　　Tyler Keith

"You know, what he did to you."

"What do you mean?"

"You don't even know, do you? I told him you didn't know. He wanted to make sure. And of course if you ever found out …

"What the fuck are you talking about?"

"Your father. He killed your father, Ronnie. Or he had him killed. I don't know the details. He tried to talk your dad into working for him. He wasn't interested. He's buried over there somewhere in Holmes County."

He looked at me.

"You know what I'll do for you, Ronnie? I'll kill your old piece of shit uncle after I kill you. The man is 82 years old. Believe me, he won't be missed. But then, neither will you."

He raised the gun and pulled the trigger. It clicked. He looked at the gun and back at me.

"Well what do you know. I should've checked to see if it was loaded. But who keeps an unloaded gun? Oh yeah, a woman."

I took the second he paused to rush towards him and tackle him as hard as I could, slamming him into the mud on his back. He grabbed me and squeezed my neck with one hand. Then the hand with the gun pounded me on the head three hard times. My eyes went blurry. I managed to clutch his windpipe. I squeezed as hard as I could. I could hear it crack and he started to choke. He grabbed me by my shoulders and threw me off of him, and got to his knees clutching his throat with one hand, his other hand with the empty gun stuck out in front of him. I ran at him and smashed him with my fist as hard as I could in the temple. His eyes blinked and he fell over on his side still clutching his throat. I looked around, saw the gun laying in the mud and snatched it up. I hammered the side of his head with the butt. After the first two hits, I could hear his skull crack and see inside his skull. He made a spastic shiver and a low moan. Blood came out of his mouth and he fell over into the mud.

I collapsed next to Travis' body. Trying to catch my breath. I cried a moment, then got up on my knees. I picked up some mud and threw it back down. I looked at my other hand and realized I was still holding the bloody gun. I looked at it. I washed off the handle in a puddle of mud, staggered up and stuck the gun in the back of my pants.

The rain and the wind seemed to be getting worse. The tall pines bent and debris flew through the air. Sarge's body lay close to the bank and the water rose towards him. It was easy to roll him in. Travis was dead weight, and already heavy. I dragged him a few feet, then rolled him to the edge, too. I fished the keys to the Camaro from his pants pocket. With a final heave I pushed him into the bay. Both bodies seemed to move quickly away from shore into the dark bay, almost like they were swimming. Maybe I imagined it. I heaved a few deep breaths.

I ran back to the office, and I cleaned up the desk quickly, trying to hide the sign of a struggle. I grabbed the briefcase and ran to the car. As soon as I got in, I opened the briefcase, tore open a carton of the cigarettes, ripped one out. I lit it, and took a long drag, smoking almost half. I started the Camaro and sat for a moment. *Where was I going to go?*

There was only one place.

29

I PULLED OUT of Camp Eden and whipped the Camaro onto Highway 98 headed east. The wind whistled through the crack in the window and howled though the pines and scrub oak. The trees bowed to me again. My body shook, my skin wet with sweat and dirty rain. Mud. Blood. The top of my head throbbed. I could see Travis' face as he pounded me with a determination to destroy or to live. I'd squeezed his throat with the same determination. Him or me. In that moment, I felt no fear, just the urge to live.

But now, I felt my body loosen for the first time since I'd charged Travis by the bay side. A shiver ran through my bones. I started to cry. Weep. A long moan formed in my throat. I banged on the steering wheel. The rain fell harder and the wind pushed the Camaro around like a little toy. I could barely see the road. It snapped me back to the present, to what I was doing. I saw no one else on the highway except a highway patrolman screaming by towards Gulf Breeze.

Can't be nothing involving me? I thought. Too soon. Nobody was down there. Nobody saw anything. I passed Navarre Beach. The wind eased a bit. Still no one on the road. A few miles up, I turned north onto 285 Eglin Parkway. My thoughts turned to my uncle and the last meeting I had with my father. His "mission" he's talked about. He was headed back to Holmes County, to his brother, my Uncle Albert. Maybe he knew he wasn't coming back. Or he didn't want me to know what he'd be doing. Or maybe he had something he had to do. An event came to my mind as I drove towards my Uncle's place.

My Dad came down to Holmes County to some kind of homecoming service, a triumphant return. It was not long before the last time I saw him. It was in the little chapel he'd grown up in, Crooked Run Chapel. The church was packed with his friends and all his kin. My cousin, Albert Jr., and my Aunt May.

I still remember part of his sermon, " 'Vanity, vanity: saith the preacher. All is vanity!' Ecclesiasties 12:8 and 14. 'For God shall bring every work into judgement, with every secret thing, whether it be good or it be evil.' "

The people swayed and shouted as he almost screamed the verses. "Vanity, vanity. All is vanity!" he shouted again and again. I sat in the front row with my mother. She shouted and raised her hands in the air. My father looked down at me from the pulpit like a towering giant, wiping his face with a white handkerchief.

"Everything that is hidden will one day be exposed!" he shouted.

The piano player and the organist answered each other and answered the man in the pulpit.

"Judgement day is upon us!"

"Amen!" the congregation shouted.

"If you don't keep your word! If you lie! Be sure your sins will find you out!"

Some shouted in tongues. Some prayed, repeating a phrase over and over again, "Praise him, praise him …" Aunt May and Junior each raised a hand and shouted, "Amen!"

I looked at my father that day with awe and wonder. He held the Bible in the air and spouted its words, never looking inside its crumbling black binding. At the end he began to sing *Crying holy to the Lord.*

Everybody started clapping and singing along. After a few verses, a weariness came upon the service. The whole thing wound down like a spinning top wobbling

                                        Tyler Keith

to an exhausted end, the music coming to a stop with my father slowly raising his hand, and he quietly finished with a prayer.

After the service people flocked to the pulpit to talk to him, some telling him their hardships. A few of the ladies looking at him like a famous singer after a concert. They had food prepared and laid out on tables in the grass next to the church in front of the small graveyard. After a few plates, me and Junior ran around with some other kids getting dirty and sweating. My father sat in a chair by my mom and Aunt May.

Out of this quiet scene, the loud sound of a late '40s truck broke the peace of the dinner on the grounds. Uncle Albert slid in to a stop in front of the church in his black Ford. He got out leaving the truck running and his door open. He was drunk. His shirt hung open and he wore a straw cowboy hat cocked to the side. Junior stopped in his tracks when he saw his dad like that. He turned white, and walked towards his father and the truck like he knew he'd be leaving.

Albert stumbled up to Aunt May and stopped in front of her, swaying.

"Get in the car," he said in low deep voice.

She didn't move.

He grabbed her arm with his big meaty hand. Junior stood by, closely watching.

My father stood up and said, "Albert, I'll bring her home when we're done here."

Albert looked him in the face with a blankness that turned into something like hate. Everyone at the church stood like statues, a quietness descended.

"Don't you tell me what to do with my family," he said, pulling Aunt May up by the arm.

She was afraid.

"Don't …" she said to my father.

"Junior, get in the truck," she said, shaking off Albert's hand.

He let her go, still looking at my father. Junior ran towards her and they got in the truck. He grabbed my dad like he was giving him a hug, his powerful hand on my father's neck. He whispered something in his ear. With his free hand he gave him a short, almost invisible punch in the gut and pushed him back onto his chair.

Albert walked back to his truck, Aunt May and Junior just looked straight ahead.

As he climbed aboard the Ford, he turned around to the congregation and shouted, "You can all go to hell!"

He skidded off down the road throwing dirt into the air. My father stormed off behind the church, kicking up dust on the dirt road. My mother and the other folks packed up the food like nothing happened.

Was this a provocation? The beginning of a feud. The end of it. I thought. My father was a proud man. The embarrassment must have angered him. Maybe my father thought there had to be some kind of righteous showdown, some sort of reckoning. Maybe that was the reason he went back to Holmes County.

What was I going to do? I thought.

I remembered the gun. Took it out of my pants and laid it on the seat beside me. No bullets. But he wouldn't know that. Then I understood that I was going to Albert's house. I felt the bloody wound on my head. Caked with mud. *I need to talk to him,* I thought. Confront him. Didn't know what else I may do. I wasn't going to the cops. Never crossed my mind. I remembered right where he lived.

The house on stilts on the banks of the Choctawhatchee River, just before the bridge and the boat dock and picnic area. The place in my dreams. I'd been on that river many times with Junior. That spot. The dirt road by the bridge would lead to the house. There weren't many houses by the river because it flooded so much.

I wondered who would be there. Probably just my Aunt May. She'd been with Albert as long as I could

　　　　　　　　　　　　　Tyler Keith

remember. There was a rumor of a first wife but I never knew her. Aunt May was a tender and sweet woman. Always kind to me. She made me come over and eat with her when Albert wasn't around. He didn't like visitors. Didn't like her to see people. Let her go to church, but not much else.

I hit 90 and headed east, the road clear. Rode through Defuniak Springs, the town dark, stoplights blinking yellow. I took 83 north, through more pines. A few bait and tackle stores. Sign for Holly King Lake with a bass on it. Past Vortex Springs, the deep spring with roped-off swimming area and a scuba diving school.

For a moment my mind went blank. No plans. No more memories. Just clutched the steering wheel. Turned right onto Highway 2 heading east. A few miles down, I crossed from Walton County to Holmes County. Then I thought about Aunt May and a few other good folks I once knew here. These folks watched as people ran shine and weed and threw bodies in the river. Ran people out. Not speaking up. Not stopping things. But the number one law down here was, "mind your own business."

Maybe that made the silent ones just as guilty. I don't fucking know, but I was more like them than the others. I let things happen like a coward.

The road curved and I could see the Choctahatchee River bridge up ahead. The rain had slowed, but the wind still blew heavy. I took the dirt road just before the bridge. Someone just driving by might not notice the turn. The road curved around, coming just about twenty yards from the river. The road was rutted and muddy. I slowed the car to a crawl. Knocked out a cigarette and lit it up.

About two hundred yards down, I could see the house. I eased up close and cut the lights. An old black truck and a light blue Ford Escort were parked under the stilted house. One dim light shone in the back by the big glass double doors. The house was a simple A-frame with a wrap-around porch. The stilts raised it about twenty feet off of the ground.

I parked the car off to the side of the house by a clump of pines. I grabbed the gun and quietly opened and shut the door. I could hear the river rushing by, close. The water was high and made a great swooshing and shattering racket. And there was the eerie woosh of the wind, like a deep whistle, or sound you hear when you blow on the top of a Coke bottle. The old man wouldn't hear me coming. I didn't really care if he did.

I crept up to the bottom of the stairs by the side of the house that led to the wrap-around porch. A little handicapped elevator ran up the side of the steps. I could see the seat at the top. He was home. I slowly ascended the steps, creaking of the wood buried in the sounds of the river and the storm.

At the top of the stairs I could see through a glass door. A figure in a wheel chair looked out the back window towards the river, his back to me. I tried the door. Unlocked. The light in the house came from a lamp on a table by an old black vinyl couch. I opened the door slowly. When I was inside the wind sucked the door shut with a loud slam. Uncle Albert swung around in his chair to face me. I hurried towards him with the gun pointed at him. He lowered one hand down the side of his wheelchair like he was reaching for something.

I moved closer.

"Don't do it," I said.

He pulled his hand away, and put it back on his wheels. I held the unloaded gun in his face as I reached down and retrieved a .38 snub nose tucked by his side. I stuck my unloaded gun in the back of my pants and backed away a few feet. I checked the .38 — it was loaded.

"Hey, Uncle Albert," I said.

"You decided to come visit your uncle, huh?"

His voice was ragged and gruff. He smelled like a sick

                                        Tyler Keith

man, stale sweat and Bengay. His sagging face was rough with stubble.

"Where's your friend, Travis? Is he not with you?" he asked.

"No. He's dead. I killed him and threw him in the ocean," I said.

"I didn't know you had it in you, son." He smiled briefly, then his face sank back to its original, decrepit hardness.

"I guess it runs in the family," I said.

Neither of us spoke for a minute.

Then I said, "You killed Junior. Everybody knows it. You drowned your own son."

"The boy was a willful child. Disobedient. He was soft too. Always hiding behind his mother. He wouldn't obey me. Don't you know the Old Testament, son? A father has a right to deal with a willful child."

The old man seemed still angry with his dead child.

"And you killed *my father*," I said.

The hand holding the gun began to shake.

"Travis told me. You killed my father. Your own brother," I blurted out a bubbling cry. "Why? Why would you do that? He was a good man. A preacher for God's sakes."

"Your father was a hypocrite. He went around with his preaching. His bullshit. I needed him. But he didn't want to help. I brought him up."

He pointed his crooked, thin finger at me.

"I put food on our family's table. When the whole world had nothing to eat, I put food on the table."

He rolled closer to me and leaned forward in his chair.

"He didn't respect me," Albert continued. "He came back like he was going to do what I asked him to. But he was planning to stop me. Turn me in. After all I'd done for him. He was going to bring me down. He thought he was some kind of prophet, bringing down God's judgement."

I heard someone behind me. I turned around. Aunt May stood in a long housecoat and robe.

"What's going on in here?" she said, moving closer. She pulled her glasses out of her housecoat.

"Ronnie?" she asked.

"Stay out of this, May," Albert said.

"Hey Aunt May. I came to see Uncle Albert. I just got out of prison."

"What are you going to do now, son?" Albert asked.

"Shut up," I said looking back at him, pointing with the .38.

"You killed my father. He killed my father!" I screamed and looked at May. "He killed Junior, too. Drowned him. He killed your son!"

She looked at me and back at Albert but said nothing.

"What are you going to do?" he asked again.

I heard the first tinge of fear in his voice. Two glass double doors stood behind him. I walked around the side of him, still pointing the gun at his head. I opened the double doors. Pushed them all the way open. Wind and rain poured in. I grabbed his chair. Turned him around, I pushed him onto the porch next to the railing. I kicked at the railing to see if it would break, but it just cracked a bit. I looked around to see if I could find something to break it. A small pile of kindling lay a few feet down the porch. A hatchet lay on top of the pile. I grabbed the hatchet with my free hand.

"I've got money, Ronnie," he said. "Lots of it. Cash."

"I don't want your money, old man."

I took the hatchet to the railing, chopping with a fury. Tears filled my eyes.

"Don't," he said, almost pleading new. "I've got lots of money."

The railing cracked and split. I kicked it a few times and a small opening appeared. A few pieces of wood fell to the ground below.

Aunt May moved to the open doorway, hanging half inside and half out, eager to see what was happening.

"Stay back, Aunt May."

I got behind Albert and brought the chair to the edge, dangling the front wheels off the edge of the porch.

"Don't," he said, reduced to a sad whimper.

"You know the Bible? Right, Uncle Albert? Remember this verse, 'For the wages of sin is death.' "

I pulled the chair back and then pushed him over the edge with a heave. He let out a warped cry. The crashing sound was loud even over the wind and the rain.

I looked over the edge and saw his body lying in a heap in the mud, the upside-down wheelchair's wheels spinning futilely, close to the river's edge. Aunt May walked to the edge and looked down at the broken body. She grabbed hold of my arm. She leaned over and spit towards the body of her dead husband.

We stood there for a moment. I struggled to slow my breath. We both slowly backed away from the edge of the porch. The rain picked up, really pouring now. Aunt May led me by the arm back inside the house.

"You'd better get out of here, Ronnie," she said softly.

"But what about ..." I jerked my head in the direction of the porch.

"I'll take care of it, son."

She looked at me with wet eyes. "Do you need a car?" she asked.

I looked around, thinking about my current predicament.

"Yes, ma'am," I said softly. "I've got this car ..."

"I'll take care of it," she said again. "Do you need money?"

I thought for a second, remembered the briefcase in the Camaro. "No, ma'am."

She walked to the door, took a set of keys from a hook above the door. She opened the door.

"It's the blue Escort. You'd better go now," she said. I

took the keys, dazed, and walked down the steps. Got the briefcase out of the Camaro and left the keys on the front seat. I went back to the Escort. When I turned on the headlights, I could see my uncle's crumpled body by the river's edge. I pulled out of the driveway, drove back down the dirt road and turned onto Highway 2.

I took 2 to Highway 7 just before Graceville, then south to 90 at Bonifay, just above Vernon. Took 90 east.

It would be days before they knew I was missing. They might not even find the bodies. Maybe I'd be someone lost in the storm. But, no. They'd be looking for me soon. But Florida is a good place to disappear. I'd head south. Maybe the Everglades. 10,000 Islands. Miami. The Keys. I had a few thousand bucks and a forgettable face.

After Cain killed his brother, God sent him away. Set him to wander. He put a mark on him. Maybe it was something like a birthmark, or a tattoo. Maybe it was something that people felt just by looking at him. But God made it clear, that, no matter how much someone might want to, or how much Cain may deserve it, you couldn't kill him. It was a mark that set him apart. And just like Cain in the Bible, I'm set apart.

Nobody can kill me.

30

THE BAREFOOT MAILMAN Motel. A little motor court off of Highway 1 just south of Palm Beach. The kind of motel where other guests don't look your way when you pass their room, and expect the same from you. On the way down, somewhere near the Suwannee River, I picked up some stuff: a couple of fishing poles, tackle box, cooler, an old man hat, a net, and a bucket. My hair and beard are growing out now. The beard's coming in grey.

I go down to the pier every day. Hit a Cuban cafe in the morning. They don't speak English. The fishing's good here: speckled trout, sheepshead, snook, red fish, pompano, snapper. I read the newspaper. Watch the local news on my old black and white set at the motel. Keep my radio on the old country station, listening for any news, listening for my name.

People are friendly, but if you keep to yourself they get the message. They leave you alone. That old man I glimpsed in the mirror back in Holmes County that drunken night is almost here with me now. If someone looks close they may see I'm not a complete old man, but nobody looks too close down here. There's a sea of old fishermen on the boardwalks. I'm just a craggy face in the crowd.

But I want to hear my little girl's voice again, and I want to see my granddaughter. But I can't go back. I see the kids playing in the surf and I can't stop weeping inside. The Florida Southern train rolls through town every morning at three. The train cars rattle and shake in the quiet darkness. Sometimes it blows that lonesome whistle.

It lets me know I can always head further south to Leisure City or Homestead. Key Largo … but not much further.

Hell. I guess there's always Hell. That's about as far south as a man can get.

ACKNOWLEDGEMENTS

I WOULD LIKE to acknowledge, first and foremost, Tim and Susan Bauer Lee for their unwearied efforts on this book: Tim's many edits of the manuscript and Susan's excellent work on the graphic design and layout.

I would like to thank the many readers of this novel, chiefly, James Tighe, who read, corrected and advised from the beginning to the final draft. Anne Evans also read early drafts and gave many helpful suggestions. Ace Atkins, Lisa Howorth, Max Hipp, Melissa Ginsburg, David Shirley, and Bram Riddlebarger all gave close readings, corrections, and advice. Special thanks to Rosalie Riley, my mom, who read the book and gave me much encouragement. Thanks to Tracey Thomas for moral support.

All these people took this project and me seriously, and for that I'm truly grateful.